The Color Play

A novel by

Eartha Holley

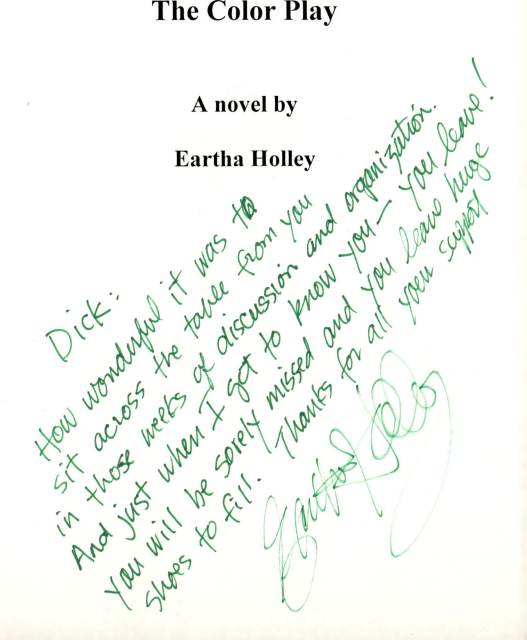

Dick:

How wonderful it was to sit across the table from you in those weeks of discussion and organization. And just when I got to know you — you leave! You will be sorely missed and you leave huge shoes to fill. Thanks for all your support!

ISBN: 0-7596-8589-4

This book is printed on acid free paper.

1stBooks - rev. 03/27/01

1

Woodrow

I never really had much use for whiteboys. Didn't have nothing against them. It's just that anytime I saw one in North Philly, he was usually asking for something. Trying to hustle me, or collect on some damn bill. Anyway, whiteboys made me nervous. Always think they got something you want. Acting like you're the Brute Negro or something. That's why it tripped me out that me and Mark Berens ever got as close as we did.

I mean, even if I wanted to hang out with some devil, why choose him? We ain't got nothin' in common. I'm strictly from the streets. He's some spoiled Air Force brat whose biggest crisis before he met me was probably trying to *gank* his Pops; trying to cheat him out of spending change. Wouldn'ta lasted ten minutes where I come from. I met him at Delaware State College down in Dover.

I didn't know nothing about college. Barely got outta high school, but I was certainly ready to get away from the streets and them crazy-assed gangs running 'round killing everybody. My boy Andrew went the year before me, and when he showed me how to get a government grant to pay for it, I was in there, Jack.

Delaware State College for Negroes (or DelState for short) was put together right after the Civil War to do something with all them recently freed niggas loose everywhere. Couldn't send them to the University of Delaware with decent whitefolk. So, they built this "coon college" just north of Dover. After Civil Rights and *Martha Lutha King* (as my friend Bobo calls him), we got "free at last." So, DelState dropped that "Negro" part, and started sucking up to white people in town and at the Air Force base. Had an open admission policy too. And if you was slick enough, you could even register your pit-bull and he could be a freshman for a semester. The perfect place for a "non-traditional" brother like me.

If I ever thought high school was full of meaningless, pointless bullshit that nobody would ever use in life, I was shocked at college. Stuff like World Literature, World Civilization, and here's a good one, Intro to muthafuckin' Logic! I mean, cain't nobody teach you how to be logical. Either you stupid, or you ain't! And if you are, classes damn sure won't help. And if I ever need to know the literature of some foreign country, I'll read it in the plane on the way over there. Now, I'm supposed to take this seriously, right? Some of it was so boring, you'd be listening to a lecture one minute, then you'd just pass the fuck out! Like somebody had farted sleeping gas or something. Slob be drooling all on the desk. Strangers hafta wake you up. It was embarrassing. But at least it was keeping me off the streets. And I had to admit that this was way better than living at home. The part I liked best was that you were exposed to so much: concerts, plays, exhibits, lectures. I got to see Jesse Jackson, Ray Charles, Nikki Giovanni, Wynton Marsalis, Gil Scott-Herron you name it. All I had to do was walk across campus. And boy, more honeys than you could shake your dick at.

What got me over in class was that I'm a good reader. If you could get thru 256 *Marvel* Comics, you's a fairly literate dude. I can't write worth a goddamn, though. I can do letters and little essays, but not too much over three pages. My thoughts just won't stay still that long. I could keep up enough to get C's and occasional B's. And since all these other dorky chumps were passing every semester, I knew I could hang for a little while at least.

In my sophomore year I signed up for a class in *Play Production,* just for the sheer hell of it. Enough with all this egg-head stuff—let's have some fun. Hell, I been an actor all my life. Been acting like a college student for a whole year now. Besides, I knew that I could *play the moment,* play it for all it was worth. When me and my young brother used to play make-believe as kids, I could pretend with so much emotion and conviction, I'd have Tim laughing, crying and pissin' all over hisself. Would just fuck him up. So yeah, let's try some Play Production. Well, that's when I met Mark Berens.

2

Mark

How did I end up in Dover, Delaware? Well, the Air Force brought me here. I know Woody's probably told you already how I'm this know-nothing, spoiled, pitiful whiteboy, right? Well, Woodrow is prone to exaggeration, if you can't tell that already. He's partially right. I am a veteran and so was my father. But I see that as an advantage. I got to see quite a bit in the Force. Been to the Philippines, Germany, Alaska, and all over the United States.

Besides, my motivations for enlisting were, how shall we say, *unconventional?* I guess you could say I have this *thing* about authority. I don't know what it is. It's just that misused power infuriates me. Maybe it's because I've seen so much of it in the military. Maybe it's because my father always had this little regimen mapped out for my brother and me. Greg could always figure out how to please Dad. He was the golden child of the family, and Dad wanted me to emulate Gregg. But I'll be damned because, they're fakes; the both of them. When I got into my teens, me and Dad fought about one thing after another, all the time. For a while there, I was hell-bent on defying every single rule anyone had ever given me. It got so bad that the MP's on base knew Dad's phone number and duty roster by heart. Finally, Dad had enough. Told me that he couldn't take the dishonor any longer. Either I would enlist in the Air Force and try to make something of myself, or I'd have to leave his house. That next weekend he helped me put my bags on the plane to Lackland Air Force Base.

The military did nothing to domesticate me. If anything, it had the opposite effect. Man, we did more drugs, had more sex than I ever did at home. I used to let my fingernail grow out so I could use it as a coke-spoon. Back then, there was more acid available than coke. One day my CO asked me had I been painting my nails because my pinky was purple. I couldn't tell him that it was from all the purple micro-dot I had crushed up and snorted, so I told him it was mimeograph ink. With all the girls sneaking in, the barracks were busier than a Holiday Inn during a hooker's convention. Plus, Staff Sergeant Steve Hemmig and Airman Don Reed shared more than just a room together, if you get my drift. Everybody knew, but nobody cared. And all this was happening right on base.

By the time I finished my tour, I had been transferred to Dover, and all I wanted was a little peace and stability. This disciplined military life was just too fast lane for me. So when I got discharged, I rented a little trailer in the woods. See, if I enrolled in college full-time, my veterans benefits would pay more than I could make on minimum wage. So, I went to DelState as a professional student.

I've always had an easy time in school. Too easy. Maybe that was the problem. I'm a voracious reader and history buff. Reading has always been a way to escape for me, a way to cope. So, whatever the subject, I was usually ahead of the rest of the class. Made me restless and bored in high school. College was more bearable because at least they treated you like an adult. But whoever designed the curriculum missed the whole point if you ask me. Seems like they went out of their way to make it as excruciating as possible.

Case in point: If you want to introduce new readers to literature, why start with the museum pieces? Why not start with something enjoyable to read like Hemingway, or Richard Wright, even Steven King? But no. That would make the whole process too pleasurable, wouldn't it?

Another thing that I found hard to take, some of the History Department's faculty didn't know much more than I did. A couple of professors were as scholarly as they come. But there were a few whose knowledge of European and American history in particular was weak. And these guys were doctors? It was very difficult for me to take a grade from some guy who couldn't answer questions as well as I could.

And then there was this *black college* thing.

It was common knowledge on base that DelState was a *black college,* whatever that was supposed to mean. I overheard a couple of airmen, whose necks were of the redder persuasion, refer to it as "Watermelon U" and "grade 13?" But what did I care? As long as I could get my VA benefits, fine. And being in the military, I was brought up around minorities; no problem. Oh, but things are a little different at a *black college.*

Well first, all the buildings have historic African-American names like *Harriet Tubman Residence Hall,* and *Martin Luther King Jr. Student Center.* Cute, right? But the biggest difference is the attitude on campus. There seems to be this fear among black people. There's this great insecurity that anything they've gained can be arbitrarily taken away from them. At least that's how I see it. So, whatever happens, race is always a factor.

Now, I understand how centuries of abuse makes you like that. I mean, I've read Malcolm X and Frederick Douglass. But that attitude keeps unsuspecting whiteboys like me in a constant state of confusion and frustration. So much so, that you want to give up after a while and quit trying to associate. For example, I was told never to use the word "nigger," but Woody uses it around me all the time, some times with affection even. But let the word slip from my lips. You'd think I was the spawn of Hitler the way he would carry on. So what do I use this year, Colored, Negro, Black? African-American?

Then, Woody can call me anything he wants, and it's supposed to be okay. Here's my updated list: whitey, whiteboy, stupid whiteboy, skanky whiteboy, pecka-wood, blue-eyed devil (or "devil" for short), the great Satan, white trash, po' white trash, Euro-trash, redneck, hunkie, buckra, beast, leper…need I go on? And you'll go out of your way to be friendly and helpful, and it'll be construed as a racist hostile take-over.

Another case in point: A group of us commuters were sitting around the lounge one day trying to car pool and arrange rides for people. We came up with the idea of organizing a Commuter's Club. Stupid us. We thought this would be a great service for the school. We selected a president, vice president and officers. Well, when the student government got wind of our idea, you wouldn't believe what happened.

They called a protest demonstration, mind you—not a meeting. Marched over to the commuter lounge 100 strong (There were only eight members in the club, for god's sake!), and demanded that this racist organization be disbanded. It was something out of the 60's. The student government president must've thought he was Martin Luther King or somebody, because he had the act down pat. He was ready to go on the road with it. He would take that self-important stance, roll his eyes up to heaven, and then preach to you the way Jesse Jackson does.

Well, I was dumbfounded. Race had never been mentioned until now. Never mind the fact that the vice president and five of the eight members were all black. It was I, the blue-eyed devil who was the president, and we were coming to re-enslave their children. Hey, fuck this noise! I've got a car! So, I put my rosy pink ass in it, and drove off. They could figure out how to get to class on their own.

That's not to say that every moment at DelState was a replay of *Birth of a Nation*, but I'll tell you things could get tense. The Theater Department was different though. It's something about putting on a character that's like putting on a costume. You have to strip bare first, before you can wear either one very well. When we were working on the shows, the racial tensions weren't so pronounced. Theater is one of those activities, like sports and religion, where you can transcend your race and gender. And that's where I first met Woodrow Tyler, back stage at the Humanities Theater, auditioning for a part in the musical *Hair*.

3

The Audition

Hair? A rock-musical? And I could get three credits for singing and dancing 'round a stage? Yo, I'm down. Where can I sign up? I found everything I needed to know on the bulletin board in the Theater Department. So, I shows up back stage, like ten minutes late. There's this hallway right off the stage where I guess everybody was warming up. These folk looked like they just escaped from Ringling Brothers or some damn where. Homeboy was over in the corner doing jumping-jacks. Another brother was lying flat on his back talking to the ceiling. Whitegirl was doing splits on the floor, and girlfriend was squatting next to the wall barking like a dog. I musta got the wrong door, that's it. As I start to leave, I check out this whiteboy sitting in a chair near the stage door. He's got a cigarette and a can of coke in on hand, and a clip board with an open paperback in the other. Maybe this is the dude I needs to speak to. I walk over, throws on my white voice and say, "'Scuse me, but is this where they're auditioning for the play?"

"Yes, you got the right place," he says kinda snooty. "But first, Ms. Raleigh wants you to fill out this form," and he hands me this sheet wanting to know my name, room number and schedule.

"You got a pencil or something?"

"Sure I do," and he hands me this pencil from a bundle he has under his chair. He's got this look on his face like he just knew I was gonna ask him for one. "Don 't forget to fill out the back, and uh...Ms. Raleigh wants me to ask everybody to try to be on time, next time. Okay?"

"Yeah, right," I say. See there? I don't like this already. Fuck a Ms. Raleigh. She don't know me. That's what I want to say. But instead I squat down next to the barking woman and fill out this form.

When I hand it back to him he says, "Ms. Raleigh does group auditions. She's got one in there already, and she'll be back for the rest of you guys later. What part are you auditioning for?"

"I don't know. I'm not that familiar with the show. What parts are available?"

"Well, the lead characters, the chorus, or you can be on the tech-crew like me."

"Oh, you on the crew?" The way he was acting, I woulda thought he wrote the damn show.

"Yeah, I took the class for credit last semester and liked it so much that I came back."

"Well, what part did you play last semester?"

"I worked tech last semester too. Look, I'm no actor. I'd mostly like to get into directing and writing?" With this last comment his mug broke, and he cracked a little smile.

"What part would you suggest?" I asked him.

"You might as well go for one of the leads. You got as good a chance as anybody else."

Of course he was right. Then I kinda whispered, "What's up with everybody here; did I miss something?"

"No, they've just had Ms. Raleigh before, and they know the kind of exercises she does. Don't worry. She'll show you what to do when you get in there."

'Well, wish me luck."

"Good luck, uh…Woodrow Tyler," he said as he looked at the info sheet. "But, I don't think you'll need it."

"Well, what's yo' name?"

"I'm Mark. Mark Berens," and before I could shake his hand the door swung open and about ten people came out.

Then I heard somebody say: "Mark, send the second group in please. Are they ready?

"Okay, you guys. You 're on."

Mark herded us thru the door. The theater was empty except for three people around a small table about three rows back. Then this white babe steps up and starts to talk to the eight of us on stage. She's a healthy white woman, kinda chunky with nice tits. And she sounds like she might be from overseas 'cause she's got some kinda accent. On the real tip, I suspect that she's just some lower Delaware babe who's been to New York one too many times.

"Mark, do you have the vitae on these young thespians?"

He gets with them at the table, and they huddle like they in the Rose Bowl or something. I'm thinking, what's a *vitae*, and who is she calling a *thespian*?"

"Good evening, ladies and gentleman. I am Ms. Jane Raleigh, director of the show and instructor for Play Production. First we want to do some stretching and relaxing exercises. Next, we'll do some improvs together, then I want to see you perform individually. I ask that you play along with me in some of these exercises. They might seem strange at first, but I guarantee that if you participate in full, it's the best way for me to see your talents. Any questions? Let's begin."

I've never been to an audition before, but this babe had us doing some of the strangest stuff. I couldn't tell if this was theater, or physical therapy. First, she had us get in a circle. Then we reached out to massage the neck of the person directly in front of us. We turned around and did the same to the one behind us. I didn't know what this had to do with acting, but it did feel good.

Next, we laid on our backs and did breathing exercises. Nothin' new here. I been breathing for years. After that, we stood and touched our toes and had to exhale and inhale when she said.

"Come on now, thespians." I can hear her now. "Stretch and undulate, stretch and undulate. Mr. Tyler, you're not undulating properly."

I'm thinking, Yeah baby, I got yo' undulation. But I say, "What you talkin' about *undulate?*"

"Just bend your knees and flex your back as you stand up. This keeps your creative energy from blocking." Okay, so I undulates my ass off."That's it," she says. "Now you're getting it. Now, assume a position from the undulation and create a character from it."

"Do what, now?"

"Take that energy, and create a character from it. And remember to vocalize, like this." She bends over, touches her toes, and all the while she's moaning and carrying on. Oh, excuse me—she's *vocalizing*. She don't straighten up but stops about half way with her flat little butt sticking out and her back humped over. She walks over to me and starts babbling in this cartoon voice. "Hello, young man. I'm the widow of Abington, and...blahsay, blahsay, blahsay." She goes to the others and runs this on them too. And then she leaves the stage like she did something.

Now, I'm really confused 'cause I don't feel no creative energy flowing no goddamn where. Everybody else acts like they know what she's talking about, and they start to undulate too! What characters are these? Who is the Widow of Abington, and what the hell she got to do with anything? So, I don't bug out; I just chill. If undulation is what she wants, that's what she'll get.

So, I bend over and vocalize, and I come up as Slim Weston, the numbers runner from my neighborhood. It's an impression I've done a hundred times, but nobody here has ever seen it. I cop this *gangsta lean*, hook my hand behind my thigh walkin' like a pimp, and start talking in this Mickey Mouse version of Slim. Well, Ms. Raleigh, Mark and the rest of 'em around the table come outta their little huddle and starts staring at me. Oh, they likes this, huh? I really get into it then. I pimp across stage and get up in everybody's face, and they start doing characters right back at me.

By this time, Ms. Raleigh is thumbing through papers, writing down notes. Man, they eatin' this up. All the while I'm thinking, y'all ain't seen nothing yet.

Next, she wants to see us individually, so she gives us these little scenarios to do. She told whitegirl to walk in from the side of the stage and speak to one of us like she's angry, except she wants her to use the words from *Mary had a Little Lamb*. Whitegirl looks more confused than angry.

"Mr. Putnam and Mr. Mack," she says to two of the guys. "I want you to face each other as in a confrontation. Mr. Putnam, you're requesting. Mr. Mack, you're denying. And the only words I want you to use are 'yes' and 'no?'" They begin, and before you know it, they're up in each other faces like they gonna pimp-slap each other. Just like two dudes. She breaks in, "No, guys. What you're showing is anger. I want to see request and denial, not anger. Do you understand the difference?" They try again, but this time it's more laid back. "Very good," she says and starts writing in that notebook again. Next it's my turn.

"Mr. Tyler, I want you to pantomime the actions of potting a plant, a big plant. And the emotion I'm looking for is exasperation. You're fed up with this whole activity, and I want you to use the words from…the *Pledge of Allegiance.*"

"You want me to do a character?" I ask her.

"Why, yes. That would be nice," she says kinda surprised. Then she adds, "Could you do a female character?" And she shoots me this sly smile.

Oh, this 'spose to fuck me up or something? So, I do the impression of Miss Josephine from my block. I don't come off all mean and sissified, cause I know that's what they expectin'. I pretend the tree is too big for the pot, and one of the branches hits me in the eye. I carelessly throw dirt all over the place, and I use my voice rather than prance around all limp wristed. Before I can finish, everybody just bust out laughing.

Ms. Raleigh says, "That's fine, Mr. Tyler, thank you. And I want to thank all of you for auditioning. Call-backs will be posted on the bulletin board by the end of the week, and I'll see you all in class on Tuesday."

That's it? We all leave the stage. I look back at the table where Mark Berens is standing, and he shoots me a smile and a thumbs up.

4

The Cast

At the audition, I had wished Woody good luck even though I knew he probably wouldn't need it because last year, when we'd done the play, we had problems just casting the darn thing. Like me, the usual theater clique would turn out for any chance to work on a show, but when I saw some new blood auditioning, I knew that if he wasn't crippled, lame or mute that he was a cinch for a part. At worst, we could install him in the light booth or on the tech crew. As it turned out, Woody was an exceptional actor. Easily the best I'd seen at DelState.

What impressed me the most was his presence. When Woodrow mounted the stage, he filled up the whole auditorium. He wasn't physically big, but there was a smoldering intensity about him. He had huge expressive eyes, quick, strong movements, and it was hard to take your eyes off him. As it turned out, Ms. Raleigh cast him as Claude, the lead character. No one was concerned whether he could sing because with presence like that, he could certainly sell the song even if he couldn't sing it.

Hair was the perfect show for a college like DelState. Most of the students had never seen a stage play before, so doing one of the *classics* from Shakespeare or Tennessee Williams would've been kind of silly. And because of the loose structure of the play, concerns like race, gender, acting and singing ability weren't as much of a problem. I mean, can you imagine Woody doing Othello? No, let's not.

Theater attracts the oddest assortment of people, everybody trying to working out some fantasy...or some deep pain maybe? Among the cast was Dessa Everett, a mousy student who needed some stage experience to help her ascend to the ranks of prima ballerina. She was in the chorus, mostly as human wallpaper, but she helped Ms. Raleigh with the blocking and the dance steps. Pam Brock and Tina Peich were two tom-boy types. They were lots of fun, and quick with some comic relief whenever things got tense. They helped build the set, and I swear to god they could handle a hammer and saw better than any five men I've ever seen.

Jodi Ewing was a fair-skinned redhead who, after five minutes at the beach would've burst into flames. Sunblock #457 wouldn't even help. She had a ripe, well-fed, curvy figure that was just bursting at the seams—much like her sex drive. She seemed hell-bent on screwing everything she could: male, female, black, white, vegetable, mineral—it didn't seem to matter. Bill Putnam was a History major with a face like Howdy Doody and a mushy-mouthed voice to match. This guy was so anal retentive, I'm sure he could've created blue diamonds with his sphincter. He was always the butt of jokes (no pun), and god knows what trip he was on. Our Pillsbury dough boy was Harry Woznicki. I found out later that he was the oldest member of the cast, but there was something disturbingly boyish about him. He was obviously a grown man, but still owned Micky Mouse towels and *Archie* comic books. One time, we went to McDonald's and this guy actually ordered a Happy Meal! I'm serious.

Neicy Dixon was rough edged black woman who would take no crap from anyone. But beneath that hard exterior she had a heart as big as her bust line. She wore her hair short and reminded me of Nell Carter, the actress from TV. But she could really blow you away with her singing. She'd already made a reputation for herself on campus soloing in the gospel choir, and she could take over a stage damn near as well as Woody could. But Neicy's performance was crass and gaudy. You had to always tune her down a notch. And please, don't get this woman angry. I saw her almost come to blows with a guy on campus, and had they fought, I bet money she would've kicked his ass!

I'd known Tamara Lawrence from last semester. She was a luscious, dark chocolate popsicle with a taut, lean body atop two long shapely legs. Her skin was clear and smooth like a Hershey bar, her lips full and plum colored. She was elegant and aloof, with a sultry, smoky voice, an honest-to-god singer. But the most interesting of all the black girls was Karen Malone.

Karen was attractive enough, nice face and figure, but she was light-skinned, a *redbone* as I heard one of the fellows say. She had brown hair and light brown eyes. What fascinated me was how the other black guys in the cast fell all over themselves for her. Now, I thought that Tamara would've been their favorite. After all, she was gorgeous. Reminded me of Nefertiti from the Egyptian drawings. But no, the brothers preferred Karen. I realized then, that this *black pride* thing only went so far. This was a constant source of irritation to Neicy. And Tamara tried to pretend it didn't bother her, but I could tell that it did. So much for *black power,* guys.

And speaking of the black guys—let's talk about them. Woodrow seemed almost refined compared to some of them. At least you could calm him down enough to hold an intelligent conversation. They all walked around with chips on their shoulders, ready to find the worst in every situation. I couldn't figure out why they were so angry, so loud, and so very full of themselves. But I would find out plenty about that later.

This one guy was nicknamed *Swine,* and to this day I can't remember what his real name was. Now personally, I'd never accept a name like that, but he wore it with pride. And I guess when you looked at him you could understand why. He was short, fat and had the face and disposition of a...well, of a hog. Somebody tell me, what the hell was a man named *Swine* doing in a stage play? Then there was Donnell Robinson who had obviously watched too many reruns of *Lady Sings the Blues* because he had a Billy Dee Williams complex, complete

11

with greasy hair, soft prissy speech, and a different outfit for every day of the week. I wasn't that crazy about working with him because he made everything so damn difficult. I think he was just an attention freak, and being contrary and difficult all the time got him more attention.

Jerome Mitchell was second-string linebacker on the football squad. He was six feet five or so and built like a gladiator. And he acted like one too. Jerome couldn't just disagree with you. Any conflict had to be an all out war to him, so I didn't have much to say to him either.

As I said before, the race factor wasn't as pronounced here as it was everywhere else on campus, but you could feel it just the same. At least I could. The black guys always seemed to have something going on among themselves. Sometimes they would burst out laughing, slapping five to each other. Neither Woznicki, Putnam nor myself would ever understand who or what the joke had been about. Other times, I would walk in the dressing room where they were hanging out, and when they saw me, everything suddenly got quiet. Ms. Raleigh deserved some kind of United Nations award for just keeping everything together.

For example, once when Dessa was helping with the choreography, Neicy spoke up and said, "Ms. Raleigh, we can't move like that. That's the way white people move, all stuck-up and tight butt and everything."

Of course, the black guys broke into laughter and a hearty round of hand slapping.

"I'm hep," said Swine. "Can't we do some dance steps that ain't so corny? Something a little more funky?"

"There are no such things as *black* movements and *white* movements," Bill Putnam explained.

"Man, if we do some ol' tippy toe shit like that, I guarantee you they'll laugh us off the stage," returned Donnell Robinson.

"Well, I'm open for suggestions," Ms. Raleigh said. "Show me a step that you would feel more comfortable doing."

"I got one," Woody said. Why don't we do something like uh...the New York Hustle where you go, step two three four, turn two three four, and back two three four," he demonstrated.

Bill Putnam complained, "Oh god, now we're on *Soul Train*."

"Well, it looks better than them ballet steps," Swine said. "That stuff makes my feet hurt..."

"Let's try this," Ms. Raleigh negotiated. "We can start with Woodrow's move, put in Dessa's crossover step next, then finish up with the second half of Woodrow's sequence. How's that?" Silence. Then mumbling approval.

And that's how the choreography, the blocking and the directing got done. Every time Ms. Raleigh made a suggestion or criticism, she had to prove that it wasn't somehow racist. I don't know how she handled it myself.

Oddly enough, that's when me and Woody started to get close. For all his black unity and pride, whenever Woody needed help with his performance he always turned to me. One day after rehearsal, Ms. Raleigh had just chewed him out for not knowing the lyrics to the song *I Got Life.* There was this part where he had to list about twelve or thirteen body parts, and he had been screwing it up all week. I pulled him to the side.

"You keep messing up on that part of the song, Woody. What's wrong?"

"I don't know. I get to saying, 'I got my hands, I got my arms, I got my this, I got my that,' and I forget where I am."

"Can I make a suggestion that might help you out?"

"Damn skippy!"

"Just forget the way the parts appear in the song and list them in a way that makes sense for you."

"Won't that throw everybody off?"

"Not at all. The band doesn't care what the lyrics are as long as you end up on the beat with them. The audience won't know because they have no idea what the lyrics are in the first place. Just start with your head and work your way down. You know, 'I got my hair, I got my head, I got my eyes, I got my nose,' and so forth until you've listed enough to finish the song."

"Damn, that's logical as hell. And it's so much easier than tryin' to learn it the other way?" He looked at me surprised, like he had never really seen me before.

"How come you could make a suggestion like that, and Ms. Raleigh can't?"

"Well, Ms. Raleigh's got a lot on her mind right now. Plus, like I told you at audition, I've got a director's eye, which is why I'd rather help out behind the scenes and not on stage. I make a much better director. Well, assistant director"

"Let me ask you something else. In that one scene I've got with Putnam. The way he has to turn, I can't understand a word he's saying. He throws me off so much that I miss my cue."

"I know. Bill's rhythm is way off."

"Yeah, just like a whiteboy," Woody said and we both laughed.

"If you're depending on him for your cues, you going to mess up every time. Don't even listen to him. When he stops; that's your cue. And if he doesn't, then listen for the music. When the band plays, start singing regardless of what Bill is doing."

"Dig it. If he won't give me my cue, I'll just hafta take it."

"Yeah, just like a black man," I said and we both laughed even harder.

"Tell me Mark, how did you learn so much about directing and plays and stuff?"

"I don't know, Woody. It's just something I got interested in, and what you're interested in, you usually get better at. I could ask you the same question. How did you learn so much about acting and performing?

13

"I'm not sure that I know that much about acting."
"Well, I'm not sure about directing either."
"Well, look I got a test tomorrow. I'll check you out later."

5

Rehearsals

I really dug rehearsals. That feeling of community surprised me sometimes. Man, there was this whole gang of people waiting on us, making us costumes, and building us sets. There was this unity between us. We helped each other study and write papers. You almost had to, just to even have rehearsals. And you couldn't hide much when you were rehearsing. With your feelings out in the open like that, you started to realize things about yourself.

For example, I realized early on that I wanted to get busy with Dessa Everett, the ballet babe. Straight up! I mean, any woman who could do splits and turn her body in them kinda positions had to be a freak. Plus the fact that she was white— I ain't go'n lie. I never stroked a white girl before, and I was curious about what it felt like. I didn't want to marry her or nothing stupid like that. I would just like to take her out, fuck her tough, and that woulda been the end of it. You could just feel the tension sometimes. Neicy Dixon didn't like it one bit neither, but to hell with her. I can't help it if she ain't gettin' no play.

To be honest, I coulda screwed every babe in the cast. I'm an equal opportunity muthafucka like that. But Jodi Ewing was just too slutty, Pam and Tina were probably screwing each other, and with Swine, Donnell and Jerome hawkin' Karen so tough, I didn't feel like waiting in line. But I'll tell ya, the one who coulda sent me through some serious changes was Tamara Lawrence. That babe was bad! Not only did she have that strong, wiry body, but she was so damn slick and cool. None of the shit that bothered the rest of us seemed to affect her. She'd laugh it off. And I wanted to break through that cool, cause I knew there was a fire on the other side, but she wouldn't have nothin' to do with me. I cracked on her a couple of times, but she played me off as cool as any dude.

"Well, Woodrow. I have to admit that you are sexy?" she told me. "But I know the kind of guy you are. Better yet, I know the kind of woman I am. It would be hot as hell, but we'd end up hating each other in the long run. Either that or we'd be so wrapped up with each other that it would feel like hate. So, let's not even go there, okay?" Of course that just made me want her more.

Of the two whiteboys, I could tolerate Harry Woznicki. He didn't start no shit, and he laughed at my jokes, so there was no problem. But Bill Putnam? I wanted to blast him in his mug. Just once, for the satisfaction. He was a squirmy, nervous little muthafucka. He couldn't just chill out like normal folk, always had to be fixing this and re-arranging that. And if things didn't go the way he thought, you could see him start twitchin' and shit. We'd all be sitting around back stage or in the dressing room and Putnam would start cleaning up, sweeping the floor! Just like some damn woman. If you ask me, it was that blonde hair and them blue eyes. Had that Euro-mania. Probably woulda tried to colonize the dorms if nobody was looking.

Now, Mark was a cool whiteboy, but he had a way of popping in on me at the wrong time, and then would feel all hurt when I ignored his ass. Once, me, Jerome, Swine and Donnell were in the dressing room about to go run some ball, and in walks Mark. Sorry, Mark. But you don't come up on a bunch of brothers who are in full *nigga-mode* and expect *We are the World*.

This was Swine, "Aw boy, you can't play no ball. I'll drive yo' ass like power steering. You ain't got no jumper, and if you do come in the paint, I'll send that weak shit back to Jersey where you found it."

Jerome added his two cents, "Yeah, you can talk shit if you want to, but ask Woody what happened the last time you tried that okey-dokey, 'Bama bullshit. You found your fat ass gettin' up off the floor, didn't you?"

"That's cause you play like one of them Camden criminals," Swine complained to me and Donnell. "Man, I put this funky move on him, faked the nigga out his drawers, and he got so mad he lowbridged me!"

"Damn man, that's some low rent shit," me and Donnell agreed. "If you gonna mug him like that, Jerome, you might as well take his wallet," and we bust out laughing.

"Yo, Donnell. You still beggin' what's-her-face for some pussy? Ain't you stroked that young girl yet?" said Jerome. I seent your ass hawkin' that girl the other day, beggin' like Barry White...'Oh, please baby, baby. Just let me listen to it.' I bet you done tasted the puss too, haven't you?"

"Aw, man. Don't tell me you eatin' at the *"Y"* like some whiteboy? Not me," bragged Swine. "When I go at it, my tongue sits on the bench, and my dick starts. And so far, dick is still in the game?"

That's when I had to interrupt, "Wait a minute, I know I done had more pussy than both of y'all times two, and I'll eat, lick, sing, dance...whatever it takes to get the job done, junior."

"Tell 'em 'bout that shit, Woody," Donnell agreed and he slapped me five.

"And if you ain't takin' care of business, I bet I can pull your woman any day. Jerome, who you goin' with now?"

"Well..uh..."

"Just like I thought. Talking all this shit and spending your nights with them hard-leg niggas on the football team. You need to quit."

Now, in the middle of all this, who walks in but Mark Berens.

"Hey, fellas. What's up? Did you see next week's rehearsal schedule?"

"Yeah, yeah, yeah..." Donnell said. Swine and Jerome didn't say nothin'.

"We checked it out already, Mark." I tried to rescue his ass. "What's up with you?"

"Well, me, Pam and Tina are going over to the Finish Line for a couple of beers. You guys want to go over there and close the place down again?"

16

Naw, we gonna run some ball," said Swine. "You play any basketball, Mark?"

"Yeah, I play a little, but I didn't bring my sneakers with me."

"That's too bad, cause I woulda enjoyed doggin' you out."

"Yeah, I bet you would," Mark said and then reached in his bag and handed me a book. "Oh, Woody. Here's that book I was telling you about, *The Method Actor* by Stanislavski. You might be able to use some of the techniques." I looked at the book, then I looked at the fellas. The fellas looked at me, and then they looked at Mark.

"Thanks, man. I'll get this back to you in a couple of days."

"Take your time." Then he gathered up his shit and walked out. You know, like he suddenly remembered he had somethin' urgent to do.

"What's up with you and the whiteboy," Jerome couldn't wait to ask. "Y'all gettin' real tight. Y'all be up under each other at rehearsal and shit. I don't know?"

"You don't hafta worry, Jerome," I said. "You still my main bitch and there's plenty of this left for you," and I grabbed my dick. Swine and Donnell just fell out.

"Ooooh! Damn!"

Needless to say, nobody asked me about Mark Berens again.

That's how I had to deal with 'em. You can't blame Mark, though. How could he know? He's white. Hangin' out with me musta been a first class education for his ass. Because I told him some shit that I know he never thought about before. He didn't know whether I was lying or what. One afternoon, Ms. Raleigh asked Mark to run up to Wilmington to get some supplies. I rode with him, and while we were up there, he wants to treat me at this restaurant he heard about.

"I don't know, Mark. I'd just rather go to Mickey D's and grab a hamburger or something."

"Well, they got burgers here too. Plus we can get some drinks. I'm treating you, so what's the problem?"

"Will it be cool if I'm dressed like this?"

"You're not dressed any differently than I am. C'mon, Woodrow, this is not about how we're dressed. This is about you not wanting to be seen with some whiteboy, isn't it?"

"Naw man, it's just..."

"I'll tell you, Woody, you and the black guys are just too hung up on being black. You guys are more prejudiced than the white people. Everything's about race with you; I mean, how Ms. Raleigh directs you, dancing, singing, everything. Look at you. You haven't even been to this restaurant, and you're convinced that there's a Klan meeting going on inside. Lincoln already freed the slaves. You have a right to go anywhere you want to."

"First of all, Mark, you don't know what the fuck you talkin' about."

"I know what I see, and I see that you make an issue of race when it's not an issue."

"It may not be an issue with you because you's a whiteboy. You can afford to buy into this 'freedom and justice for all' bullshit. I can't. If I forget for one second that I'm just another nigga, that's my ass. Look Mark, racism is routine. That shit happens all day, every day, twenty four-seven. The only reason you don't see it is that you're not around when it's happening. And you probably wouldn't recognize it if you were lookin' at it. Look, we just came out of a supply store right? If I went in there by myself, I woulda been treated completely different."

"Different how, Woody?"

"First of all, the clerk woulda been on me like *Dragnet*, afraid I'd be tryin' to steal something. Second, I would hafta prove that I was actually who I said I was, before he would ever let me walk outta there with these supplies."

"Don't you think maybe it's just you, over-reacting?"

"Maybe some of it is, but most of it ain't."

"I don't know…"

"Well, I do. And you're just gonna hafta take my word for it. Between the two of us, I think I have more experience in being black than you do. I mean, if we were talking about how it feels to conquer somebody and take their country, then I'd hafta take your word for it."

"Cheap shot, Woody."

"You're right. I'm sorry, okay? But you're pissin' me off. You say you don't know, but when I tell you what the deal is, then I'm hallucinatin' and shit."

"How can you possibly know whether a restaurant is racist, when you've never even been in there?"

"I can't know. That's why I gotta assume that it is, until I can find out different. Causes a lot fewer problems that way."

"Well, let's say they are racist. They can't just refuse you, can they?"

"Naw, Mark. They're slicker than that. They can't refuse me outright, but they can ask for five pieces of ID that they know I don't have. They can charge me a ten dollar cover charge that just went into effect the second I walked in. Then if we do sit down, I might hafta deal with some waitress with a bad attitude. Yeah, I guess I could put up with all that. But hell, I just want a hamburger and a soda. I'm not trying to integrate their sorry-ass restaurant. That's why if you don't know beforehand whether it's cool for brothers to be up in there, I'm gonna be nervous about it, okay?"

"Well, it sounds so complicated to me."

"Yeah? Tell me about it. Why do you think niggas so pissed-off all the time? Why we got the highest blood pressure of anybody on the planet? So, it's not about you personally, okay?"

18

After that, Mark backed off. Realized there's a lotta shit happening that he don't know nothin' about. So now when the issue of race pops up, at least he don't roll his eyes, all exasperated like he used to. I know he still don't like it. But hey, the truth hurts, don't it? So, driving back from Wilmington, he's all friendly and apologetic. Wants to understand more about us now. I wanna say, whiteboy please! You just feeling guilty because you realize that you's a prejudiced muthafucka, just like everybody else.

"I read that book you gave me, Mark."

"*The Method Actor.* Really?"

"Don't act so surprised. What, you thought I wouldn't check it out?"

"Well Woody, you don't come across like this driven scholar, y'know?"

"Surprised you, didn't I? I figured if this was important enough for you to give me, it was important enough for me to read."

"So what do you think?"

"I think he's absolutely right. The best way to act is to use the emotions that you've already felt before. It just surprised me that this is such a big realization. What other way would you act? It's the only way I can. And they're conducting experiments about it, writing books and shit. Makes me feel like I been doing something right. Makes me feel, uh…"

"Validated."

"Yeah, validated. Thank you, Mark."

"Working on *Hair* has showed me the same thing."

"The deep part about it, sometimes you dig up experiences that you had forgot about. Forgot about on purpose."

"Like what, Woody?"

"Well…uhhh…I don't know…like…like the way Neicy Dixon acts in that scene we do together reminds me of the way my Moms looked when we was kids. Every Friday night she would get drunk and threaten to kill my Pops. She would wake us up and explain all logical. 'Now, boys. You know I love you, and you know I love your father, but I'm go'n hafta kill him. Yes, honey. Ain't nothing else mommy can do. So, I wanted to tell you boys so you wouldn't be mad at mommy, okay?' Then she would stumble down to the kitchen and boil some water so she could do one of them Al Green, hot-grits-in-the-bathtub chumpies on my Pops. But, she'd fall asleep and either me or Tim would hafta get up, go downstairs, turn off the stove and put the pots back in the cabinet. She'd wake up and swear to god she'd been cookin' something. Then, she'd pour another drink and start all over again. All the while, my Pops ain't even in the house. He's hangin' out all night. Me and Timmie used to take shifts, 'Aw man, it's your turn. I went at one o'clock.' 'Well I went at two thirty.' 'If you go this time, I'll double up next time.' When Neicy does that part, she reminds me of my Moms, big time. And it kinda pushes a button in me. That's why that scene

19

works so well. I betcha, I remind her of somebody too. My Moms could be a crazy bitch sometimes, I'll tell ya."

"Don't feel bad, Woody. Everybody's family fucks 'em up some kinda way. That's what families are for. With me, it was my father and my brother. Greg could do any crazy shit he wanted to me or anybody else, and as long as he apologized, pretended that he was sorry, and went back to playing military, Dad would kiss his ass. They gave him more for fucking up than they ever gave me for not causing a problem in the first place. Then when he'd aggravate and torture me, Dad would say, 'Somebody has to have some sense.' Meaning, it was my fault for being too stupid to figure out a better way to take the abuse. And I'm like you. Something unexpected can just set you off sometimes."

So, with me and Mark Berens cruising over the St. George's Bridge on our way back to Dover, I realized that Jerome was right. There *was* something between me and this whiteboy, this part of our lives that we could talk to each other about, and apparently, only to each other. Can you see me admit some of this to Jerome? Neicy? Timmie? No, I can't neither.

6

The Performance

Sometimes you can get so wrapped up in the details that you forget the big picture. That's how it was with this play. After two months of rehearsals, planning and anticipation, tensions were rising, and everybody had started to get on each other's nerves. And if this play didn't go on pretty soon, we'd all kill each other. So finally and unbelievably, it was opening night, and we had a few surprises for the crowd. I didn't know that the crowd had a few surprises for us too.

To say they were "responsive" is putting it too mildly. There was as much pageantry in the audience as there was on stage. The show was a campus event, a place to see and to be seen, and everybody had been rehearsing. First, there were the fraternity pledges, the Groove Phi Something and the Something Psi Dogs. These guys' costumes were better than ours; they wore sunglasses, berets, combat fatigues (in purple, now), boots and walking canes. They had insignia carved into their hair, and were led around by a Big Brother, who's now treating them like the scum he had been only last year. They didn't just arrive, they made an entrance.

They chanted and stomped a few funky steps with the requisite pelvic thrusts ("Hunh," one time!). Jump up, spin around and stomp some more (two time say, "hunh-hunh!"). Then the other frat would do the same kind of step, only lower and nastier, or they'd march up the aisles with it. They'd primp and pose, someone would call out the pledge's name, and the girls would scream and swoon.

Next, the campus characters made their entrances. One guy showed up wearing a white, silk, three-piece suit. Someone in the crowd barked, "Mack Daddy! Work 'em, brother." Then a couple of guys dressed in African clothes walked in and you heard, "Kahliq the Freak!" and he waved at the crowd. The football squad arrived next. "Jay Tee!" the crowd chanted for a couple of seconds. "Jay Tee, Jay Tee." Students were climbing over seats and parading down the aisles. I wondered if we could ever get them settled down.

My job was basically done at this point. Everything would either come together, or it wouldn't. This was where I could just sit back and enjoy. The band kicked in, and immediately the audience clapped to the bass and the snare, rhythm junkies all of them. The curtain opened to show twelve faces spotlighted in darkness, each cast member singing a line. Some of those faces were at eye level, some suspended in air. The audience was disoriented and enjoyed the effect. "Ooooo Stop!" Someone yelled, "Ha!"

By the time each of the cast had sung their introductions, the lights came up enough to reveal them standing in a maze of painter's scaffolding four levels high. They climbed and sang like kids on a jungle gym. They pointed to the pit, and the spotlight struck a caped figure ascending from below stage (we had sneaked Woody down there about ten minutes before). The figure climbed and climbed until he reached the top of the proscenium, billowing his cape along the way (Ms. Raleigh had found about twenty yards of light muslin in the dressing room and was determined to use it somehow). The crowd cheered at the sheer spectacle of it. Woody stood there in the spotlight like some king. The ham!

The cape fell, and magically slid away into the pit, as Woody joined the ranks of the cast. They made patterns with their bodies on the scaffolding, none of which were quite the ones we had rehearsed though. Then on the third level, Harry Woznicki raised his hand, bellowed for a few bars, and jumped! A voice from the audience screamed, and two men bolted from their seats. But, Woznicki had fallen safely, gymnast-like onto the interlocked arms of the cast members, a stunt I thought we'd never get right, because he'd always freeze up and giggle like a frightened kid. I expected him to revert back to infancy right there, but Woznicki was exhilarated, and in no time, the first song was finished.

"Wood Dee! Wood Dee!" Somebody chanted and the audience cheered.

Backstage, I could tell the cast was shocked at the hearty reception. Putnam and Swine actually slapped five. Neicy hugged Dessa and congratulated her while Tina and Jerome guided each other, hand-in-hand, through the backstage darkness. Well, sir. I guess anything's possible.

I was proud at how the cast rose to the occasion, because the audience was both the kindest and the cruelest I'd ever seen. Bill Putnam had tripped over a couple of lines (surprise!) and they barked at him mercilessly. A voice screamed "Duh, duh...daf all folks." The crowd exploded, and it was the biggest laugh of the night. Putnam just crumbled and never quite regained the audience's respect. There was something phony about him, and they could just smell it. After that, whenever he had lines, someone (everyone) would just yell, "Duh, duh, duh..." Putnam would drop his lines again, and everybody would crack-up again. They had written their own show!

Then on the other hand, Pam sang *How Can People*, and she was singing her little heart out. She lost her place and had to start over, but between takes some matronly voice spoke up, "Honey, that's all right. You just take your time and sang that song." Someone else actually said, "Ay Man!" like they were in church. Pam began again, and when she finished, she got one of the night's biggest ovations.

This crowd was determined to have a good time. If anything was lacking, they quickly filled in the blanks. It was fresh and raw and we loved it. Neicy Dixon was the biggest moon-faced, Pearl Bailey impersonator you ever saw. Whenever the pacing lagged, she'd mug to the audience or roll her eyes, anything to get a laugh. When the white girls sang *Black Boys*, the dance steps didn't seem as sultry as we had rehearsed. It came out frumpy and comical. Jodi Everett's round body was as out of control as her hormones. She thrusted and gyrated like Mae West on steroids. The audience didn't care. Just give 'em a show.

Woody's performance was amazing. The band cued up for *I Got Life* and he was off like a down hill skiier on the brink of disaster. He hadn't learned to breathe properly, and couldn't keep a regular pace. He leapt and cartwheeled across stage, keeping the beat, and singing on key most of the time. He was into serious oxygen deprivation, and we all watched transfixed to see if he would finish the song or crash pitifully into the pit; either one would be a glorious spectacle. Somehow he finished, and he was just as exhilarated as Woznicki had been.

The cast was seeing the show come together for the first time. Even during those horrible tech rehearsals, we never saw that the show had a flow to it, a rhythm and movement. Probably not the one the authors intended, but one nonetheless.

Ms. Raleigh had even more surprises for the second act. The house lights went down and the band began, the audience impatient for the curtain to open. Suddenly from all around, flashlight beams searched the house, and the cast members walked through the audience to the stage singing, *Oh Great God of Power*. The crowd was wrecked. They reacted with various Ooooo's and Ahhhh's and cheers.

During *Walking in Space* the cast attached white elastic bands to their feet and hands. When the blacklights, positioned at various points on the scaffolding, were switched on, everybody looked like cosmic marionettes dancing and dangling in the florescent light. And when *What a Piece of Work is Man* was sung, we all saw two angels flown in from the loft dressed in billowing white robes (cameo appearances from Mr. Hasten and Miss Phipps, two English teachers adorned in bed sheets). For the finale, the entire cast gathered for the curtain call and tableau, except for the character played by Woodrow. His conspicuous absence gave the ending the right element of pathos and drama. The audience went crazy as the final curtain came down. They cheered and stomped their feet and some sang the show tunes they could remember. Well, the cast was just ecstatic. You couldn't tell them they weren't on Broadway. The experience couldn't have been any richer even if they had been. And for the actors who weren't hooked on theater before, they certainly would be addicted now.

7

The Cast Party

The show ran for three days, Thursday, Friday and Saturday. And for that entire week I didn't give a damn about nothin'. When you could be the star on campus, or go to class, which one would you choose? Yeah, that's the one I chose too. Man, after Friday's show, I was treated like a movie star. Brothers would stop me on campus, gimme five and congratulate me on the show. People be wavin' from their dorm windows. Once, I was across the street at Denny's and this old couple, looking like somebody's Moms and Pops, walked over to our table, started sniffin' around us like we celebrities or something. Hell, I thought they were go'n ask us for our autographs. This went on for weeks after the show closed. Man, I certainly likes this! I mean, how could you be expected to study and go to class when all of this was happening? It's a good thing that Ms. Raleigh sent letters to our instructors excusing us from class, or we all woulda screwed up that whole week.

Saturday night was like a reunion because that's when everybody's family and friends showed up. You ain't heard no applause like what you get from yo' Momma and Daddy. The feeling of family got stronger than ever. Not only with the cast, but the band members and the tech crew too. I mean, Dessa wanted me to meet her Moms. I even got to shake hands with Papa Smurf, the name we gave Putnam's father. A sense of sadness set in because we realized that the party was over. No more midnight rehearsals. No more bitchin' and moanin'. No more family!

That's why there was such a funky vibe at the cast party. Most of us knew this would be the last time we would be hangin' out together, so we tried to pack a whole lotta emotion into those final few hours. After we struck the set and cleaned off the stage, Ms. Raleigh held the party in the lobby of the theater. Good move, because it gave the groupies something to do after the show. And if you can't help clean up, don't be tryin' to *bogart* the party. This way we got some of the football crew and fraternity freaks to do most of the work.

The lobby was hooked up. Three long tables with pizza, Kentucky fried, cold-cut platters, two punch bowls, chips, pretzels, the works. Somebody passed around a hat and collected money, went out and bought a keg. We weren't supposed to have liquor on campus, but since everybody was cool about it, it wasn't no problem. There were chairs and couches so you could sit down, and like I said, it was hooked. At first we watched the video tape of the show, giggling and bustin' on people as we stuffed our faces. In no time, the food was gone (if you slow, you blow!), and the faculty and parents started to leave. That's when folk really started to get blasted. Pint bottles appeared, and funny packets of white powder. And if you walked up to the light booth, you woulda swore it was a Rastafarian convention from the smoke up in there.

It's a good thing that the keg went dry and the food ran out, because I don't know what woulda happened after that. I could make some pretty good guesses though. Campus security showed up and told us they had to lock up the building at one o'clock, and we'd hafta leave in a few minutes. The party was so sentimental that nobody was ready to go home. So, we asked Ms. Raleigh could we have an after-party at her crib. She had this nice home with a big-ass basement. Why can't we come over there for a couple of hours? She resisted at first, but we promised her that only the cast and crew would be invited. She saw how hard up we was, so she agreed. Now that's when things really got interesting. Well, all of the cast didn't make it to Ms. Raleigh's. And some who did weren't in the cast. Woznicki didn't show because it was way past his bedtime already.Neicy Dixon had to sing with the gospel choir that next morning. I saw Jodi Everett slink away from the lobby with some redneck, so I knew she wouldn't be there. Jerome couldn't come either. One big surprise was that Ms. Raleigh was hitting on a biker from a motorcycle gang called the *Pagans*. I knew there were some dangerous lookin' whiteboys running the sound equipment, but it tripped me out to see this pseudo-cosmopolitan babe all up under some lower-Delaware, biking dude. But the surprises were just begining.

Pam Brock and Tina Peich showed up, and they had some dude with them. I don't know what the deal was, but I was betting that there was something freaky between them, like he was either their leather master or their sex slave. He was supposed to be with Tina, but you could tell from the way they were acting that something was going on with Pam too. I mean, you can tell when two people been fucking, used to fuck gonna fuck or wants to fuck, just by the way they talk and stand next to each other. I gotta admit though, the thought of these two vamps in bed together made my dick harder than Chinese math.

Donnell and Karen showed up together and you woulda thought they were married the way she was up under him. Obviously, Donnell had won the Redbone Pussy Sweepstakes and beat out Jerome and Swine. Swine rode with Mark and Tamara Lawrence. But he had been at the Rasta convention in the light booth, and was the first in line at the keg too. So he was sloppy-pissy-drunk already. He sat in the corner, half passed out laughing and giggling to hisself. I copped a ride with Putnam, and he was just as nerdy at the party as he'd always been. He wouldn't drink or smoke or nothin', just sat around like a poster boy for Alcoholics Anonymous.

Now, Mark Berens and Tamara Lawrence were just *too chilly* at the party. Oh yeah, they drank and smoked a little herb and were having a good time, but they didn't seem caught up in the party the way everybody else was. Mark stood in the corner while Tamara sat on the couch next to him. They both looked like they knew something the rest of us didn't. But hey, that's the way Tamara always be acting. So, I didn't think nothing about it. Mark was Steven Spielberg or some damn body. Y'know, like he's directing the whole thing.

Dessa Everett showed up alone. She wasn't that drunk, but she was buzzed enough to be all over me. She'd find every opportunity to rub her little tits up against me, or touch me some kinda way. And she wasn't hiding nothing, like she just didn't care anymore. At one point we were sitting around a card table crackin' jokes, and I felt her hand on my leg up under the table. I wasn't sure what to do, but my dick was. It shot straight up. Plus, I was half high anyway. Nobody seemed to mind anymore, like they expected us to just walk over to the corner and screw each other right there on the floor. And what could anybody say now, anyway? Ms. Raleigh was with her skanky whiteboy. Donnell and Karen were holding on to each other like they were stuck together. Pam, Tina and their sex-stud already had their scenario for the night. So, why not a little freaky-deaky with Dessa?

Dessa pretended like she was going upstairs to get some more chairs, or paper plates, or some bullshit like that.

"Woody, could you give me a hand?" she asked me. I looked around the table and everybody was egging me on, you know smiling, winking, tilting their heads. I got up, put my hand in my pocket so my dick wouldn't embarrass the hell out of me, and followed Dessa upstairs like a sheep to the slaughter. She led me into this walk-in closet that Ms. Raleigh had right off the kitchen. She clicked on the light and closed the door behind us. And man, this girl was on me like stank on shit.

"Hold up girl. We can't do nothing in here. Somebody might find us."

"Don't get shy on me now, Woody," she said pressing her body up against me, rubbing my chest and stomach. "You weren't shy all during rehearsal when you were flirting with me. What? You think I didn't notice how you looked at me every time I'd try to dance or something. Everybody knew. And now that we can do something about it, you're scared? I don't believe that for a minute." By this time her hands had found my zipper and she was strokin' my jones through my jeans. My dick was so hard it was aching. She started to nibble at my neck, and I felt her hand grab my naked dick. Then suddenly she jumped back, smiled all wicked and said, "Well, Woody. What are you going to do?"

I knew there was no turning back now, and she knew it too. So, I stepped to her and ran my hand under her sweat shirt. She wasn't wearing no bra, and I felt-her-up ungodly. Her tits were little, but firm. And her nipples stuck out like pencil erasers. I licked them from up under her shirt, and the fact that I was about to bang out this white girl made me hornier than ever. The difference between her and the sisters wasn't all that great. I mean, a babe's a babe. But there were some little differences that I didn't expect.

The smell was different. How can I describe it? There was a flat, tangy odor about her, and her skin felt funny; not rough, but like she had permanent little goose bumps or something. Her hair was all over the place, all in my face when we kissed. When I ran my hand down her jeans, she had a vise grip on me, pumping and strokin' like a trooper. I wanted to hold back, but she wasn't trying to hear that. So, before I knew it, I shot off right there in the closet. No sex, no romance, just a slutty orgasm. *Ugh!* I felt so…so used!

As we zipped up, and buttoned down, she had this look on her face. "Now, that wasn't so bad was it?" like she had been in charge all the time. She got her stuff together, and bounced downstairs like nothing happened. Then, here I come, all dazed and confused, stumbling down the stairs like a wino.

"Damn, Woody. Are you all right?" Putnam asked.

"I couldn't find no paper plates, but here's some cups." I said all stupid. Good thing I had sense enough to sit my ass down somewhere, until I could get my shit together.

By this time everybody was either into to their own little thing, tired or passed out. People started to leave. First was Dessa (thank god!). Then Mark Berens and Tamara dragged Swine to the car. Pam and Tina kissed and hugged everybody, knowing this was probably the last time they'd see us for a while. Finally, me and Putnam left.

Putnam dropped me off on campus. I knew that I wouldn't be able to sleep, so I got out where I could walk across campus and stretch my legs. I remembered that I left my World Civ book in the dressing room. So, I was gonna check the Humanities building to see if the security guard would let me go in and get it. That's when I saw Mark Berens pull up to the side parking lot, all close to the building. Mark and Tamara Lawrence got out together and stood in the shadows between the car and the building. Mark pulled Tamara to him and kissed her tough on the lips! And I don't mean one of them friendly, little good-by pecks, neither. I mean one of them tongue-packin', tonsil-tastin' chumpies.

I couldn't believe what I was seeing. My mind was struggling so hard to understand these images that I couldn't move for a second. Then, I ducked back so they wouldn't see me. Mark Berens was *the man!* He held her and stroked her on the face with the back of his hand. He whispered something in her ear, and she giggled. They kissed again, and she walked away. Mark got in his car and drove off. I stood there all shocked and confused. Mark Berens and Tamara Lawrence? Was that actually Mark standing there, cool as ice, clocking a babe that's done already rejected *me?* Me! No way, naw, uh-unh! My mind rebelled so that I wouldn't have to accept what that meant. Because, if that was true, then…I don't know whiteboys as well as I thought I did. Plus, I don't know…(damn, do I hafta say it?)…*women* neither.

Then I got pissed. Damn, Mark. Like that? I thought we was boys. You coulda told me. And Tamara? That's some low shit. You can run with some white devil, but you can't get with no brother, huh? Naw, that's all right. Fuck both of y'all then. Days later, I had to finally ask myself, what's wrong with you?

Don't neither one of them owe you a damn thang. They can screw whoever the hell they want. Quit acting like a bitch, Tyler. That's when I knew I could talk to Mark about it.

"That cast party was a trip wasn't it, Mark?"

"That whole week was a blast, Woody, but I'm glad it's over. Leaves a damn nice memory though."

"Yeah, the way we was partying so tough, we had to finish up at Ms. Raleigh's and everything."

"Yeah, that was great too."

"Did y'all make it home all right with Swine? He was kinda fucked up when y'all left."

"No problem. He came-to when that cold air hit 'em."

"So, like…where else did y'all go?"

"I went home. It was going on four in the morning."

"You and Tamara didn't go nowhere?"

"Like where, Woody?"

"I don't know. Driving, maybe parking?"

"What's this, cross-examination?"

"Look, Mark. I accidentally saw you and Tamara when you dropped her off after at the Humanities building after the party."

"Yeah?"

"No. I mean, I *saw* y'all."

"Yeah?"

"Well, I didn't know that you was into sisters, Mark."

"Now you know. So what?"

"Nothing. It's just that I wondered why you didn't mention it to me or something."

"Well frankly, I didn't know you'd be interested. Not to mention that it's none of your business."

"I know it's none of my business, but I thought we was cool like that. You know, me telling you stories about my Moms, ol' Crazy Francine. You telling me about your brother Greg and your Pops."

"Well, Woody. You never tell me about the women you're having affairs with."

"Well, you can tell me."

"And in return, you'd tell me about who you might be sleeping with, right?"

"Of course…"

"Great. At the cast party, what happened when you and Dessa went upstairs?"

"Aw, that? Nothing happened."

"You came down those stairs like something happened."

"I'm telling you, Mark, it was nothing."

"Then nothing happened with me and Tamara either. See, I knew you were bullshitting."

"What I mean is that we didn't have no sex. That's why I say nothing happened."

"Just because you didn't screw her doesn't mean nothing happened."

"You want a blow-by-blow description?"

"No, Woody. I'd just as soon talk about something else. You're the one who came in here begging to talk about our sex life, remember?"

"Okay, okay. Soon as we got up there, she pulled me in that little closet and grabbed my dick. I slobbed her down, she jacked me off, and that's it."

"You didn't get in them panties?"

"Naw, I'm telling you, Mark. We just felt each other up, she grabbed my package, and that was it. Square business. I didn't even get my finger wet."

"That really wasn't nothing."

"I told ya. Okay, you tell me; what's up with you and Tamara?"

"We've just been seeing each other."

"Now, who's bullshitting? You knockin' them boots or what?"

"Okay, Woody. If we start talking about this, I don't wanna hear no racist bullshit. How I'm this Nazi dog, trying to mess over black women. I don't want you bragging to Swine or Donnell about it either. This is strictly between me and you."

"C'mon, Mark. You know me."

"That's why I'm telling you this. It's precisely *because* I know you. Now, I don't want to hear any anger, any blame, and no resentment from you. You hear what I'm saying?"

"Deal!"

"I'm serious, Woody."

"Me too. No really, man. I ain't gonna fuck with you. Swear befo' god. I see now there might be some things I can learn from you, other than Stanislavski."

"What do you want me to tell you? That we're seeing each other? Yes. That we're having sex? Yes. What?"

"How'd y'all get together?"

"I knew her from last semester. We were friends, one thing led to another. You know how things can get."

"So, what do you think about being with a sister? Tamara only likes white guys?"

"See, now you're being racist. Tamara's a good woman. She's got a good heart."

"Damn, man. You sound like you in love or something."

"Maybe. I respect the woman. It's not just about sex, like your little episode with Dessa in the closet."

29

"Aw, man she started it. What was I supposed to do? So, you got a thing about black girls?"

"Damn, Woody."

"What you laughin' at?"

"You think that if a white guy and a black woman get together, it's got to be about sex. It's got to be freaky or dirty, or that she hates black men or something. Yeah, maybe I do have a curiosity about black women—the forbidden fruit and all that, but that's not what keeps you together. First, I knew Tamara as a person, somebody I could be with."

"You know, I cracked on her once and…"

"And you're shocked that a whiteboy like me could have a woman who turned you down. That fucks with you, doesn't it, Woody?"

"Well?"

"Can you blame her? Listen to how you and the fellas were talking that night in the dressing room. What woman wants to be with any man, black or white, who would talk about another woman like that?"

"We wasn't talking about her."

"She made sure you'd never have the chance."

"Well, you's a cool muthafucka, Mark. I didn't suspect nothing. Damn. Whiteboy, running the sisters."

"See? It's not about running the sisters."

"I know, I know. So you in love or what?"

"I don't know."

"Well how do you like it? How is it, with a woman of a different race?"

"I don't know, Woody. You tell me."

"Well, uh…it's different."

"Yeah, *different.* Let's just leave it at different, okay?"

"Cool."

8

After the Party

I didn't know what to tell Woody. I was just as surprised about my relationship with Tamara as he was. I can tell that he's looking at me differently now, like I'm this Don Juan or some sophisticated playboy; either that or some warlock or vampire. Apparently he had confused my shyness for slickness, but I really didn't have any answers for him. Being with Tamara wasn't like any other relationship I've had. There wasn't that usual push-pull you get with women. It was really easy with her, no stress or strain—just friendly! That's why I didn't know whether or not it was love. You're supposed to be stressed-out and bouncing off the walls when you're in love, right?

Tamara didn't want us to be "all up under each other" as she would say. So, it wasn't this heavy emotional thing. Sometimes we would go for days without seeing one another, and that was just fine for both of us. It started out innocently…well, unsuspectingly, and god knows that I wasn't trying to have an affair with a black woman. It never crossed my mind really. But after getting to know Tamara, from last semester, from our being in World Lit together, from the show, from us talking on the phone so much, I started to see that she really is a gorgeous woman. She must've seen the same thing in me too. I'm not Tom Selleck, but I'm no slouch either! I'm 6-2, a little on the lean side, but I can look good when I have to.

After that, the sex part came easy, no surprises, no expectations.

"So what are you going to do, Tamara," I finally asked her, "stay in school or go back home?"

"I don't think I have much of a choice, Mark. Mom's sick and can't get around by herself. With this new job, I'll be making good money. I can finish up at City College, maybe. At least I won't be struggling and trying to make ends meet like I am now. I love college and all, but I'm just tired of scrimping and scraping, especially now that I've got a chance to do better."

"Are you going to be all right?"

"Oh yeah, sure."

"Even about us?"

"Oh, Mark. You so sweet. No honey, I'm fine about it. Are…you…?"

"Well, this is kinda all-of-sudden. But…you're right. If you gotta go, you gotta go. Can't we see each other though?"

"It wouldn't be very easy for you to come see me where we live. So, I think this ought to be it, Mark…a clean break, you know?"

"I can call, can't I?"

"That would only keep us both hanging on."

31

"What's so bad about that?"

"Mark, you're not making this any easier…"

"Am I supposed to be?"

"Look baby, we can't go on sneaking around, seeing each other on the sly. We both deserve more than this. It's better just to quit now."

"You've always been the one who wanted to keep it a secret. You know I don't care."

"That's just it, Mark, you should care."

"Hunh…you're sounding like Woody now. That's other people's problem, Tamara, not ours. You're letting the race thing come between us."

"It's always been between us, Mark. I thought that was obvious. It's just a matter of accepting it. Or for me, not accepting it. Look, I don't know how I would've got by without you. And I'll always love you for it."

"Why do you want to give that up?"

"Because if we take it any farther, it won't stay nice and easy like it is now. The stuff we'd have to go through would ruin it. You'd be treated different, resentments would set in, and we can't have paradise with resentment."

"But…"

"Don't make me fight you, Mark, please. I might not see you again before I go. Can't we at least leave on a good note? Because baby, after all is said and done, I still got to go. There's just no other way around it…"

A couple of weeks after that, she was back in Baltimore managing her cousin's construction company. I wish I could say it didn't hurt, but I missed Tamara; not so much the sex, but the friendship. After all, we were friends first. It pissed me off that she could sacrifice a friendship which could've lasted indefinitely for a romance which only lasted a few months. But that's what usually happens to friendships when sex comes into the picture, isn't it? If the romance doesn't survive, then nothing does. What probably bothered me the most was that I couldn't see it coming. How come she could break it off so suddenly, so completely, and I was the one left hurt and angry…again? No, I wasn't devastated, but it stung like hell for a long time; too long.

After that, I started to get bored with school just like I always do. And when that happens, I start to skip classes. I'd only show up for playwriting class with Mr. Hasten. Now that I'd seen the process, I wanted to do a play myself. I couldn't sit back anymore. It was time for me to try something on my own.

I remember reading somewhere that Shakespeare said, "The plays the thing," but he was mistaken. If you ask me, "The performance is the thing." At DelState, that's what the audience and the cast in *Hair* showed me. A well crafted play is important, don't get me wrong, but an excellent performer can save a badly written show. Nothing makes up for a shitty performance. If an actor is mesmerizing, then it really doesn't matter what he's saying. Ask any cult member that. But if he's a spastic, stuttering, wall-flower trying to act, then even Shakespeare himself can't save your play, mister.

I had developed a taste for simple plays, performed plainly and direct. My favorites were *Our Town, Spoon River Anthology* and *For Colored Girls.* There's a simplicity and grace about them that cuts through the pretense and the clutter (There's that rebellious streak in me again). No sets, simple costumes, a handful of excellent performers, a good story and a little magic. That's all you need, really—that and an audience. I decided that those were the kind of plays I wanted to write.

In Mr. Hasten's playwriting class, we used to do script reading of the one acts we had written, and I was amazed at how much you could tell about a script just by having it read aloud. For one of the first assignments, I collected some of my old poems, distributed the lines among three characters, and had members of the class read it aloud. Well, it worked! I mean it wasn't a play, but it was a good foundation to build from. What I needed was some dialogue and a story line. I also knew this would be the perfect project that Woody could help me with.

I invited Woody to come over on a couple of weekends so we could have a few beers, smoke a joint or two, and put this play together.

"I like your spot, Mark. I didn't know a trailer could be so nice?"

"From the inside you can't tell that you're in a trailer, can you?"

"And you got this nice quiet spot in the woods. This is hooked up. So…how you want to get started on this play you writing?"

"I don't need you to act or anything. I just need some more characters and plot lines. You know, different from mine. So, just tell me about your past; that's all really."

"Cool, what do you wanna know?"

"Like, how did you grow up? Tell me about life in North Philly when you were a kid. How was it?"

"Rough man, very rough."

"Like how? Give me an example."

"It's just that everybody's trying to get a piece of you, and if you let your guard drop, they'll fuck you up."

"Well, let me ask you this, Woodrow. What do you remember as your most…uh…yeah, humiliating moment. Some crucial moment when things changed for you."

"Why you ask me some shit like that?"

"Good question, huh?"

"I'll tell you about this one time in the eighth grade with this dude named Charles Patterson. He was a big thug. You know, seventeen and still in the eighth grade? Loved to fuck with people. Get you mad and then kick your ass. One day, he stopped me on the way to school. 'Yo, little muthafucka, what's yo' name? You got any money?' Then he'd pat me down and take my lunch money. I didn't eat lunch for weeks behind that. So this one time, I was walking with Twylah Gordon. I'd been hawkin' this girl for weeks, and she finally walks home with me. We're on the way home, I'm talkin' cash shit to Twylah, and outta nowhere steps Charles. He snatched me up against a wall and started searching my pockets, looking for *his lunch money* as he called it. Man, did that piss me off, and now there was no way I was gonna let this stupid punk just bitch me out like that in front of my woman. Well, Mark, I snapped-out! I swear to god. The next thing I know, somebody's pulling me off him, and blood is everywhere. I couldn't tell if it's his or mine."

"Get outta here."

"I'm serious, Mark. He was so scared, he started crying like a baby. This big punk scared of a little blood. After that, things changed. People at school started treating me with more clout. I had Charles bringing me *his* lunch money."

"All behind that one fight?"

"Oh, I had plenty of fights after that, but the word got out, and I guess that people saw a change in me. I wasn't scared no more, and they saw a serious change in Charles too. I took his heart, man. And you could just see it on the both of us."

"So, you were the new Mafia Don then?"

"Naw, man. I wasn't about that. I just wanted Charles to feel what he made me feel. Payback's a bitch."

"What did you do to him?"

"He'd try to avoid me. Once, I caught him shakin' down some other little eighth-grader, so I kicked his ass in front of the kid, and told him that he had to buy lunch for both me and this kid, until I got tired of it."

"Did he do it?"

"If you just got your ass kicked and dogged out, would you?"

"Yeah, I guess I would, for a little while anyway."

"There are moments in your life where you gotta do what you gotta do, and whatever happens, happens. That's when I realized the power of the moment, Mark. Nothing's more important than the moment."

"That's all it takes, huh? Just you believing for the moment?"

"Most of the times, yes. But it damn sho' won't happen if you don't believe."

"Well, this is true."

"Like one time, I was with my girl, Rene. When we'd used to get it on, she'd love it when she could make me come. So, I *pretended* to have an orgasm, wait ten minutes, and start bangin' her tough again."

"Pretend how?"

"I'd make faces, moan and groan, twitch my dick like I was squirtin'. And she'd buy it like it was on sale for a dollar. Then she'd be so amazed and proud of herself cause she knows she can't make nobody else orgasm twice in a half hour. Oh, she was crazy about me after that."

34

"But all the…the deceit. How'd it make you feel?"

"She loved it, I loved it. Hell, I felt good about it."

"Aren't you putting a lot of pressure on yourself? What if you can't keep up the act?"

"That's a moment I'll deal with when it gets here. And anyway, shouldn't you be writing some of this down?"

"I don't have to, Woody, believe me. There's no way I'm going to forget this."

If different experiences was what I wanted to hear, then Woody was the right man to listen to. Even when he would tell his stories, I didn't always understand what the hell was going on with him. Quite often, I didn't believe him either.

9

Two College Dropouts

I didn't know it at the time, but me and Mark both were having the damndest time staying in school. With me, it was my bill. I got so wrapped up in that play, I forgot about doing the paper work for my grant. I'm still not sure what went down, but some kinda way I didn't fill out this form, my grant didn't come through, and I couldn't register until I paid DelState $724. 61. Plus, I had to re-apply for the grant. So, I knew what I would be doing for the summer, and for the fall and winter too—stayin' my ass out of school. And I guess it was just as well because my heart really wasn't into it. And after a point, all of that has a way of gaining on you, like a brick. And now that Mark's done got me all hyped about this play, that's all I want to do.

I'm not sure how he's gonna put our little therapy sessions on paper, but I read that play he wrote for class, and the shit wasn't half bad, and I'm thinking, what better acting role can you have than one you done helped write for yourself? So, I did kinda beef-up the stories a little bit. Like, I didn't really kick Charles' ass that first time. In fact, he kicked mine. But the ass whippin' wasn't nowhere near as bad as the humiliation. So after that, Charles knew it was go'n be a chore to shake me down. Then, when I wounded his big ass, he left me alone. We ended up bein' boys, but everything else about the story was true. So, that ain't really lying, is it? Same difference.

I enjoyed those weekends at Mark's. After a while, a dorm room starts to close in on you. Mark was the kinda guy you could talk to. I knew that whatever kinda wild shit I would tell him, he wouldn't judge me about it. We'd smoke a little weed, drink a few brewskies, and he'd play show tunes and explain how they were performed. When I heard this one, *Sweeny Todd* about some deranged whiteboy in England, who'd slit peoples' throats while they in his barber's chair, then he'd ground up the bodies so his woman could sell them in meat pies; I thought: well that's white people for ya. What kind of person could dream up some gruesome shit like this? But really, the show ain't no different than watching a horror movie. And, it is a good show. So damn, I guess you can make any subject into a play. But of course, I had to fuck with Mark about it.

"Yo, Mark. What's up with you whiteboys?"

"What is it this time, Woody?"

"Naw, I mean why y'all always be snappin' out and shit?"

"Y'all who?"

"Anytime you hear on the news about some nut who done killed everybody in his family including the dog, and been selling them as tacos, you don't have to ask what race he is."

"So, what are you saying, Woodrow, that white people have cornered the market on insanity now?"

"Naw, I'm not sayin' that brothers can't be crazy. It's just a matter of degrees. But when it comes to that demonic, ghoulish shit, y'all pretty well got the market wrapped up."

"And why is this, Woody?"

"I don't know. That's why I be askin' you. You're my Ambassador to Caucasians."

"Well, maybe it's because when it happens among black people, nobody gives a damn, so it doesn't make the news."

"Damn good point, Mark. See, you surprise me sometimes. But you do have to admit that white people are some serious zoom freaks."

"Why do I have to admit that? See, If I said something like that about black people, you'd bitch and moan about me being a racist."

"I might bitch and moan, but you always been a racist, and so have I, and so has every person in this country for that matter. How you go'n grow up in America without being one? You can't—it's impossible. The difference is that I'll admit that I'm racist. Yeah, fuck it! Let's talk about it then. White people won't admit that shit for nothin' in the world. But you can't deny that every time you see somebody skiing down a mountain at a hundred miles an hour, or skydiving out a plane, or breaking the land speed record, it's a whiteboy."

"But I'm not sure if that's about race, Woody. Could it be that black people don't have the money and access to the ski clubs, and the private planes?"

"I don't think so, because when brothers do get money like that, it's the last thing they want to spend it on. Give twenty grand to a brother and a whiteboy. Tell them to buy their fantasy car. Brother will come back with a grande, deluxe, brougham, luxury edition with the gold chrome and whitewalls. Some whiteboys might go that way too, but if you look in the driveway and see a monster truck with tires big enough crush houses, then you can rest assured that a whiteboy bought it, not a brother. And see? You can't even admit to me that's true."

"It's nothing I have to admit. You can see that for yourself."

"Well, what's up with all that?"

"Look, I drive a used Bonneville, so I guess I'm not the right zoom freak to ask. But usually when someone tries to collect power, it's because they feel they don't have any. They're afraid or insecure about something, and I guess it's a way of compensating."

"But damn, y'all got everything."

"Why do you keep saying *y'all?*" I'm not part of these people."

"Relax, damn…look, I don't mean nothing personal. I 'm just saying."

"But why is this always our ongoing, unending conversation, Woody? Makes me feel like you're ashamed of something."

"Either that or you're feeling guilty. See, brothers can own up to our bad side. That's probably why we call ourselves 'nigga' the way we do because we all know that sooner or later we'll have to feel like one again."

"Why does it just kill you then, when white people say it?"

"Because y'all ain't niggas! You don't know what that feeling is. When y'all say it, the word don't have no heart. Hell, y'all can't even pronounce it right. It's not 'nig-*ger.*' Ugh! That '-*er*' sound makes my fist wanna swing."

"How do you pronounce it then?"

"It's 'nigga.'"

"Nig-*gah?*"

"See what I'm sayin'? No heart, no cool."

"Ne-*gah*, Nig-*gar?*"

"Mark, just forget it, okay? But see? I gotta pour out my guts to you for the play, but when I ask you an honest muthafuckin' question, then you're all offended. But, I know what it is. You're scared that if you say what you really feel, then I'll peek your hand and find out how prejudiced you are. Well, I already know you's a prejudiced whiteboy anyway, so there really ain't nothing to hide."

"Okay, Woody, what's this honest muthafuckin' question again?"

"Do you think that white people are into speed and power sports, more than black people? And what is that all about?"

"I never thought about it, Woody. But yes, I would agree there aren't many black people at some place like...uh, the stock car races at Dover Downs. What does that mean? I don't know. But here's what gets me. Underneath all these questions is this hidden little accusation, like all this is just to show how evil white people are."

"Well, you know that's what some of the Muslims think."

"I've heard, but coming from the Muslims, somehow that doesn't surprise me."

"They say white people came from this outcast African tribe who had leprosy. That's why y'all's skin turned white. There was like this big headed, brainy dude who led the other lepers in a revolt. So, onion-head and his boys went to the mountains where the cold air felt good on their white skin, but the weather only made them evil, and they swore an oath to Satan and shit. And that's how Europeans were invented, grasshopper."

"Well, I heard it told this way, that white people were descended from Africa true, but it wasn't until they moved north did they actually become human. And now this new, improved, highly evolved model was the only true human. The Africans we had evolved from were actually chimpanzees by comparison, nature's rough draft, the missing link? Now, I don't believe that blacks are apes any more than I believe whites are devils."

"Naw, but you gotta admit the differences."

38

"Sure, I admit the differences, but since nobody knows what they mean, why bring 'em up? From what I see in sports, blacks are superior athletes. So what does that mean? That black people are super humans or lowly animals? Which one? And if you are god's greatest physical specimen, what does that make whites?"

"Coaches."

"Oh, so the blacks belong on the field while the white man is calling all the shots. Somebody sing *We Shall Overcome* because this sounds like slavery to me. Look, Woody; if you want to call white people Satan or lepers or zoom freaks or whatever, go ahead. I guess we've got it coming. But don't pretend that these little stereotypes you've made up are based on any science or on any truth...okay?"

Well, I guess Mark told my ass, didn't he? It's just that I'm telling him stuff I ain't never told nobody. And the fact that Mark is a whiteboy, I'm not sure what to expect. That's why the questions. But Mark knows how to get you off his back, don't he. I likes that. He was right, though. Nobody really knows what all that shit between the races means. Well, we know what some of it means, don't we? But like, how are you *not* gonna talk about it, especially when you're talking about every damn thing else? And really, I guess for any black person to become friends with a white person, they have to have that conversation eventually.

We had been shut in all weekend, and we both were gettin' rammy. Mark drove me back on campus, and we stopped by the gym for a little game of round ball. That's right, a little one-on-one with the whiteboy, see what he's made of. When we got there, the place was damn near empty except for a three-on-three game at the other end. The bottom part of the bleachers were pulled from the wall so we had some place to sit, and three or four basketballs were sitting around in all the dust on the floor. So, Mark pulls off his jacket and starts stretching and shit. I pick up the ball and immediately dribble downcourt and do a monster slam, just to let him know what the deal is. I do a couple of lay-ups, and finish off with a few jumpers from outside.

He gets the rebound and shoots from the top of the key, and I was surprised. You could tell he could play. He had good form, and he could knock that shit through. When he'd do a few lay-ups, the same thing, textbook form and accuracy, just like a whiteboy. I knew I'd shake him all outta that, as soon as I put some defense on his ass.

"So, Mark. Are you coming back to school in the fall?" I asked him as I passed the ball.

"Probably not. I'm failing in a couple of courses, and the VA won't let me come back." He shot that weak looking jumper again.

"So, what are you go'n do?"

"There's this insurance company called National Securities. Wants me to be a claims adjuster up near Baltimore. They were recruiting in the King Center the other day, but I'm not sure really."

"I heard about them. But didn't they just want graduates?"

"Graduates or veterans."

"What's a claims adjuster do?"

"I'm not sure myself, except they pay good."

"What about the play?"

"Oh, I'll always be scribbling stuff down. Did I tell you? I got with the program board at DelState and they scheduled us to do the play in Evers Dorm in about six week."

"Six weeks? That's hyped. You go'n be finished by then?"

"Guess I'll have to be. That's the only time they could schedule it in. You ready to play?"

"Shoot a do-or-die for the take out." I said as Mark stepped to the top of the key and shot that robotic-looking shit, all strings. Whap! "Take 'em out," I told him. He had a little routine where he'd come to the top of the key, hesitate and then bust his move. And from there, if you tried to play him left, he'd go right, take away his jumper, he'd play you down low. Mark was kinda smooth with the ball, could finger roll it soft into the nets. And I could tell from his rhythm that he could probably dance a little bit, too.

He didn't know what to do with me though. Now, I'm almost six feet tall myself, except I got them Jimmy the Greek, slave thighs. So, I'm much quicker, and I could outleap Mark. I'm as quick as anybody. I truly believe that my first two steps can zoom by anybody in the NBA. So, what I would do is put my big butt in Mark's gut, back him down under the basket, turn around and bang my shot straight-in off the back of the rim. Clack! Well, after the fifth time I did that, and after five times listening to Mark say "Good shot, I can't stop that," it wasn't fun no more. So, to make the game interesting I agreed not to shoot that one.

About halfway through the game, I saw how sneaky Mark could be. He's the best counterpuncher I've ever seen. He would take the shot straight up in yo' face, and when you went to block it, he'd switch the ball in mid air to the other hand. Something simple like that would just make you look stupid. Once, he dribbled down the right side like he was going all the way, and I could see he was gonna take a jumper, but he threw me a head fake instead, and I leaped up like Air-Jordan. Just knew I was gonna reject that shit. Mark faked me out so tough, he had enough time to walk to the basket, climb a ladder, and roll the ball in if he wanted to. I felt stupid; not out-played, just out-foxed, and the fact that the shot kissed off the backboard with such a soft touch, just pissed me off all the more.

The way he played defense totally messed up my shooting rhythm, especially since I agreed not to post him up. Instead of checking you when you go up to shoot, Mark would try to block the ball when you'd pick up your dribble, or just as you're about to make a move. He never stripped me, but just seeing his hand get in so close when I wasn't expecting it was enough to throw my rhythm off.

So, I'm shootin' bricks, the score's tied at twelve apiece, and we're going to fifteen. He takes the ball out, steps back in, and dribbles in place bent over like he's tired. He ought to be, I been rough-housing him really bad the last couple of plays. Then he shoots...no, he *launches* one from way outside. Hell, you don't check nobody from way out there. So, I run up to get the rebounds, and I arrive just in time to hear the nets snap as the ball goes through.

"That's thirteen, right?" he asks all smart.

"You're one up." I said, "Take the ball out." Next, he steps in dribbling but to his left side this time. I knew he could go to his left, but his strongest moves were always to his right. The more determined he was to run that way, the more I would deny him. When I lunged to strip him, he spun away, took two dribbles and slammed it in! I kid you not, that whiteboy slammed that shit in my face. It wasn't no monster jam, he barely got it over the rim, but he stuffed it in there with much gusto. I had to just laugh and say, "Damn good shot, Mark."

"Thank you very much," he smiled as he took the ball out. "This is game point, right?"

"Just play," I told him.

Mark drove right to where I was standing. I saw him coming, and had no idea of what kind of okey-dokey bullshit he was gonna pull outta his ass this time. Once, he shot a reverse. The time before that, a hook. Then one of them head fakes of his. But I wasn't gonna lose the game off no bullshit move. He dribbled to me, stopped and shot...no fakes, no stutter steps or nothing, all while I just stood there. I felt the ultimate stupidity then, so goddamn confused, I'm paralyzed now. I watched all goofy as the ball soft-touched off the glass and fell through.

"Died like a bitch," I said disgusted with myself. "Run it back."

"Take a break," he said as he collapsed on the bleachers.

"C'mon run it back, before you cool off too much."

"Wait a minute, dammit!" He's huffin' and puffin' like he's gonna die.

"It's them cigarettes. Told you about that smoking." I was just pissed that he beat me while I stood there with my dick in my hand. He was lying on his back, and his chest was heavin' up and down. I wanted a rematch, but I could already tell I wouldn't get a good game out of him now. He shot his load. But fuck that, you gotta give me a rematch.

He finally dragged his ass up start the next game. This time I was gonna play him straight up, no bullshit. Quit lettin' him dictate the game. I was gonna see if this *Negro as Ape Theory* had any validity to it. This time when he would dribble in, I didn't try to strip him or block his shots. Instead, I'd just beat him to the spot, and make sure he didn't launch anything uncontested. I didn't go for none of them herky-jerky head fakes of his neither, just solid defense.

I didn't have to post him up to score on him. I found other ways to capitalize on my speed. I knew that I couldn't dribble as well as he could. So, I'd just throw the ball in front of us and outrun him to it. That's not dribbling exactly, but serves the same purpose. You just can't hide good talent. I'd beat him to the rebound and be back up with the tip-in before he even knew the ball was off the rim. About half way, the game was lopsided. Mark was so damn tired 'till he stop puttin' up any defense. He was too weak to even take it to the hoop. The victory wasn't sweet, though. It still didn't remove the bad taste of how he beat me.

10

Chesapeake Trailer Park

I knew Woody would be shocked that I could hold my own against him. Little did he know that I was all-state forward in high school. And when I defeated him, it probably broke his little heart. So, after the first game, I didn't care if I won another one or not. I had already made my point. I guess I could've played harder in the second game, but now he'd know that all white guys aren't the rhythmless, physical wrecks he wishes that we are. And if we ever played again, he'd know I was somebody to be reckoned with. What I'd really like to see is both of us playing on the same team. We'd make much better team mates than opponents, just like we were doing with the play. It was a blast having him over on weekends and putting that play together. There was a sense of accomplishment and purpose, and much of the fun of mounting a show is in the anticipation.

Well, it was spring and I'd finally finished the damned thing; a one act about forty-five minutes long that I titled *A Gentlemen's Journal.* It had dramatic scenes built around the monologues of three male characters. The guys would recite soliloquies based on my poetry, much like I had seen in *Colored Girls.* The dramatic scenes were done with the two female characters, and the whole thing was performed without a set. We used only three chairs, and we pantomimed the rest. The plot focused on the lives of the three male characters as they told in diary form how their marriage had failed, about problems at work, or about dealing with women.

For all practical purposes this was my only connection with DelState now. I had stopped attending classes. Since I was doing my own show, Mr. Hasten had said it was more important than anything I could learn in his class. I'd stopped attending my history and math classes, so going to rehearsals was the only reason I would even be on campus now.

Casting the show was easy. Donnell and Karen from *Hair* signed on. They were such big hams (especially Donnell), I knew I could depend on them for a good performance; even if out of pure vanity. I got Jeff Wiggins and Bonnie Standifer to play parts too. Neither had the time to do *Hair* last semester, but both had acted with me in the children's play last year. I promised them only two rehearsals a week, plus the nights we'd perform, and they agreed.

The show was ridiculously easy to produce. Didn't have to worry about costumes, sets or props. The dorm auditorium only held 40-50 seats max, so there were no big seating or stage concerns. The lighting would be simple—lights up, and lights down—so, even I could handle that. And with just five cast members, we would only need to rehearse for a couple of nights a week. By the fourth week, we started to string the parts into scenes. The play was taking shape, and opening night would be next weekend.

That was about the time I signed on as a claims adjuster with National Securities. Basically, all they wanted was somebody who could read, write, put sentences together, and show up on time. Everything else was part of their training program. For a few weekends a month until June, I would be in their program and collecting $200 dollars each time I showed up. Then, I would be ready to work in Harford County, Maryland just outside of Baltimore. The two-grand-a-month salary would kick in just as my veterans' benefits would stop. Sure, it was a regular nine to five; and yeah, I would have to relocate. But hell, for two grand a month, I could do it. That's why this chance to get *Gentlemen's Journal* performed was so important now. I didn't know when I'd have resources like this again.

Since June was just a couple of months away, I had begun driving around Harford county just to see the kind of area I was moving to. Only fifty minutes from Dover and about fourty-five minutes from Baltimore, it was the usual suburban sprawl. But the more sophisticated attitudes of the city hadn't quite seeded this far out yet. And, although the layout was nice, the feel was decidedly rural. For me that was fine. After all, I loved living in the country. And since my first trailer had been such a nice place, I wanted to find another one out in the woods.

One Saturday, I passed a small wooden sign that looked like a park entrance: *Chesapeake Trailer Park.* I followed a gravel road around a thicket of bushes and saw several secluded trailers nestled in lots on either side of the road. These weren't pull-behind campers, but modular housing actually; looked like you could enjoy your home in complete privacy. Yet, you still had a neighbor close by for any emergencies. Well, if you've got to live in Harford County, this seemed like as good a place as any.

I drove around Shangri-la until I saw another sign on a mail box which read *Rental Office.* The lot hid a mobile home with aluminum siding and a peaked, shingled roof. A patch of lawn out front was well manicured, and held back the woods with a row of split-rail fencing. Parking the car behind a pick-up truck, I climbed the cement porch and knocked on the door. A voice commanded, "Come on in."

The living room was spacious but ordinary, and a counter had been built in front of two office desks and a row of filing cabinets. At one of the desks sat a stout, white-haired man who looked like the lost clone of Mr. Greenjeans; had the overalls, the plaid shirt, the works.

"Hello, sonny. How can I help you?"

"Good afternoon, sir. I'd like to speak to someone about renting a place here, if one's available. I'm moving to this area soon, and I'm looking for a nice spot in the woods."

"Well, I'm Harlen Passwaters, the proprietor." He stood up and walked to the counter with surprising energy. "First, I'll need to get a little information from you." He pulled an application from under the counter, wrote my name and numbers from the drivers license I'd given him, and said, "What kind of work do you do, son?"

"I'll be working for National Securities; its headquarters is over on Marlton Road."

"You say you *will be working*. What are you doing now?"

"I'm in college now. But I'll tell ya, it doesn't seem like the right thing for a veteran like me." I added that to impress him, just in case this was some kind of pissing contest.

"You're a vet, are ya?"

"Yes, sir. I was discharged from the Air Force about two years ago. I'm in college on the VA bill, but around June or July I should be moving out this way."

"I'm a vet myself," he said proudly. "I was in Korea back in '51. Nobody wants to remember that one, but we kicked as much ass as they did against the Germans. Were you honorably discharged, son?"

"Oh yeah. I was just a first termer, but I left as an E-5."

"Well, look Mr. uh...Berens," he read from the application. "You seem like a good kid. Anybody who can get through this government's military is okay by me. Now then, we have some lots back in "C" sector, or you can rent one of the units we already got set up."

"If you already have one set up, it would make things a whole lot easier."

"Well, follow me and I'll show you." He grabbed a ring of keys from the wall and escorted me along a path around back. A hundred yards or so to the rear was a trailer that looked identical to his except it was smaller. It had a bedroom at either end with the kitchen, living room and bathroom lined up in the center. The yard wasn't a lawn per se. Instead, a gravel walkway had been carved through ivy which covered the ground like a lawn. Not too much to mow, I thought, and plenty of room for a bachelor like me. Lots of peace and quiet too.

As we walked back to his office, Harlen Passwaters told me, "Now son this is a nice, quiet place. Folk here in *Chesapeake* don't like a lot of noise and disturbances. I know you're a young colt and still might like to kick up your heels a bit. But just think about your neighbors and be courteous, and that's all anybody can expect."

"Well, you don't have to worry about me Mr. Passwaters. Most of my romping days are behind me." The thought of me throwing a wild party was comical. Hell, if that's what I wanted, what would I be doing in this time warp called *Chesapeake Trailer Park?* I followed him back to his office and gave him a $500 deposit so that he would hold it until June, or until he could find another renter. I drove away feeling more secure. Knowing that I would be living in such

45

a nice place would make relocating much easier. Now, I could concentrate on *A Gentlemen's Journal.*

The play was well attended even though it was in a cramped auditorium which formerly held only dances and house parties. We had borrowed four portable bulletin boards and set them up in a box shape at one end of the big room to make entrances and exits, and so we could have a backstage area. The chairs were placed around the bulletin boards in a makeshift thrust stage providing about ten feet of playing space. Fortunately, lights were built into the ceiling and were on their own dimmers, so the lighting would be relatively simple.

By the time we started, we actually had to turn students away because there was no more room. The antics weren't as dramatic here as they had been in the Humanities Theater, but the air was just as energy charged. We all had those same pre-show jitters that didn't stop until the show started and all six of us were in various positions on stage. Here we each took a line just to introduce our faces. Yes, despite my own objections, I acted too. There were two cameo scenes I picked up because the blocking wouldn't permit any other characters to do them. They were just brief scenes though, which allowed me to spend most of the time offstage jockeying the dimmer switch or managing things behind the scenes.

I made the mistake of giving the weakest actor the opening lines. I thought the scene could build to the stronger actors, but by the time Donnell and Karen had butchered their lines, I knew the show was dying; dead at the starting line. When my lines came around, I was so damned nervous that, honest to god, my leg was trembling. The audience probably thought it was impatience rather than the abject fear I was feeling. I'll have to admit that sitting there exposed and emotionally naked before that audience, listening for any sign of acceptance had to be one of the most frightening moments in my life. The fear of rejection is so great! It's one thing for someone to reject you because of your looks or your race, but if someone rejects your art, your expression of yourself, it feels like they're rejecting your soul and your very essence. Now was a fine time to be realizing all this.

Finally, it was Woody's turn, and I knew he could tell what was happening because he delivered his lines forcefully and comically, different from any of the rehearsals. The audience laughed, or better yet they sighed, and sat back in their seats a bit. That simple act had broken the ice, and it was like a cold slap in the face for the cast. The rest would be easy now. Thank god for Woody because I thought I was *surely* dying. I was starting to see the bright light in the tunnel, angels flapping their wings, the whole nine yards.

Then the pork factor kicked in, and everybody turned into the hams they'd always been, no longer intimidated by the show or the closeness of the audience. I could also see some of the more private feelings of the cast in their performances. Donnell and Jeff Wiggins couldn't stand one another. Each thought he was the BMOC (big man on campus), or as Woody would put it HNIC (head nigger in charge). So every scene they had together became this heated competition, like some dick measuring contest. Each would be more dramatic than the other until the rehearsals got more and more out of hand. Then for no reason, Jeff went in the other direction. He started to underplay his scenes, giving his performance a dignity and elegance that Donnell couldn't match. So, Donnell compensated with more melodrama. Their performances would've worked better without all that tension, but what the hell could I do about it now?

Karen and Woody seemed to be having their own little *thing* going on too. There was a scene, based on one of those stories Woody told me, where he'd get fresh with her, and she'd slap him. Then he'd overpower her into submission. Well, in rehearsals, we had practiced a stage slap, one that was loud but without much sting. But no, Woody insisted on having Karen actually slap him; his being the method actor and all. Towards the end there, Karen was getting better and better, until the blow looked more like an overhand right to the jaw rather than a simple slap. And Woody's reaction would always be the same. First, the pause of disbelief where everybody would think, damn she fucked him up! His eyes would go evil, and he'd snatch her down and slowly advance on top of her; then lights out.

Well, tonight when she whacked Woody, she drew blood. I don't think the audience saw the drop trickle from the corner of his mouth, but Karen did; and when he jerked her down, she lost it! She was kicking and screaming, and it took us several uncomfortable moments behind those bulletin boards to calm her down. After a while she laughed like she had been joking all along, but even then, we weren't sure how strong her composure was. The audience gasped at the blow then giggled embarrassed as the lights went down. There was something greasy about the whole scene, as if whatever dark, private moment they shared was not meant for public viewing. Later we would get the most complaints, especially from the ladies, about that particular scene. Woody told me that he believed Karen had actually been raped once, and this was her way of working it out. I thought, okay Woody, that explains what's going on with her, but what about you? I didn't ask him because I wasn't sure I really wanted to know.

Just about every scene was welcomed by a hearty round of cheers or jeers, the women responding to the female characters and the guys shouting "right-on" for the male characters. The audience enjoyed the exchange; some even complimented it as being *deep,* but there was something cartoonish about it that I didn't like. I couldn't put my finger on it, but something didn't ring true. The cast bowed for the curtain call without me. Gladly, I was on the dimmer switch.

Well, the crowd bought it like it was on sale for a dollar, as Woody would say, but I think their enthusiasm was for what the show tried to tackle, for its directness and for the issues it raised. They had never seen these topics approached in a play before. Me? I was much more critical.

11

Back in North Philly

I wanted to tell Mark not to give the opening lines to a prissy little bitch like Donnell. That nigga was too concerned with tryin' to look pretty and playing that Billy Dee role. Oh, he'd be fine after the play got started, but I knew sooner or later he'd choke just like he did. And Karen was so intimidated by the audience all up in her face that she couldn't carry the load either. And I didn't know what the hell was going on with Mark. He was shakin' and tremblin' so bad, I thought he was gonna explode right before our eyes. Damn, Mark, like that?

Well, when my lines came around, I knew what I was gonna do. So, I kicked it in rough and ready, and it was just what everybody needed to get their shit together. The play woulda fell flat on its face if it wasn't for me. No, there wouldn't even be a play if it wasn't for me. By the time we finished, I couldn't tell who had enjoyed the show more; the audience or us. And seeing a project go from a bull session around Mark's kitchen table, to a full blown play, had to be one of the hippest things I ever did. I couldn't believe that this audience was actually gettin' off on my acting and my own story.

I knew that when we performed again we couldn't depend on Donnell to get us started. We'd have to give the opening lines to somebody talented and forceful, somebody who had the balls not to be intimidated by a close crowd or a strange stage. Somebody like...like me goddammit! As a matter of fact, Mark changed the script that same night. He wrote up an all new opening for the show, and we were behind the bulletin boards the next night trying to learn the new lines before the last performance. I found out something else I didn't realize; that a show ain't really a show until it's performed. I'd always thought that novels and books and plays fell out the writers ass complete and whole, like a turd. But nothing is ever final about a play. Even when you think you got it the best it can be, you'll still find little ways to improve on it. I didn't know about Mark Berens, but I wanted to do this again, a lotta mo' times.

After the play ended there were only a coupla weeks left in the semester. Going back to class after a performance was hard enough as it is, but since I knew I wouldn't be coming back to DelState for a while (if ever), it was really difficult now. So, I just packed up my shit and left without even taking any finals. Hell, I couldn't study anyway, and besides, school wasn't what I wanted to do now—theater was. When my report card finally came, I think I failed two courses, got a "D" in one and a "C" in the other.

Coming back to North Philly wasn't easy either. There were just us three guys now; Cool Will my Pops, my brother Timmie, and me. Everything seemed so small and closed-in after being away for almost two years. My bedroom wasn't big enough anymore, and it was hard for me to feel rested and comfortable with two other grown men in the house. And I gotta admit that coming home without a degree made me feel like a failure. I was sure everybody was saying behind my back, "Yeah, Woody thought he was big shit going to college, but look at him now. He's back here with the rest of us."

I tried to get up with Mark whenever we could, but since I didn't have no car, I had to wait until he could drive up here and pick me up. We still got together, but he was so busy moving to Maryland with his new job, that I couldn't depend on him, not the way I did down in Dover.

Being at home was definitely a crash landing after the show, and I had to deal with all the bullshit that made me want to leave in the first place. The neighborhood wasn't as dangerous as it had been a couple of years ago. After enough women, kids and cops got shot behind all that gang bangin', things got better. While I was away, people had formed a neighborhood watch where folks would spy on each other and call the police every time they had a gripe with somebody. They even installed a mini-police station around the corner and put two black cops up in there. So, at least all that crazy stuff was gone, but I felt like a stranger on the streets sometimes. People acted like they didn't know who I was anymore, and because I dressed halfway decent and could throw on a white voice when I had to, some of the bums actually thought I was a narc or some kinda undercover cop. They'd be hangin' out on the corner smoking or drinking or snorting or whatever the hell they'd be doing, and when they'd see me coming, they'd hide their shit or duck behind a parked car or something. I wanted to say, "Negroes, please! Yo, man, pass the joint!" But I didn't because I *was* the outsider now.

The situation at home wasn't much better. Pops was almost retired now. He'd been working for the city on various jobs for damn near 30 year, so that staying-out-all-night bullshit had caught up with his ass. Ol' Cool Will was a slick dude, don't get me wrong. He'd still go out to the New Tech Club or over to the Kitty Kat Cafe, and his wardrobe and car was still slick enough for me to want to borrow them. But Pops had changed, wasn't as lively as he used to be, and most Saturday nights he'd just sit home watching TV and sipping *Wild Turkey*. I guess living with my Moms, Crazy Francine, had finally wore his ass out.

I didn't have to worry about rent or groceries, because Pops always told us that we had a place to stay and food to eat as long as he did. But damn man, I didn't want to be a burden on my Pops. Hell, I wanted to be supporting him now. That didn't seem to bother Timmie, though. See, he never lived anywhere else, so mooching off people was all he ever knew. It bothered me that Tim didn't have no more determination than he did. I mean, he didn't wanna do nothing but sleep all day, and then run the streets all night like some damn vampire. Tim was grown now, even had a little daughter by Angie, his girl from high school. Thank goodness Angie's Momma was keeping them, cause if they had to depend on Timmie, they all woulda starved.

After about a month of this shit, I was ready to lose my goddamn mind. If I hadn't got up with my boy Andrew who also dropped outta DelState, I don't know what I woulda done. He turned me on to a job at Master Guard, a rent-a-cop service that hired security guards for the corporations downtown. The money was just a little better than minimum wage, but hey, it was something to do.

The job was easy as hell, and it didn't take me no time to settle in. You'd be assigned to one of three or four buildings, and just sit there behind a desk at the door all night. You'd get to talk to some of the regulars and meet the visitors who signed in, which made it a little more bearable. And if it got too boring, I could always find a corner of the building where my supervisor couldn't find me, and crash out for an hour or two. Then I'd have all day to do whatever I wanted. This wasn't no fast track career move now, but I did feel good when I could come in, and hand my Pops a couple of twenties every now and then. I didn't give Timmie shit though. Hell, we'd been trying to hook him up too, but he couldn't show up for work on time three days in a row, so to hell with him.

The more I sat at that desk acting like the Maytag repairman, the more I wanted to get back on stage. I got tired of waiting for Mark, so I started to read the classifieds and the entertainment section to see what I could find happening in Philly. Then the *Daily News* did a story about a place called the Bohemian Art Gallery who was asking for scripts to produce. You had to bring in your play, do a reading, and if they liked it, they'd hook you up.

On my next day off, I went to one of the readings figuring the best way to find out was to buy a ticket and see for myself. The Bohemian Art Gallery was on South Street, a couple of blocks from Old Town. I liked that area because that's where Philly's weirdos hung out. And being an All-American weirdo myself, it had a special appeal to me. I found the address, and tipped into the little art gallery they had set up in a store-front. Behind a counter in the lobby was some old rickety white dude and a middle aged white babe who was *baldheaded.* I'm serious as a heart attack; Miss Lady was bald as a cueball. She had the perfect round head, wore a lotta makeup and big heavy earrings, and was all speedy and energetic and shit, kinda like Flipper the dolphin.

I'm staring at this alien woman and the old guy says with an accent, "Welcome sir. I am the director of the Playwrights Workshop, Adolph Grumann. How do you do? There's a five dollar donation we ask to help fund the workshop. If you would like to be a Bohemian Patron, you can sign up for a season pass for twenty dollars. It's all tax deductible." While he's running this on me, Flipper fumbles through a stack of brochures and hands me one.

"Naw, one ticket will be fine," I say.

"Well, thank you, and we hope you can support us in the future," and he escorts me away. The gallery itself was a big room which they had painted charcoal grey everywhere; had the same ceiling lights on dimmer switches just like in the dorms. The room only held about forty chairs, but it was hooked. The gray walls, the lights and the little black curtain they had as a backdrop made it like a mini-theater. As expected, I was the fly in the buttermilk again, the only nigga in the vicinity. So, I tried to look cultured and shit, you know, crossed my legs, studied the program like I was a critic or something. Everybody else was mumbling to theyself, and taking the whole thing just way too serious for me. You woulda thought they was performing brain surgery up in here. Finally, this lanky Alfalfa lookin' dude introduced the two plays for tonight. One was supposed to be a domestic drama, whatever the hell that is, and the other a comedy. Cool, I thought, a little bit of everything. Well, I must've missed something with the first one; and even if I did, the play wasn't entertaining worth a goddamn. It was this little Moms, Pops and wild-child story where everybody's pissed at everybody else, but nobody wants to say nothing. The actors were dull, the story was dull; just dull, dull, dull. It was worse than sitting through World Civ. At least in class, I could drool on the desk if I wanted to. Here, I had to pretend like I was all intellectual, like everybody else was doing.

The next play wasn't much better, but it was more entertaining. Hell, if you gonna bring these people out here, you gotta at least give 'em a good show. All that deep, psychotic shit can come later. The comedy script was just a sitcom really, straight off TV, about a Jewish family whose daughter was dating a black guy. Oh, it had a lotta other plots too; but of course, that was the one I remembered. It was all right I guess, but most of the humor was from cheap shots and everybody bustin' on each other. It was so much like watching *All in the Family* until I was like, waiting for the commercial breaks. So, after sitting through two hours of this, I'm thinking; Damn, Mark, they need us bad.

Adolph stood and led the group in discussion about the play. I had to stick around for this. Let's just see how the writers were gonna justify putting us all through this bullshit. Well, Adolph was just ruthless with 'em.

"There is a woeful lack of structure in the first script," he told the one. "Neither the plot nor the characters are focused at all…"

"But I was trying to communicate a mood, an atmosphere. Not just provide the usual characters, tradition bound to linear plots and stories…"

"Well fine," interrupted Adolph. "Do that, but at least make a statement. Make it big and obvious, and then take us on from there." That's right, I thought, tell him about it, Adolph; making us sit through that bullshit.

"But at least you took chances," he dogged-out the other writer next, "which is more than I can say about our second reading. The entire idea for the script, its very *raison d'etre* is predictability and contrivance. It would have been perfect as a television comedy." Damn, he spoke my very thoughts. "The humor was…rather abusive really, not clever a'tall. And you rely entirely too much on the one-liner, the punch line. Why not situational irony or character irony? You

51

understand the difference, no? The script calls attention to you as the writer, not to your characters. We laugh at them, but not with them, you see?"

Well, I'll tell you, Adolph impressed me, more than the writers or the plays or anything else; the fact that he pulled no punches with these dudes, and told them about themselves straight to their faces. I finally got with him after the reading. He was eager to schedule a time when we could do *Gentlemen's Journal*. He wrote us in for the first of the month, and I couldn't wait to tell Mark.

"Wait, slow down Woody. It's two in the morning."

"Oh, did I wake you up?"

"No, I had to get up anyway; the phone was ringing. Now what's this about blacks and Bohemians?"

"I just got back from the Bohemian Art Gallery, the place on South Street I told you about?"

"For the playwrights workshop, yeah?"

"I got up with the director and he scheduled us in for a reading of *Gentlemen's Journal* at the first of the month. That's three weeks; can we get it together by then?"

"Shouldn't be a problem; everyone said to just call 'em. But what's the African American part?"

"If they like it, maybe we can get a week's run at The Drama Center in their Black Drama Festival."

"You want to do *Gentlemen's Journal* at a black drama festival?"

"Sure, why not?"

"Well, mainly because it's not a black play. I mean, I'm the writer and if you haven't noticed, I'm not African American."

"Well damn, Mark. It never occurred to me that it was anything other than a black play. All the actors are black, the audiences have been black, the stories are partly based on me, and I'm black. The only thing white about it is you."

"But, it just happened that way. I didn't write the parts especially for black people, or white people either for that matter."

"What difference does it make? They're offering us a chance to do a week's run at a legitimate theater, and you're asking questions? Did Steven Spielberg call while I was away or something? We go down there, do the show, and let them make the call. They ought to know what they need for their own festival."

"It's not being honest…"

"Oh, I get it. The big problem is that you don't like the label *African-American* associated with your nice white play. That's it, ain't it? You don't want no little mulatto script running around here with your name on it."

"Oh, here we go."

"You done gone and done it now, Mark. You been laying with them niggers so long, now they gonna think you are one. You done crossed the line son, and you might not be able to come back now!"

"Is that what it is, Woody?"

"I been saying you's a prejudice little muthafucka all along."

"Hey, whatever, Woody? But I still say it's not a black play. Because as a white man, I can't speak for black people. It's not just because it will *nigger-rig* my play."

"Nigger-rig? What's that mean?"

"I thought you'd like that one. It means uh, shabbily done, fixed for the moment. You know, a muffler swinging from a wire coat hanger is nigger-rigged; a Cadillac with missing hub caps is nigger-rigged."

"That's what y'all call it?"

"Oh, you're offended now? After all that venom you spew at white people? Well, if I am considered a nigger now, then I guess I should be able to use the word, right? At least with you."

"Well, just don't let nobody else hear you say it. If you do, you're on your own. But I do know what you mean; *Gentlemen's Journal* is a white play. That's true because you wrote it, but it's a black play too. And anytime you hook that *black too* onto something, that makes it black period. And no, I wouldn't like it either if I got complimented for being the best *black* actor, or the best *black* this or that. Why can't I be the best period? Hell, I didn't like that it was a Black Drama Festival, but I'm not stupid either. I realize that I'd rather be in a black festival than in *no* festival. And that's what you gotta realize too, Mark. Take it wherever you can get it, buddy. So, you gonna do the play or what?"

"Well yes, I got to. But I'd much prefer..."

"Yeah, yeah, I'd much prefer a lotta things too, but hey that's racism for ya. It's enough to make a fella angry, isn't it?"

"We can have this discussion some other time. Look, we need to get together this weekend to work on the script. I'll pick you up Friday night about nine, okay? I gotta get some sleep. Good work, Woody."

"Thank ya, massa."

"Aw, fuck you."...*click.*

12

Mark's Visitors

Maybe it *was* prejudiced for me to not want the play to be in an African American festival, but it's human too. If we were talking about entering the same play in a European-American Festival, Woody would bitch and moan worse than I did. And all that other stuff about me being an *honorary nigger,* or whatcha call it, *coon by association* is so crazy let's not even talk about it. He was right though; if we go down there, do the play, put our cards on the table, and they still choose us? Well hell, then I wouldn't care if it's the Martian Drama Festival, and neither would Woody.

After a long enough time, I finally moved to my new trailer. It took forever, but I was finally getting settled. With all the confusion, I hadn't realized how secluded and cozy the park actually was. I knew I could get to like it a lot, if I could ever get settled.

The training weekends at work were finally over, and I had been assigned to the regional office for about three weeks now. I used the term *training* loosely because basically the whole process was learning the codes and regulations about insurance claims. We all would start out coding and processing individual claims, then maybe in a few years, we could work our way to some of the corporate accounts where the big salaries were.

The office was one huge floor of a building with about twenty-five or thirty desks sitting in rows. At the front, three offices had been partitioned off—where our supervisors worked. And the lowly coders like me would have to work our way from the back rows to the front until we could be promoted; where I guess we'd start the process all over again. I'd seen this kind of ranking system in the military so I knew how to fit right in. It did seem sad though, because that's one of the reasons I left the military. If you want mindless regimentation, you can't beat the Air Force.

The routine would be the same every morning. You arrive at 8:30 or 8:45, dressed in your JC Penney's Classic Collection wool blend suit, you get coffee and donuts at the canteen, you bullshit with the guys about the Orioles, you gossip or read *USA Today* for another fifteen or twenty minutes, then you go through the unending task of converting the IN stack into the OUT stack. You verify venders, you check policy codes, you add, you subtract, you do the Hokey-Pokey, and you leave at 4:30. It had only been a couple of weeks, and the tedium was beginning to set in already. But like I say, I'm a vet so I could handle it.

If you wished, you could play office politics, and maybe move up a lane or two in the rat race. Go to a party with this one, a ball game with that one, kiss a little ass here and there. But being the new kid on the block, I didn't know the players well enough to choose sides yet. Besides, I'm not much of a joiner anymore. The top dogs who had their own offices were Linda Courtney, Account Assistant; Thom Cooper, also Account Assistant; and Craig Dempsy, District Manager in the big office. Linda and Thom were male and female versions of each other. Both were strictly business, married with kids and expert brown-nose specialist. Both just loved their little status in the office and worked with mindless efficiency. The office HNIC (damn, Woody's right, I am turning black!), was Craig Dempsy a bearish Irishman whom I liked the moment I met him. He was relaxed and unpretentious, but he could get you to perform for him with what seemed like the smallest amount of coaxing. His easy-going manner was infectious and made the regimen of the day much more tolerable. Sometimes I wondered why a guy who was obviously so at ease with himself, chose a job like this one? Then I thought about myself and why the hell was I there. When I first got to the office, I got things clear with Craig Dempsey.

"Well Mr. Dempsey…"

"Please, call me Craig."

"Very well, Craig. What I want to say is that occasionally I'm going to need a little time off. I'm actively involved in writing and producing stage plays right now. Most of the time it won't be a problem. It's just that when we have a performance, I might need an afternoon or evening break here and there."

"Oh, you're into theater are you? I'm an old song and dance man myself."

"You, Craig?"

"Yeah, I did several years of summer stock when I was a kid like you, and even did an Off Broadway show once."

"Really?"

"I can still sing a little bit too," he laughed heartily. "But frankly, Mark, I don't think that's going to be a problem. As you know, we're on flex-time here so if you don't finish in the afternoon, you can finish the next morning. If anything does comes up, just let me know. The thing you really have to guard against is letting your hobby affect your responsibilities here."

"Well, I don't think that'll happen."

"Neither do I, but I'm glad you mentioned it; shows initiative."

Me and Woody got back Friday about midnight and stayed up damn near dawn bullshittin' each other, smoking pot and drinking beer. This had become our little ritual. Before we could write, or do any work, we always had to have a bull-session first. What do you call that, *male bonding?* We finally woke up in the afternoon of the next day. I made some breakfast-hash from potatoes, eggs, onion and bacon; which just astounded Woody that it could taste so good all mixed together like that. Then I asked him to help me set up the antenna outside, and maybe we could watch some *Star Trek* or a game later on.

Woody was obviously the city boy; you could tell he didn't know how to lift or carry or do outdoor work at all. And he was so damn worried about getting his clothes dirty; a grown man afraid of a little dirt—unless, of course, he was playing football or clowning around. After we finally got the antenna up, Woody found my old football and we played catch in the driveway.

"Yo, Mark. This is how those old school whiteboys run it. Larry Czonka takes the hand-off, third and short." Woody held the ball with two hands and did a hilarious imitation of an out-of-control tank. "Czonka would run head-on into whoever tried to cover him. He'd even go outta his way to fuck-up somebody." Woody bounced off nearby trees and imaginary linesmen to make his point. Laughter stabbed me in the gut.

"Then there're the pretty boys," he demonstrated. "Brothas who could run the ball and just look so damn gorgeous doing it. Chicago Bears are second and 30 from their own five yard line, hand-off to Gale Sayers! You ever see him run in a ballgame? He was the prototype of the broken field runners you see today like. He goes up the right side; but no, it's closed." Woody mimed a runner hitting a brick wall, dazed. "He reverses the play ladies and gentlemen, and what's this? Sayers throws two head fakes, smiles for the cameras, leaps like a gazelle, and I think he's going all the way." Woody spun and slid like James Brown, wiping away tacklers. "Sayers scores, ladies and gentlemen! And the crowd goes crazy folks…" I was paralyzed laughing, and amazed at how much of a natural impersonator Woodrow was. "I always did like the brothers who could just *throw down,* and do it with so much style," he continued. "Of course the king was Muhammad Ali. Now, back in the day, Ali talked mo' shit than a little bit, and his opponents and the press and Howard Cosell, everybody bought it, like it was…"

"On sale for a dollar," we said together. He danced around mimicking Ali, sneaking jabs at me the moments he could look the coolest.

"First, Ali started with that shuffle," Woody did a stutter step, "then that bullshit bolo punch," he looped his left three times and shot two comical jabs at my face. "Then the ultimate mind-fuck, the rope-a-dope for when he was too washed up to fight anymore. He used that shit against George Foreman and knocked his ass out." Woody pretended to be sagging on the ropes then suddenly unreeled a flurry of punches.

"That's what I be tellin' you about playing the moment, Mark. Ali knew what that was about. But he stayed too long when he fought Larry Holmes. Ali was slow, and Holmes was beating him to every shot." Woody puffed his cheeks and threw two jabs and a balloon right; but in mid-stroke, an imaginary punch collided with his jaw. The impersonation was utterly convincing; the look of surprise in Ali's eyes, his attempts to counter which only got him hit twice more; even when he bounced off the canvas in slow motion and flopped around like a drunk trying to get up, Woody had me on my knees laughing.

"Damn that's funny, Woody." I said when I finally caught my breath. "You've got him down pat. Man, you ought to be doing stand-up. I'm serious!" Then we broke into another laughing fit.

We came in, and I made some sandwiches and Kool-Aid. I asked, "How do you like my new spot?"

"It's fine, but you know how I am about being back up in the woods. When I see too many leaves, I have one of them slavery flashbacks. I start seeing torches in the night; I hear yelping bloodhounds and people in sheets screaming 'Yee-hah!' But other than that, it's nice."

"I like the feeling of coziness and seclusion," I added.

"Seclusion my ass! *Isolation* is more like it. End up like them dudes in the movie *Deliverance.*"

"Well, I've been here about a month, and I haven't seen any Klan rallies or cross burnings yet. Here, get your mind on something constructive," and I handed him the rewrites for the opening of *Gentlemen's Journal* .

> I've come to sing,
> To shout my song out loud; to be heard.
> I'm here to tell you about myself for myself;
> So that we can know myself.
> I've got strong songs, anthems of sorrows,
> Melodies of forgotten times and places,
> A chest full of pride, and a heart full of sorrow.

"This opens the play? Damn, Mark, I like it. It's poetic as hell, but it still kicks. I mean, you can bring a lotta attitude to these lines."

"Here's what I need to know, should we have a single character say the entire stanza, or should we divide the lines. The advantage with giving everybody their own line makes it moves quicker, picks up the pace so we won't have that fiasco we had with Donnell."

"Give the whole stanza to a single character," Woody suggested. "There ain't gonna be no fiasco, because I'll be doing the lines; so we don't hafta worry. The second reason is that splicing and dicing the lines like that destroys the poetry, fucks up the flow. If you want action, move the actors around rather than the lines; see what I mean?

"Yes, I do. And if the actors cross the stage when they speak, then it'll be even more interesting to look at."

"Besides, it's easier to act when you're moving around and not standing still."

"So, I guess I'll have to come up with four or five more stanzas like this. And, oh yeah. I wrote myself out of the play. Jeff takes my part in the first scene, and you take it in the second."

"You're not gonna act at all, Mark?"

"Too much to do."

"Wow, it's really a black play now."

"Yeah, right. One other thing. I picked up these forms from Mr. Hasten; it's time we got the play copyrighted, don't you think?"

"What all does copyrighting do?"

"It just registers your play with the Library of Congress so it's legally yours. Later, if we get paid or somebody uses *A Gentlemen's Journal* without our permission, we can prove that we own it. Now let's see, I already put our names and addresses on here. What year were you born?"

"1960, and you?"

"'58."

"You just two years older than me, Mark?"

"Remember to respect your elders. What else, *citizen of?* What country are you from, strong Mandinka warrior?"

"From the Republic of North Philly."

"*Domiciled in the same?* Yes. *Briefly describe nature of this author's contribution.* How do you want to describe it?"

"Written by Mark Berens and Woodrow Tyler."

"Well Woody, you haven't actually done any writing. I mean like now, I'm the one who has to figure out the specific words to use. That's writing isn't it?"

"Just because I didn't type the damn words on the paper, you make it sound like I'm a consultant or something. There wouldn't even be a play without me."

"There wouldn't be a play without either one of us. Relax, would ya? I'm just asking, what's the distinction between what you did and what I did?"

"Why you gotta be making distinctions now?"

"I'm not! The Library of Congress is. Look; to me, what I did to create the script is different from what you did. Is that not true?"

"Well, yes and no…"

"Then how do you describe it? That's what this thing wants to know…"

"I gave you ideas for the characters and plots."

"So, do you want me to write? *Developed ideas for characters and plots?*"

"I guess so."

"Woody, I'm asking you."

"Yeah, then."

"Well, since you're so sure about everything, here. You can take the instructions home and read them for yourself. If I don't hear from you by next weekend, I'll go ahead and mail it like this. Fair enough?"

"Cool."

Whew! What the hell was that all about? There I was trying to fill out the form as honestly as I could, and Woody's pissed because I'm telling the truth? I was glad to let him take the five pages of instructions home for himself if he thinks I'm doing such a bad job. And when next Friday rolls around, Woodrow wouldn't have even read the first paragraph.

I knew what revisions to make on the script, so at least most of the work was done for tonight. But there was this tension in the air now. We were relatively quiet for the rest of the evening, watching a rerun of *Star Trek* that we'd only seen five times. Just before the Orioles game came on, there was a knock at the door. What I would find on the other side was the first in a series of events that would change me in some very fundamental ways. I opened the door, and it was Harlen Passwaters, the landlord.

"Oh hello, Mr. Passwaters. Come on in."

"No thank you. What I got to say will only take a minute." I stepped outside and closed the door behind me. "Well Mark?" He grinned like he was about to tell me my fly was open, "I...uh, well..?"

I tried to help him, "It's the stereo isn't it? I know I play it a little loud but..."

"No son, your music is fine. Y'see, I'm the proprietor here and I have to look out for the best interest of every body."

"Yes sir..?"

"In the past hour or so, I got several calls about..." he heaved a big sigh and said, "about that black man who's visiting you. Folks don't mean no harm, but they're just afraid son, that's all."

Well, I was staggered by this comment, and I refused to believe what I was hearing. I needed instant clarification. "You mean my friend Woody?" I thumbed quizzically towards the trailer. "You're afraid of him? Why?"

"It upsets people son. They're not used to a lot of strangers, and they wanted me to speak to you about it?"

I felt my jaw hit the ground. After all, what do you say to a man who knocks on your door to tell you that your guest isn't fit enough to be there. He couldn't even look me in my face to say the words. And when he did, he saw my expression and started babbling again.

"Now, I hope you don't take this personally, because its not about just you. Last summer young widow MacFarland over in "B" section was working with a black man on her job, and he would drive her home from work everyday. Then the next thing we knew, he was bringing his family over to visit her family."

I felt my face flush; anger and shame rose up in me so quickly, I knew I had to shut this stupid prick up right now. "I don't know who the hell you think you are, Mr. Passwaters; but whoever I decide to bring in my home is none of your goddamn business."

"Aw, son. Don't get angry, now..."

"And if you and your racist friends don't like it, you can all kiss my rosy pink ass." I stared at him disgusted. "Is that's all you got to say to me?"

"Well, Mark; I hoped you wouldn't..."

"Good!" I shouted. "If you'll excuse me, I have a house guest." And I left him standing there with that shit-eating grin on his face. As I opened the door, it occurred to me; I had to tell Woody about this now. Why was I so embarrassed?

"Damn, Mark. What was that all about? Thought I might hafta come out there and kick some ass."

"That was my landlord…"

"What did he want? Trying to find out who's that escaped nigga you got hiding in here?" Woody spoke in complete jest, but when he saw my expression, that I wasn't laughing, his eyes widened and he said, "Get the fuck outta here! Your landlord came to your door and asked you about me? What did he say?"

"Said he got calls from the neighbors."

"What fuckin' neighbors? Who even knows I'm here?"

"Apparently everybody. I guess they saw us outside."

"Kiss my ass! That's a strong move. I've seen some prejudiced shit go down in my time, but ain't nobody ever come knocking on my door asking me questions about who I got up in my crib. Well, Mark," he grinned, "are you…*angry?*"

"Look, Woody. Don't fuck with me now, okay?"

"Damn man, you're messed up about this, ain't you? Well, what you wanna do? You wanna leave? You wanna go fuck somebody up, what?"

"I don't know, but I'm not leaving; I live here. I just can't believe this. It's almost the 1990's, and I have to move into this redneck time warp. What do you think I should do, report it to the police?"

"Fuck no. Just forget it. Cops don't give a damn, and really ain't nothin' they can do. Besides, these crackers can't kick nobody's ass, not tonight anyway, and tomorrow morning I'm outta here."

"But I'll still be here. How are we supposed to rehearse now? How am I supposed to feel safe knowing that the Aryan Nation has me under surveillance?"

"Maybe you could hide me in the trunk and back up to the door next time."

"Woody this isn't funny."

"Yes it is! I can't believe you're so shocked by this. That you can be as old as you are, and have never come face to face with real racism before. How can you be damn near thirty and not know there ain't no Santa Claus?"

"I never lived in Mayberry RFD."

"All you gotta do is live in America. Mark, you my boy and all, but it's hard for me to feel sorry for you. Black people hafta go through this shit all the time. Okay, take that anger you got right now, and how you're feeling all watched and targeted and shit, and multiply that over a lifetime then you get some idea of what it feels like to be a black man in this country. And you wonder why we're angry and heart-attacking all over the place?"

"How do you stand it?"

"That's all we know. It's like that story about the woman who didn't know her husband was a drunk 'til he came home one night sober. There's a guy I went to school with who's a Muslim now, and he said that when he went to Africa for the first time and could walk through the streets and didn't have to feel like a criminal, like a suspect—like a *nigga;* he went home and cried like a baby. I think I know what he's talking about. It's like when I finally fought Charles, the bully back in junior high. I felt sad that I was like that to begin with. That first trip overseas fucks up a lotta brothers like that; Malcolm X, Muhammad Ali, them soldiers in World War II. Hell, Richard Pryor stopped using the word *nigga* after he came back. So this kinda shit ain't new to me, and whatever you want to do is cool. If you want to work on the play somewhere else, that's fine. If you want me to get my boys and we kick some ass, that's cool too. Make it easy for yourself because you can't make it no easier for me."

I should have listened to Woody and just dropped the whole thing, but I couldn't. I had been violated, and if that's how Woody wanted to handle it, fine. But I just couldn't let it go. I didn't tell him this, but after I drove him back to Philly, I came straight home and made a few phone calls. To whom? The cops for one, then the housing commission for another; but the story was always the same. "Sir did he threaten you?" No. "Did he attempt to evict you?" No. "You can come down and fill out a complaint if you wish, but other than that, there's nothing we can do." It got so bad that in a fit of desperation, I called the Harford County Chapter of the N.A.A.C.P.

"N.A.A.C.P., may I help you?"

"Yes, there's been a racial incident, and I'd like to know what actions I could possibly take?"

"Well, sir, tell me what happened."

"I'm new to this area, and I just moved into Chesapeake Trailer Park..."

"You mean off Route 44?"

"Yeah, that's the one. How did you know?"

"We already got a stack of complaints about them."

"About discrimination?"

"Yeah. As a matter of fact, I'm surprised they finally did let some black people move in there. Do you have a family?"

"Well, that's just it. I'm white."

"Excuse me?"

"I'm not black, but a buddy of mine is. He was visiting for the night and the landlord knocked on the door and told me that he had been getting calls from the neighbors."

"So, what do you want us to do about it?"

"I don't know, that's why I'm calling. Isn't there some action we could take against him?"

"Well, frankly sir, *we* got people who can't even find a place to stay. So maybe *we* are not the best ones to help *you* with this. But since you think our services are so important to the community, maybe *we* could include you in our next membership drive."

Desperation can make you do stupid things sometimes, can't it? Why would the N.A.A.C.P. want to run to the aid of some disillusioned white guy, especially when he never gave a damn about them? In fact, up until now, I'd always thought they were a necessary nuisance; you know, like mosquitoes in the summer. But I was determined to address this problem somehow. The nearest chapter of the A.C.L.U. was in Baltimore, and I was ready to call the Black Panthers by now. I wasn't at peace anymore no matter how much I tried to regain it.

13

The Bohemian Reading

"I can't believe you can be so stupid, Woody. You mean to tell me that you let some whiteboy handle a business deal, and you didn't check it out first? What's wrong with you man? Makes me think you not the same Woody I grew up with. And look at what's done happened. The shit comes back all fucked up, and you been completely cut outta the picture. Well, what did you expect from a pecka-wood?"

That's the conversation I had with Andrew, two weeks later when the copyright form came back with a note attached: "Woodrow Tyler not authorized claimant. Ideas cannot be copyrighted."

"But really, 'Drew," I said. "I think it was an honest mistake. It's not like he didn't show me the form."

"I'm telling ya, that's how their minds work. They can fuck over you and not be intending to. They just so out for theyself that you get lost in the shuffle. You notice there was no problem about *his* name being on the form, just yours."

"He called me as soon as he found out. I don't think Mark is like that."

"What else could he do, hide it from you? And I'm tellin' you Woody, if you gonna deal with this devil then watch yo' back, brother. And how you let him list your name like that anyway? Thought you said y'all was writing the play together."

"That's what I told him."

"Let me get this straight now, he just happened to have some copyright forms that gotta be filled out right now. You wanted to identify yourself as the co-writer, but he persuades you to do otherwise. The claims comes back, and your name has been totally exed out, and only the whiteboy's name is legally associated with it, and you want me to believe all this was just an accident?"

It did seem damned suspicious, didn't it? And at that point I didn't know how much I could trust Mark anymore. But I couldn't weigh that against what I knew about him. I mean we was cool; in many ways I was closer to him than I ever been to 'Drew. And Mark just wasn't like that. He was unpredictable true, but I never seen him try to *play* nobody, especially me; or was all that just an act? Because here I sit with a copyright form, and my name's been cut from a script that I damn sho' helped write.

"I'm sorry it came back like that," he told me, "but I'll mail you the form, you can change whatever you want, then send back the corrections; that's all. I was just trying to be honest. In the entertainment world, they make this distinction all the time. You read *The Autobiography of Malcolm X?* Well, it was told to Alex Haley who actually wrote it. Look on any TV credits and you see the same thing. I didn't just dream this up to rob you Woodrow."

"Well, it is in your favor."

"Look, it was a mistake, okay! Why didn't you check it? You knew what was on the form."

"I didn't know."

"Well, neither did I! And now it's all my fault? Bullshit! Look, you'll get the thing in the mail, and you can put whatever you want. But I still say you didn't write the play, and I think the play suffers because of it."

"Like how?"

"Your scenes would work much better if you wrote the dialogue for them too. You know black dialect better than I do. It would be like me asking you to write dialogue between two blokes in an English pub. Which brings me to my next point; you could be doing a lot of this writing too Woody, if you'd stop being so damn lazy. You know the structure of a play, you know when it's not working and why, you know characters, and you're literate. The rest is just blood, shit and tears. You're satisfied letting me do all that, still you want it to sound like we're doing the same thing. But like I said, put what you want on it."

I really couldn't hold nothin' against Mark. But 'Drew did hip me to the fact that I should be careful with the business end. Not necessarily because I couldn't trust Mark, because it's just good business.

We didn't see each other again until the reading. We didn't rehearse until then because our show was performance ready, and the few new lines wouldn't require much rehearsing. When I finally got with Mark that night, we was like boys again.

We all agreed to hook up at the art gallery early that evening so we could do a couple of speed-throughs. And if you tried to tell us then that we weren't the *it shit,* performing in downtown Philly, you would have to kill us. We got there around 5:30, and the receptionist was expecting us. I made sure of that because I knew how terrified she'd be to find a herd of black people rushing through the building at one time.

I told everybody this was just a reading, but it still had the feeling of a major performance; and to us it was. So, Karen Malone and Bonnie Standifer brought a change of clothes, makeup, hair products and all that shit. We grouped together on the stage and did a speed-through where we would say the lines as fast as we could, but you still hafta be able to hear the words. If you got any hesitation about your lines, we found out quick, fast and in a hurry. And if you can speed-through, then you can handle any fuck ups, or when somebody decides they want to ad lib. The new lines worked fine, and I knew it would be a challenge for everybody else to compete after I stepped out and delivered those opening lines. Like Mark says, the pork factor kicks in then.

We felt *good,* jack! Before the show we still had time to stroll along South Street feeling like celebrities, but we probably were acting more like tourists. This shit was fun; things were happening. We were hyped on the possibilities of what we were doing. Back at the Bohemian Art Gallery, we hung out like it was the corner; our clothes and gear were draped all over the seats, we had bought snacks, soda, and coffee. But an hour before curtain, we cleaned that place up like the Keebler elves had been up in there. Three chairs sat on stage, and Bonnie and Karen were made-up and changed. Jerome and Jeff had their dress pants on, and I was looking good as usual; had on my black, pleated pants with a charcoal grey turtleneck, hair greased back and soft brushed 'til it was wavin' at me. And we sat chillin' when Adolph and whats-her-face, Flipper walked in. I rushed over to them.

"Hello, Mr. Tyler," he said with that accent. "You do have a reading of *A Gentlemen's Journal* tonight, no?"

"Oh yeah, we're all ready to go. You just say the word." He seemed disturbed because we was sitting around so chilly like we had everything under control, and really we did.

"Do you need any props, anything I can provide you?"

"Not really, we got somebody working the lights so you just say the word. Oh, one other thing," I remembered. "Do you have any extra chairs? The cast invited a few friends."

"Well, we have standing room for about another 15, but any more than that, and we're against code. I hope you're not expecting too many." Then he went back to the lobby.

Inside, the hanging curtain made the perfect back stage area, kinda like the bulletin boards did in the dorms. We stood around there bustin' on the building.

"Well, I was surprised how dinky this place is," Donnell joked. "Damn, when you say *art gallery,* I'm expecting this huge palace, not some little store front."

"Yeah," Karen said. "This ain't even as big as the dorm, let alone the Humanities Theater."

"But that's how all the Off Broadway shows are in New York. You might find a play in a store, a church, a warehouse, anything." Bonnie Standifer said. She was a fair actress, but she could be an air-head sometimes; I mean, truly *bubblicious.* Then she could turn around and say some intelligent shit like that.

Jeff added, "And it's not so much this performance, but what this could lead to. Maybe we'll get a spot in that festival."

I was restless so I paced to the lobby and saw Mark and Adolph wrapped in some kinda deep conversation. Mark could apparently speak comfortably with Adolph who was more at ease with Mark than he ever been with me. That's when I thought of the American Express commercial. I pictured Karl Malden holding up that green card saying, "*White people;* don't leave home without one."

65

Right around five-to-eight the place started to fill up, and even though Adolph didn't mind the five dollars a head, I could tell he didn't know quite what to make of all these black folk. When I peeked from behind the curtain, I thought I was in my uncle's store-front church except for two rows of white people sitting down front. Uncle Jake *got the calling* about two years ago, and started his *Church of New Africa* and actually got people to come listen to him. Well, this crowd looked just like them. There were a few young people, but mostly mothers, fathers and family members of the cast. Even my Aunt Earlemae and my cousin Barbara came. Neither Cool Will nor Crazy Francine could make it. I heard somebody's say, "Oh hi, honey. How ya doin'?"

"Chile, don't step on my feet, or I'll have to turn this place out."

We did the play, and I don't know what else to say but *we kicked that shit live!* I mean everything went great. Yeah, we flubbed a line here and there and Mark missed a couple of cues, but it was great, you hear me? I'm not sure what it was, but everything just came together. The cast was so cool and confident, no jitters or anything; and when somebody messed up, the audience never knew.

They were hypnotized, and at some moments during my monologue I could see them sit forward in their seats hanging on my every word. I loved it. Man, it was like eatin' honey! They seemed so surprised. The Moms and Pops in the crowd had never seen their children do anything so professional. Adolph and his group was impressed that not only weren't we the lazy, coon-show they had feared, but that our show was polished. Hell, we didn't need no scripts. But there was something else too; there was *pride.* The audience was proud of us.

Well, I knew Adolph probably never seen no reaction like this before, so I wasn't sure what he was gonna say in his critique. I don't remember everything, but he said he liked the format and how it wasn't the standard one-act. He said something about how the message was universal, and not the usual complaints about race you get from the other black plays. I thought about Mark when he said that one. He even complimented the poetry and the language.

We sat on stage and just sucked it all up. And even though he didn't announce it right then, we knew we would be back to do the Black Drama Festival.

14

Between Scenes

Woodrow's hunch was right. We were chosen for the festival and put on the bill with another one act play. Ours was to be the second one performed, so I guess you could say the other group was opening for us. Well, that's certainly what I'm going to say.

The weeks leading up to the performance were heady indeed. The Drama Center was handling all the production, and we got first rate ink in the press. We had a tiny blurb in *Variety*, were in a few underground newsletters, and the *Daily News* would even review the show once we opened. Even back in Dover we got a write-up in DelState's *Hornet* and in the *Dover Post*. Woody and I wanted to contribute as much as we could so we agreed to do the programs and the flyers for ourselves. I had experience doing graphics in the military, and I knew where I could get them duplicated for free.

When you do a show like this, it completely possesses you. Maybe not so much at first, but the closer you get to opening night, the more the play expands and fills up damn near all your waking hours, and many of your sleeping ones too. None of which helped at work either. I didn't make any major fuck-ups, it's just the minor ones that showed I was distracted.

Case in point: when an insurance claim comes in, we would identify it by stamping an invoice number in the corner. They even had a little gadget like an electric stapler that kept track of the numbers. Well, somehow I managed to stamp the wrong numbers on about a hundred different forms. Needless to say, this caused quite a stir two weeks later when people called with the same invoice numbers. The only thing that saved me was that I used the mistake as an opportunity to suggest how we could improve the system. Why not use invoices with the numbers pre-stamped on the form (stupid!) to avoid problems like this again.

It was also the time I befriended the office manager Craig Dempsey, or should I say we befriended each other. One afternoon on my break, I was sitting in the canteen smoking, drinking black coffee and composing script lines (a new ritual I had discovered). I was so wrapped up that I didn't notice someone across from me.

"You look a thousand miles away from here, Mark. Whatcha doing?" I looked up and it was Craig Dempsy.

"Oh hi, Craig. I was just trying to figure out a scene from this damn play."

"So how are things going on the theater scene?"

"I guess I didn't tell you, we got a week's run at the Drama Center in Philly. We'll be opening their first annual Black Drama Festival in October. You ought to come."

"The Black Drama Festival?"

"Yeah, it's a long story. I'll have to tell you about it sometime."

"Wow, your own play? That's great. You must be excited about it."

"Well, excited isn't the right word, but I'll guess it'll do."

"Be sure to save me a ticket. I bet a lot of people around here would want to see it; if for no other reason than to gossip about it?" He saw that I was still writing so he turned his attention to his coffee and donuts, and opened a glossy colored magazine he'd brought with him. I wanted to be as polite as he had been, after all, he was the boss.

"What's that you're reading?"

Keyboard Magazine, he told me. "I've got a small recording studio in my spare bedroom, and I'm checking out the new equipment."

"You're a musician, Craig?"

"I told you I was a song and dance man from way back."

"What instrument do you play?"

"Oh, I know a few piano and guitar chords, but now that I've got a synthesizer and drum machine, I'm doing songwriting mainly."

"Where do you perform them?"

"I don't," he chuckled. "It's just a hobby. But, if I wanted them performed, there're people I know who'd do it. Right now, I'm playing just to relax and have a little fun really."

"Got any tapes? You ought to let me hear some of your music."

"No, it's still unfinished. I'd be too embarrassed."

"Well, don't be. Maybe I could help you with them. If you need lyrics, I got plenty. Maybe we could collaborate like Rodgers and Hammerstein, or Tim Rice and Andrew Lloyd Webber…"

"Or Cain and Abel," he laughed sarcastically. "Tell you what, I'll bring in a tape, if you bring in a copy of your playscript. Deal?"

"Deal!"

Well, you know what I was thinking? I had already fast-forwarded to when Craig could maybe do an original musical with us or something. I know that's a lot to expect from one cup of coffee together, but I had always written lyrics and put songs together. The big problem was that I'm not a musician. I can sing just enough to give you a feel for the rhythm and melody, but I can't play any instrument or read music. But I do know when a song sounds like how I want it. So, between my lyrics and Craig's music, who knows?

It disturbed me how easily I'd adjusted to the office grind. In no time I'd gotten caught up in the little office community. I participated in the sports pool, I'd gone to the company picnic, and I knew the latest gossip on just about

68

everybody. For example, I knew that Thom Cooper and Linda Courtney, the bookend assistants, had actually been real life bookends. Before their current marriages and kids, they were married to each other; and some say that the career climb had split them up. They were civil to each other now, but apparently this was after the fireworks of a few years ago. Their relationship with each other didn't seem as cut-and-dry as they pretended.

I also discovered which women to watch out for. Marilee Fenner down in personnel was "open all night" as the saying goes. I was warned that anything I did with her would be on the evening news the next day, so be careful. Becky Bates, who sat two rows over, was recently divorced, a dedicated homemaker and mother, but she was hellbent on finding a replacement Dad for her daughter before the year was out. Bob Maronni in the desk across from me wanted to fix me up with some mousy brunette who worked down the hall. "She's about your age, she's smart and friendly, and I really think you two would hit it off." I guess I would've been more interested had he not been pushing us together so hard. Also, I guess I wasn't quite ready to start dating again; not with this play to think about, not with the Neo-Nazis in my back yard, and especially not this soon after Tamara Lawrence. You see, I still have a tendency to lead with my heart too much; you know, get too emotional too soon? And yeah, that's just what I need right now, more emotional turmoil. I need that like I need my throat slit.

Craig Dempsey never got caught up in the office shenanigans. I guess that's why he's the district manager. He'd participate enough not to be an outsider, appearing at a wedding or an occasional party, but he always came alone and was always strictly business. On the occasions I'd meet him in his office, I would have the tendency to be chatty, especially since I felt so at ease with him. Craig wouldn't hear of it. He wouldn't be rude or impolite, but he'd let you know that his office was no place to hang-out. He was apparently a private man because I never heard any gossip about him; well, not until later.

He did swoop-in on me a few days later at the canteen, this time carrying a hand-held tape recorder. I listened through the dinky little speaker, and the music surprised me. I was expecting to hear something homemade, but the tape sounded like a band was backing him, not just a synthesizer and a drum machine. When I began ad libbing lyrics from one of my poems, Craig's eyes widened and a surprised smile crept across his face. Apparently my lyrics fit the song. So much so, he suggested that I come to his studio and lay down some tracks. I tried to tell him that I'm no singer, but he reminded me that these were just demo recordings. He wanted to take my vocals and sketch in the melody for someone else to sing later. He gave me directions to his house, and I agreed to come over the next weekend.

"Did you have any problems finding the place?" Craig asked as he greeted me in the driveway. His house was a small but neat Cape Cod hewn out of a wooded clearing.

"No problem," I said. "Your directions were pretty clear." As I closed the car door, I almost didn't recognize him. He wore jeans, a baseball jersey and cap, and seeing him out of his business suit made him look years younger. His attitude was different too. Gone was the office formality, and he was much more relaxed and playful. As he escorted me through his front door, I saw the living room was spacious and uncluttered, the wood paneling and rustic decor making his home cozy an inviting.

"Want anything to drink?" he asked as he escorted me in. "Let's see, I've got soda, lemonade, iced tea, beer or I could brew a pot of coffee."

"The coffee sounds fine. You don't mind if I smoke do you?"

"Not at all, but just not back in the studio, if you don't mind. I spilled a soda on the mixing board once, and it cost a fortune to have it repaired." I joined him in the kitchen and sat at the table as he prepared the the coffee.

"You've got a nice place here, Craig. I'd love to find a home nestled back in the woods like this."

"Where do you live now?"

"I'm in a trailer park over on Route 44."

"How do you like it?"

"Oh, the trailer and lot are fine, it's just the neighbors I don't like. You know, my collaborator, who's a black guy, visited me a few weeks ago to work on the play. Well, the landlord came to tell me that he'd gotten calls from the neighbors complaining about my black friend. Yeah, surprised me too. And now, I don't feel comfortable there anymore."

"Maybe in a few months you can find someplace else because this area is really nice." He poured two cups and joined me at the table.

"That your kid?" I asked, pointing to a framed picture on a nearby table.

"Yeah that's my son, Joel," he said proudly. "He'll be graduating from high school in a few years."

"Looks just like you. I didn't know you were married."

"No, I'm divorced; eight years now. Joel lives with his Mom in Havre de Grace, and he and I get together quite often. He's a great kid."

"Well, did you read *A Gentlemen's Journal* yet? Whadaya think?"

He drew a measured breath and said, "The poetry is great, and the scenes look like they would be entertaining to watch. I don't know though, some of them didn't ring true. Especially that scene where the guy advances on the female character."

"Yeah, we got complaints about that one, but I wrote it with Woody, my collaborator. He suggested the scene, said he actually saw it happen like that. So really, I was writing from his experience, not mine."

"No wonder. It's difficult enough to express the truth as you see it for yourself, and it's doubly difficult to express what somebody else sees. At least that's how it is with music. If I don't understand it and feel it for myself, I can't write about it."

"I know, that's how I feel too. I even suggested to Woody that he write those scenes because I can't write in the black dialect as well as he can."

"Oh, this a black play?"

"That's what everybody's telling me. I didn't write it that way but the entire cast is made up of friends I knew when I was at Delaware State, and they're all black. And Woody managed to get us booked in an Black Drama Festival, so I guess it is."

"Hey, get it where you can."

"That's what Woody said," and I chuckled as I mashed out my cigarette and gulped the final drops of coffee. "I listened to that tape you gave me, and I've got some good ideas. Where's this fabulous studio of yours?"

"I don't know how fabulous it is, but come on back," he stood and led me down a short hallway to a small bedroom at the rear of his house. When I looked in, I thought I'd stepped into the cockpit of a 747. There were buttons, knobs and meters everywhere. A piano keyboard was set up on a stand in front of three racks of equipment which sat on a table. On the opposite wall in the corner, was a mike on an overhead boom that reached down to about eye level.

"Damn, this is a demo studio? Looks more like the Starship Enterprise if you ask me. You've got be a computer genius to work all this."

"Not really. It takes about a week to learn each piece, but then it's no more difficult than a word processor or an automatic teller."

"Well, play something. Show me how you make all this sound like a band."

He sat at the keyboard like Captain Kirk and started pushing buttons. "First, I usually start with a drum beat," he reached over and I heard the bass and snare.

"It sounds so real," I said astonished. "When you say *drum machine,* I was expecting that disco sound; you know, boom-chuka, boom-chuka, boom. But I can't tell this from a live drummer."

"Next, I usually put down the bass line, something like this..." his left hand danced on the keyboard and his head bobbed to the drums. "After that, you can put in just about any instrument sound you want," he pushed another couple of buttons and played with both hands, but this time the sound was an electric piano. "I got programs for just about any instrument you could name. Go ahead, name one."

"How about a guitar." As the bass and drums continued playing by themselves, I saw his right hand press the keys and his left hand work one of two little wheels on the side of the keyboard. The sound was a guitar, but he had to roll the wheels and play the keys like he was strumming for it to really sound like someone was actually playing a guitar. "What about a horn section?"

71

"No problem." He pushed another couple of buttons and I heard the Tower of Power horns blast from the speakers, and they got loud and then quiet as he rolled the little wheel again.

"That's amazing. You don't even need a band anymore, do you?"

"Not for making records; but if you want to do a live performance, the audience usually wants to see real human beings, not machines like this. What else would you like to hear?"

"How about uh…an Austrian fart-horn?"

"A what?"

"An Austrian fart-horn. I just made it up." He smiled and fumbled with a few more knobs, and I heard a sound effect that was so close to a fart that we both exploded with laughter. Craig was more relaxed than I'd ever seen him. Despite his bearish size and the grey speckling his sandy beard, he looked like a kid playing in a roomful of toys.

"Here's one I've been working on." He turned off the drum machine and played a moaning, soulful organ as he vocalized a melody of fragmented lyrics over the chords. He closed his eyes and rocked back and forth like Stevie Wonder as he played. Craig could sing; he had a rich tenor voice that let me know he wasn't new to this. Then abruptly he stopped. "That as far as I've gotten on that one."

"That sounds nice, but why don't you put in a break that's a little more lively or with a different tempo; then go back to the original verse. Play those last chords again…" and I imitated what I meant. "Something like boom bop a boom boom…"

"Wait, do that again," and when I sang this time he played chords that fit the rhythm perfectly. "I like that Mark; that's a keeper. Let me get some of this down on tape."

And that's how we spent that afternoon and most of the evening until we had two decent sounding songs. Craig Dempsey was great company. I appreciated his humor and playfulness, and he was quite a different collaborator than Woody had been. Where Craig was easygoing and lighthearted with his suggestions, Woody was always forceful and bombastic. Both were equally good for what they contributed, but I realized that Dempsey could be much easier to work with. What a difference a few years make.

Things with Woody had cooled too, since that incident with the copyright forms. No, there was no anger, but I could tell he wasn't settled about it yet. Not that he would mention anything, but there was a new suspicion between us that had never been there before. It was still barely perceptible, but when you collaborate with someone, you get to know them. Collaborations are really intimate that way, almost *too* intimate. I talked to Woody maybe once a week, and we got together a couple of times. I never asked him what he did with the copyright form, whether he mailed it back or what, but I knew I wasn't going to take the blame for the mistake alone, especially when I was just being honest. I guess I didn't realize it then, but I resented Woody's suspicion. After all, I'd never suspected him. When I sent him the form, he could've written anything he wanted on it; or taken anything off. I couldn't help feeling that all this was because I'm white, and lord knows that us white people can never be trusted. But one thing I can say for him, when the play starts, all that usually goes on the back burner, and we present a united front.

15

Woody Scores

Waiting for the play to start seems like it took forever. I'd bragged to all my boys: Andrew, Timmie and anybody at work who'd listen. I carried copies of the program that we made, and even cut out the clips from the newspapers that said anything about us. I hyped this play and talked so much shit until everybody was tired of hearing about it. But tough, they just mad cause they ain't got no play written up in *Variety*. I was my own best groupie. I'd hang the newspaper clips on my bedroom wall, or put them in a folder which was fast becoming my scrap book. That was the reminder I needed sometimes to keep me going, so's not get pulled down by all the bullshit around me, and believe me there was plenty of it.

On any morning, I could stumbled on Tim passed out on the couch or sleeping in his room all day. And walking down the streets of my neighborhood was so damn depressing that I wondered if I was raised here at all. Whoever said you can't go home again was right like a muthafucka. That's why I always liked to be at work. I know that sitting around a desk for hours ain't like being at Disneyland, but at least you get to meet people and have conversations. You could run into somebody who was about something other than gettin' high and hangin' out. So, I took all the overtime and extra days they'd give me; and besides, I knew when rehearsals started and I had to miss days for the play, couldn't nobody say shit to me.

I especially liked it when I could work the day shift so I could see folks come and go at lunch time and at closing. And man, there were more upscale honeys walking around than you could believe. Well, you know everybody in these office buildings was playing that corporate role anyway. Dudes had they three-piece Brooks Brothers, walking 'round with leather briefcases that probably only had a peanut butter sandwich in 'em. The ladies looked classy too. They would stop by the security desk and flirt, or when I had to unlock a storage room or escort them to the parking lot, I cracked on 'em ungodly.

There was one particular honey that I really had the eye for. She worked as a receptionist on the eleventh floor, and I found out her name was Belinda Montgomery. Homegirl was bad! Built lean and mean the way I like 'em, always dressed slick as hell and had that cool professional look. She was no knock-down, gorgeous, beauty. In fact, her smile had a few crooked teeth and she was a few years older than me, but I never liked them girls who thought they were too cute anyway. They didn't try hard enough to please nobody. They thought all they had to do was sit there and look pretty. Like that oldies song used to go, "If you wanna be happy for the rest of your life, just make an ugly woman your wife." Naw, Belinda wasn't no *dog* or nothing, but she turned me on more than just about anybody.

The first time I really had a conversation with her was when she showed up one morning and claimed she forgot her office keys, and she couldn't unlock the suite where she worked. I don't know to this day whether she was for real or not, but I know a chance to crack on a babe when I get one.

"I don't know what I was thinking about this morning," she said as I opened the door. "How could I forget the keys?"

"Oh, don't worry about it. I get this all the time, lost keys, stolen purses, stuff like that. And I won't even tell you what I've walked in on a couple of times in the storage room."

"Oh really? Sound's kinky." She arched her eyebrows like a vamp.

"Well, I wouldn't want to scandalize you. Your ol' man might come in here and beat me up or something."

"You don't have to worry about that. The only man I answer to is in the third grade and he lives with his father." She took off her coat and unloaded her handbag on the desk. "Besides, I'm a big girl now, and I don't think there's much that can scandalize me anyway. In fact, you might *get* scandalized," she shot me one of those *let's fuck* looks. Then she sat down at her desk like she suddenly wasn't interested no more.

Yeah, baby! She was so spunky, I had already imagined what she looked like with that business suit off, and I liked what I imagined. I wanted to say more, but about that time other people were coming in the office so I had to jump back into that professional role. But we both knew it was just a matter of time before I could get in them panties. I got my chance one day when I saw her standing in the lobby after work.

"Hey, Belinda. Anything I can help you with? You waiting for somebody?"

"Just waiting for the bus. My car's in the shop so I have to rely on public transportation for a few days. I hate riding the bus; it's so slow and crowded, but what else can I do?"

"It's not so bad once you get used to it. I ride everyday, and you have to find little things to pass the time. You know, like reading the paper, tripping out on the people. But when you get to your stop, it's dangerous for you to walk home, ain't it?"

"No, the bus stops about three houses from my place, so it's really pretty safe."

"Are you sure? I'm getting off in 15 minutes, and I'll be glad to ride with you, if you like."

"I wouldn't want you to go out of your way."

"Well, it's not out of my way if that's where you're going."

"Oops, here comes my bus now," she trotted to the curb but had to come back because the bus was overloaded. "Looks like I'll have to wait until all this rush hour traffic dies down."

"Tell you what; I gotta make my rounds, only take a few minutes. When I come back, we can go over to Tony's, have a drink and wait there for the traffic to clear. I'll ride with you and make sure you get home okay."

"That sound's nice, Woodrow. I'll be right here, so don't make me wait long."

Well, fuck making some rounds. I knew that Jerry Lopez, the guy on duty after me, was already upstairs changing. So, after I told him what the deal was, he covered for me, and I was sitting in Tony's bar with Belinda drinking Long Island ice teas ten minutes later. I liked Tony's because although it was a nice place, it wasn't one of them bars where you don't know what rules you might be breaking. It was friendly, and they wasn't scared of black people being up in there. We sat at a table near the window, and I'll be damned if it wasn't romantic as hell.

"Tell me, Belinda. How come a fine lady like you ain't married?"

"I was married to my son's father, but we were both young and only got together because of Jamal. Then as we grew older, we grew apart—you know the story."

"And your son doesn't live with you?"

"No, we thought it would be better if his father raised him. That's probably not a big a deal now, but I think it'll make a difference once he gets a little older. Jamal comes over all the time, and my ex has always been a good father; he just never was a very good husband, that's all."

"And you ain't found a steady yet? I thought that somebody woulda snatched you up a long time ago."

"Well, if all I want to do is go out, party and lay-up with somebody then yeah, I got plenty of offers. But I'm tired of these same ol' niggas wanting the same ol' thing. Then in a few months they're gone. What about you, Woody. Don't you have a woman?"

"If I did, would I be sitting in a public place like this with you?"

"That still didn't answer my question."

We both giggled and I said, "No, Belinda. I don't have a woman. I see a couple of ladies from time to time, but nobody regular." Even though I ain't been with nobody since the cast party (if you can call it that), I didn't want her to think I was some doofus or nerd or something who couldn't get a woman. We sat there talking for another couple of hours eating snacks and getting a buzz, and we found out quite a bit about each other. She told me that she'd been interested in theater when she was younger. She even sang in the gospel choir at her church, but really everything had been put on hold after her marriage broke up. She took this job about two years ago to get her life back together.

I lied and told her I had finished up at DelState but couldn't find anything with a theater degree. So, I was working here as a security guard and producing my own plays. She got the usual promo from me about *A Gentlemen Journal* and promised that she'd come see it when it opened. I liked Belinda, but I wasn't sure why. She was older than I was, and she seemed more settled and more adult, and I guess that's what attracted me.

She lived on the west side about an hour out of my way, but I rode with her, and walked her to her door. Her crib was hooked. She lived in a big ass, two story, brick row home with three bedrooms and a basement. Hell, her shit was bigger than where we was living. And she was up in here all by herself? Later, I found that she got the house when she broke up with that loser she was married to, but she wasn't having an easy time keeping it up.

"Would you like to come in for a little while? I could make you a sandwich or a cup of coffee before you go home." I like how she said that because she was being friendly, but at the same time she let me know that yes, I *would* be taking my ass home tonight.

I shocked the shit outta her when I said, "No, it's late and I need to get going." She probably never met nobody who turned her down like that, but I wanted her to know that I wasn't no cock hound, and I definitely wasn't like all them other losers she'd met. But just to keep the door open I added, "But I will take a rain check on that if you don't mind."

"Sure," she said with a surprised smile. "I'll look forward to it." I grabbed her hand, raised it slowly to my lips and gently kissed it. I said, "Well, I'll see you at work tomorrow, Ms. Montgomery. Good night." Then, I turned and walked away without looking back. Now, I ask you. Was I cool or what?

After that night, I couldn't keep Belinda off me. We'd meet at Tony's a few nights a week, and she'd drive me to my house afterwards. I finally did take that rain check, and by this time we both knew I would be doing more than just drinking some coffee then leaving; that in fact, I wouldn't be going nowhere until the next morning.

I liked how her crib was decorated. Living with two hard-legs, I forgot how a female touch could really make the place look good. First of all, the place was clean. Didn't have dust and shit rolling around on the floor like a house pet. It was carpeted from wall to wall, and I didn't realize how run down our sofa was until I sat on hers. It couldn'tna been more than a few months old. Wasn't no springs stickin' out the back or no sags and shit in the cushions. Plus she had little doilies and knick-knacks on the tables and shelves. On the stairwell she'd hooked up this artificial tree which was really just some branches with silk flowers glued to them. The place looked like something from a magazine.

I took a page from the Mark Berens book, and I didn't come off like no sex-fiend the way I did with Dessa in the closet. I let her know that sex was no big thing with me. She knew how much she turned me on, but if she didn't want to have sex; cool, no problem. And of course that just made her want to give me some even more.

Behind all that spunkiness I could tell that Belinda probably had been messed over, and she really didn't think she was as big a vamp as she pretended to be. Not that she had been abused or nothing, just taken for granted. So, I took my time with her. I kissed her and held her for a long time before I even touched her privately. I told her how pretty she was and what a nice body she had. Then when we finally did get naked in bed, I pulled the covers back and clicked on the lamp and told her that all I wanted to do was look at her gorgeous body for a while because it had been so long since I seen somebody who looked as good as she did. Man, I talked more shit than a little bit. I don't know if she believed it, but that didn't matter because I knew it musta felt good just to hear it. And by the time we got through having sex, she was sputtering and quivering like a car with a bad engine. I rolled over and just hugged her until she finally fell asleep. Now, after I did that for a couple of nights, I swear to god, Belinda wanted me to move in with her.

"You're over here most nights anyway," she explained. "And since I'm in this big house by myself, I might as well be putting all this space to some good use. Not to mention the time and money we could save."

"I don't know Belinda. If I move in with you, it wouldn't be the same. We'd probably get on each other's nerves. See, you don't know how moody I can be, and sometimes I just like to be off to myself for a while."

"Well, if you can't find enough space to be by yourself in this house, I don't know what it's gonna take. Now, I don't want to push you, Woodrow. I just want you to know you have the invitation."

What really bothered me was that everything was going too fast. Yeah, we had a good time and all, but if I stayed with her everyday, would I have to report in every time I wanted to go somewhere? What if I wanted to stay out all night, or visit Mark for a weekend? Hell, what if I wanted to get with some other babe? And then there's her family situation. How would I deal with her son, walking around reminding me of the loser she used to fuck? Would I have to answer the phone and deal with all of them? And what about bills? Sure, I could help her out with some of the bills, but you gotta remember that I was living for free as it was. So, *any* bills would be more than I was already paying. But she was right. Hell, if I could figure out how to be moody and alone at my pop's crib, it ought to be easy finding quiet time in this big ass house.

I thanked her for the offer, but it was something I'd hafta get used to. And what actually happened was that I started to spend two or three days a week with her, then I'd go back to North Philly and like, re-establish my independence. So for a while, that's just how we did it.

16

At the Drama Center

Me and Craig Dempsey spent another weekend working on songs and just puttering around in his studio, but somehow that didn't make us get as close as I thought we would. When me and Woody hung out like that, we talked about everything. But no matter how much we collaborated, or how playful we were in the studio, there was always this point of formality between Craig and me. At work, nobody could tell that we had collaborated at all because, like I said before, Craig was all business. That was okay; but to be honest, I wanted to know him better. Maybe it was the fact that I valued his age and fatherly wisdom, or that I just wanted to learn more about song writing, but it obviously wasn't going to happen.

The closer we got to the performance date, the more there was for me to do. First, there was the writing, which I didn't mind, because it's why I really got into this in the first place. But then came the blocking, and the directing, and designing ways for people to enter and exit gracefully. Next, I had to find somebody to run the lights. Adolph suggested a young lady he had used, but we had to pay her twenty bucks a night. That would have to do because anybody that I could find would probably want more money and couldn't run the board as well.

Then, I had to figure out a way for the cast to get back and forth to the theater, making sure those who didn't have a ride at least had car fare. And I had to do all this while working forty hours a week. I wished I had help. Woody was certainly clear enough about his status on the copyright form, but why couldn't he help me with some of this? And to ask the question was to answer it. Woody didn't have the skills in these matters that I had. He didn't know how to focus the lights, and couldn't help with the blocking because I was still finishing the script. And I certainly couldn't ask him to handle the scheduling. It was all he could do to get to rehearsals on time himself, let alone trying to get somebody else there. I realized how difficult directing actually was; and that with any production there's got to be someone with whom the buck stops. For *Gentlemen's Journal*, it obviously stopped with me.

During rehearsal week, I had scheduled my office work for late mornings so I could make the drive to Philly and be back without too much of a hassle. For the opening weekend, I'd just have to take some sick days because it would be pointless to try to work anyway. And during the following week of the performance, I'd have to wing it, and take time off as I needed it. That's one thing I can say about my colleagues at work, they certainly backed me up when I was absent, and even promised to come to the show *en masse* one evening.

The Monday before the show opened, I drove the two hours or so to Philly and picked up Woody one evening so we could check out the facility for the first time. After the Bohemian Art Gallery, we didn't have our hopes up too high because the Drama Center was only a few blocks away. As we approached the address off South Street, we were pleasantly surprised. The building was much bigger and had more of the look and feel of an actual theater. Outside was a lighted marquee with two huge posters on either side of the entrance. One was a permanent sign for the theater itself which read, *The Philadelphia Drama Center* in big bold letters, *Artistic Director, Adolph Grumann.* But the other was a professionally painted poster announcing the Black Drama Festival. And there it was, listed among the other shows: *A Gentlemen's Journal by Mark Berens and Woodrow Tyler*—our names up in lights! Well actually, they were under the lights, but let's not split hairs, shall we? Me and Woody just loved it. We beamed with pride and slapped five as we walked through the double doors of the old building.

The lobby of the Drama Center was damn near as large as the entire Bohemian Art Gallery. We could tell that the building had been an old warehouse or department store, but it was spacious and roomy. At one side of the lobby was a concession stand. Later, when it was stocked, Adolph and his crew would sell sodas, juice, chips and hotdogs for some ridiculously high prices. I guess that's one of the ways they made their money. The walls of the lobby were lined with framed posters and photographs of previous shows, and there were upholstered benches and chairs to sit on. We stared wide-eyed at posters of shows like *Hot L Baltimore, Antigone, Equus* and *Shadow Box,* and felt like we had just strolled through some hall of fame.

"Damn, Mark," Woody said. "You think we could get our pictures up here?"

"We don't have any photographs like that Woody, and we certainly don't have any posters."

"We could get some, couldn't we?"

"From where? Do you know any artist or photographers who want to work for free?"

"No, but I thought you might."

"Look, Woodrow. I've got a million things to worry about as it is. Yeah, it would be nice, but that's something you or somebody else will have to worry about; that is, if it gets done at all."

The theater itself was about three floors tall, and the chairs were arranged on a series of platforms and risers that climbed about two stories seating about two hundred or so. The stage was big enough, but oddly shaped and positioned diagonally in the space. Smack dab in the middle of it was a pole, apparently holding up the ceiling. Stage right opened to a corridor which led to an office at the top of a nearby staircase. Far left on the third level was the control booth which operated an impressive looking light grid hung precariously over the stage.

And as was usual with small theaters, everything was painted black; except the seats, which were dark blue, giving the room a solemn, regal feel. It was slick, and except for that damn pole at center stage, you could tell that the house had been arranged with considerable thought and planning. Woody and I wandered around awe struck like two kids in a cathedral.

"Ah, welcome gentlemen." We heard Dracula's voice speak from nowhere; scared the hell out of us. We looked around to find Adolph standing stage right. "How do you like our theater?"

"It's great," I said and I looked at Woody relieved. "I can't wait to get the actors on stage."

"Yeah, we were really impressed by the lobby," said Woody. "The posters and everything really look professional."

"If you like, we can clear a space if you have any photographs or bulletins to display. In the mean time let me show you the rest of the theater."

He escorted us behind the upstage wall where two small chambers had been set up as dressing rooms. And like everything else, they had been arranged thoughtfully, each room containing a wall of mirrors framed with neon lights. Two long, folding tables and a row of chairs sat in front of the mirrors. A large window on the opposite wall opened to the back alley but was icing-glassed for privacy. And just to give it a nice touch, there was a wardrobe rack made from what looked like plumber's pipes with ten or twenty costumes hanging under a plastic cover.

"These are the dressing rooms," Adolph explained, "one for the gentlemen and one for the ladies, although you will be sharing with the Liberty Theater Company. We have only the single lavatory here," he said as he pointed down the hallway adjoining the two rooms, "but there is another in the lobby as well. Each room has an entrance to either side of the stage which is behind this big partition," he pointed to the permanent flat whose opposite side served as the back wall of the stage. "So, when you change, remember that voices will travel. I recommend that you use the rear entrance to the building when you arrive because the lobby is locked until one half hour before the curtain time. You can find telephones upstairs in my office. Feel free to use them whenever you need them. If you must make toll calls however, I ask that you use the pay phone in the lobby."

"What about that pole at center stage?" I asked.

"Yes, that is unfortunate, but unavoidable. It is structural and not cosmetic so nothing can be done. My suggestion is to use it in your blocking. I've seen it used as a tree, a light post, and even the corner of a building. Ah, imagination, yes? However, you should be careful when the lights dim, for some actors have stumbled into the pole and fallen. Comical, but very dangerous."

Woody asked, "Can we keep our clothes and valuables here when we leave?"

"Certainly. I will be back stage during all performances, and we lock the building securely each night. Since you share with the Liberty company, at some point you should negotiate some rules for sharing the space. This way, there is peace, yes?"

"When will they be here?" I asked him.

"They come to focus lights tomorrow. Maybe you should come too, no? You can collaborate on settings that are mutually beneficial. They have employed our house technician, and if you agree, her fee can be shared between you."

"That sounds like a good idea," I said. "We haven't found anyone ourselves, and this should work out for both of us."

"Well gentlemen, feel free to wander around, inspect the facility, satisfy your curiosity. If you can arrive tomorrow, we focus the lights and begin the dress rehearsals on Wednesday. If you need assistance, I'll be in my office."

As Adolph disappeared up the stairs, Woody and I sauntered around the stage again, chests puffed out, quite impressed with ourselves.

"So what do you think, Woody?"

"I think this is hyped like a muthafucka, Mark Berens! Tell me, when we were gettin' high and bullshittin' around your kitchen table a few months ago, did you ever think we'd be up here in the big time kickin' it like this?"

"This really isn't the big time yet. Is it, Woody?"

"Closer than you ever been, junior."

"But not as close as I hope to get," and we laughed at each other. "Well, if we're going to set lights tomorrow, there's no need for me to drive back to Maryland. Guess I'll have to check into a motel or something. You know of any good ones?"

"Who you asking? Like I sleep at one every night."

"Maybe Adolph will know."

"If you don't mind sleeping on the couch, you can stay with us at my Pops place. Naw...wait a minute. Maybe Belinda will let you crash at her crib tonight."

"Who's Belinda?"

"She's that honey I been tellin' you about. Just chill and let me give her a call," and he followed where Adolph had gone. He returned minutes later and announced, "She said she'd love to meet you. The guest room is kinda junky, but at least you won't have to spend money on no hotel. She's short on grub, but she's made a shopping list, and we'll have to pick up a few items once we get there; but its all set. Damn this is gonna turn out all right. Now, maybe I can be the host for a change."

"What about you? Don't you have to work tomorrow, or can you come back and help me set up?" I asked Woody.

"Is this a trick question, or what? Hell, I wouldn't miss this for the world. Ain't nothing but a phone call."

We headed off to West Philly where Belinda lived, and I must admit that I was anxious to meet this lady. How could a woman who had a house, a car, and a job be this involved with Woodrow Tyler? It didn't add up, but I knew that if Woody could get along with her, she had to be fun company.

I hate driving anywhere with Woody. Since he always takes the bus and probably has never even used his driver's license, he's a piss-poor navigator. This is how he gives directions: "Oh, Mark, that was your turn we just passed back there." The next time I'll just let him drive. What the hey, I'm insured.

We pulled up to a brownstone in a surprisingly nice neighborhood that wasn't run down yet, but probably would be in another few years. I parked out front and walked up a flight of steps to the door. Belinda greeted us as we got there.

"Hello, you must be Mark Berens. Woodrow has told me so much about you."

"I deny everything," I smiled as I shook her hand.

"Well, come on in and make yourself comfortable." She was very gracious.

"Yeah," said Woody, "let me take your jacket and brief case." He pranced around proudly like the place was actually his. It was a neat clean home, nicely decorated without being cold and uncomfortable like my mother's living room used to be. That place was a museum, and I never understood why my parents even had a room that nobody could ever use.

"Would you like something to drink?" Woody asked like he was the HNIC. "Baby, what we got to drink in there?"

"Just some iced tea. You gotta run to the store for me, remember?" She walked into the kitchen, returned and handed Woody a slip of paper. "Here, I've made a list, and if you go now, the supermarket around the corner is still open."

"Here, let me help with that," I stood and reached for my wallet. They protested but I said, "No, I insist. I was going to pay it to some hotel anyway."

"C'mon, Mark. Let's make that run." Woody ordered.

"You go ahead. I've been on the road all day. Here, take my car." I tossed him the keys.

He looked at me awkwardly like he didn't want to take them, or was it that he didn't want to leave me here alone with his woman?

"Cool, I'll be back in ten minutes," he said and disappeared out the door.

Strangely enough, I was more relaxed with Belinda now that Woody was gone. No, I wasn't horny for her, although she's not a bad looking woman. But with Woody there, I felt like he was competing with her for my attention, or always trying to direct or control the conversation. Belinda returned with a tray carrying a plastic pitcher and matching glasses. She sat and poured two glasses full of tea and sat the tray on the cocktail table between us.

"Well, Mark. I feel like I already know you from what Woodrow has told me. I can't wait to see this play because it's all he talks about. He said y'all met at Delaware State College."

"Yeah, about a year ago. We were doing the musical *Hair,* and after that we became good friends. How did you two meet?"

"At work. Woody had been at the security desk for weeks before I actually had the chance to talk to him. Then one day, my car broke down and he rode home with me on the bus. We've been close ever since."

"Yeah, I know. Even though we've been friends for less than a year, it feels longer. We've been through a lot in a short time too. We did that musical, wrote and performed the play together. And when we both found out we wouldn't be finishing our degrees, we kind of cried on each other's shoulders."

"Oh you didn't get a degree?"

"I lost interest, and I think Woody had troubles with his bill. But things have a way of working out. Had we continued in college, I doubt we'd even be doing this play now."

She freshened the drinks and asked, "Well, what's this play about? Woody's tried to explain it to me, but he claims it's something you just have to see."

I gave her my usual summary about the format, the characters, and the performance; and in no time Woody returned carrying two armfuls of groceries. Belinda disappeared into the kitchen and we sat listening to the stereo with the sound turned down on the TV.

"So what kind of lighting are we gonna do tomorrow?" He asked me, "You got any ideas?"

"Well, it can't be too specific because we'll have to share it with the Liberty company. So I'm thinking about just lighting different sections of the stage. You know, up stage, center, left and right? That ought to be enough for what we have to do."

"What about a spot light?"

"That's a good option, but we'll need another pair of hand for that."

"Where will you be, Mr. Director/Producer?" Woody asked me.

"I guess I could run the spot, but we'll just have to see."

"Soup's on!" Belinda called from the dining room, "I hope you like cold cuts, Mark."

"Are you kidding me? They're a bachelor's staple," I said as we gathered around the table. The spread she'd prepared wasn't like any cold cuts I'd ever fixed. She had cheese-steaks, turkey subs and sandwiches with potato salad and slaw. All the sandwiches were cut into finger size, so everybody had a taste of everything. There was a bowl of chips, pretzels and two huge bottles of soda. I thought for a moment that I was in a deli. I stuffed myself so much until afterwards, all I could do was stare at the TV until it was bedtime.

I stumbled up the stairs to a junky guest room where a space had been cleared around the bed. A clean towel and wash cloth had been courteously draped across the pillow. She'd apparently instructed Woody to buy me that new tooth brush too because I knew he'd never be so thoughtful. I stretched out on the bed and was surprised at how exhausted I was. It was all I could do to get up again and take off my clothes; the bed felt that good.

17

The Liberty Theater Company

I couldn't wait for Mark to wake his ass up. I'd been in the bedroom all morning pissed as hell behind that dumb shit he told Belinda last night. That's why I didn't want to leave them alone in the first place. I finally heard him stumble to the bathroom, then downstairs to get the coffee that Belinda fixed before she went to work. I knew that he was up when I smelled cigarette smoke stinking up the house.

"Mark, what the hell did you say to Belinda last night?" He looked like shit, his hair all over his head, his eyes all red and puffy.

"Good morning to you too, Woody."

"Why did you tell her that we didn't graduate from DelState?"

"As opposed to what?"

"As opposed to not saying nothing at all."

"Woody, I'm sitting there drinking iced tea with the woman. I had to say something."

"It never occurred to you that I just mighta told her I had graduated, did it?

"Well I..."

"You're such a goody-two-shoes, Mr. Fuckin'-Nice-Guy. See? My boys Keith or Andrew neither one woulda never said nothing like that."

"Something always told me that I wasn't Keith or Andrew."

"It took me all night to explain that shit, man."

"Hold up, Woody. You can't possibly expect me to keep track of all your lies. How in the hell was I supposed to know? I call myself being polite to a woman who had opened up her home to me, and what? You want me to lie to her, and treat her like shit? That's your job, not mine."

"Aw man, you didn't hafta tell her nothin' about me. You coulda been polite without telling my life story. Damn, can't tell you nothing."

"Well, if you don't want me revealing your lies, then don't tell any. Either that or keep the woman away from me because I can't be deceitful and sly like that, especially when I'm relaxing with my guard down, and I'm with people who I'm thinking are my friends. So, what did you tell her?"

"Told her that you didn't know what the deal was with my degree, and that I had finished the course work, but my papers were being held up on account of my bill?"

"And she bought that?"

"She didn't have no choice, but I'm telling you Mark, don't be talking to her about me, okay?"

"Like I said, Woody. Keep her away from me then."

I was finally glad when we did get outta there to go down to the Drama Center. The way we moped around all morning it didn't look like we were even friends, let alone collaborators. Just before lunch we arrived to finally meet up with the Liberty Company; well at least with their director and tech people. As we walked in, the place looked like they were remodeling or something. The light grid had been lowered from the ceiling, ladders and tools and shit were scattered all around, chairs pushed all up against the wall. Me and Mark looked at each other like, damn, all this to focus lights?

There were two dudes and a babe running around and they were *so into* what they were doing, you woulda thought they were building the pyramids or something. The ring leader was this Puerto Rican they called Carlos. With him was this long lanky brother in braids and beads looking like Stevie Wonder with a monkey wrench. Sitting in a chair with a clip board was this dark skinned sister whose hair was cut shorter than mine. She was playing that African princess role wearing a dashiki with every color of the rainbow and big ass earrings that looked like she woulda got whiplash if she turned her head too quick. Carlos had obviously taken this directing thing way too serious because he was dressed to a "T". I mean, he had a sports jacket with a neck scarf, tinted glasses and a beret. I'm serious; he had everything except the cigarette holder, and he was walking around the stage trying to make things way more difficult than they ever coulda been.

Here he goes; "I don't know, Zavier. There's too much spill on the back wall. Can we make this fresnel a little tighter?" Zavier was the Stevie Wonder look alike; he was on a ladder bolting the light to the grid with a wrench.

"That's as tight as it'll focus," he said. "Maybe we could use the spotlight for that scene."

"Oh no, no, no!" whined Carlos like some bitch. "That destroys the ambience and the drama."

Me and Mark walked over to the the sister with the clipboard and introduced ourselves because apparently they hadn't seen us. She signaled Carlos and Zavier to come over, and they really went into their act then.

"Hi, I'm Carlos Hernandez, director of the Liberty Theater Company. These are my associates Zavier Mustafa and Katrina Ray. Glad to finally meet you; we were hoping that you'd show up today."

"I'm Mark Berens, and this is Woodrow Tyler. Looks like you're having trouble with the lights. Anything we can do to help?"

"Not really," said Carlos. "Zavier is pretty handy with that wrench and Robin's on the board." He pointed to the light booth. Up there was this fat sister in overalls and a plaid shirt, so automatically you know what I'm thinking about her, right? "You could help by explaining what kind of lighting you're planning to use."

"Well ours is nowhere near as complicated as what you seem to be doing. We just generally want the different parts of the stage lit: left, center, right, up and down?" Mark explained as he pointed.

"Yeah," I spoke up. "We already performed the show, and all we had then was ceiling lights. So, whatever you guys set up is fine. We can work around it."

"Well, what kind of a show are you performing? Is it a musical or a straight drama?" Katrina asked. She had a sweet, smooth voice and I swear to god she was flirting with me.

"Ours is a combination of monologues and dialogue. The show centers on three male characters who introduce themselves with poetic monologues. Then they have scenes of dialogue between themselves and two female characters," Mark explained. "No music or dance, just a small cast of five."

I added, "In the past, we simply had lights on and lights off for the entrances and exits. That's why whatever y'all do, we can work around. What kinda format are y'all using?" Carlos took the stage to tell us, and I thought he was gonna perform the show right there, as dramatic as he was.

"Ours is a montage of skits, songs, dance, and monologues."

"Oh, y'all got music?" I asked.

"Yes, we dance to recorded music; our songs are a capella, but we have tapes playing in the background as underscoring. It's a sort of roux to hold the action together and to spice it up."

Me and Mark looked at each other like, what the fuck is a *roux?*

"That's why it's so important to have the light cues just so, or one scene will run into the other, and we'll lose that distinction. The flavors will run together."

"So what are you trying to do with the lights?" asked Mark.

"We want to spotlight only the actor's faces as they take different positions on the stage. We need a tight focus here, down stage there, and back over here." Carlos pointed.

"That calls for some really tight blocking, don't you think?" Mark said. "Maybe it would be easier to use the follow spot from the booth. That will give the actors a lot more leeway."

Mark's suggestion was logical as hell. You could see that Zavier and Katrina both thought so from the way they raised their eyebrows. But you woulda thought Mark had slung piss in Carlos's face, the way he reacted.

"No, no, no! You obviously don't understand," he sounded like some gay queen. "We need more than just one spot; that's why just the one won't be enough."

He really got mad when Mark said, "Well, if your lights are focused that tight, then won't you need somebody on stage to know whether you're focusing on their face and not over their heads or on their waists?" That was such a logical question that Carlos didn't have nothing to say, because it was clear now that Mark knew what he was doing and Carlos didn't.

"Well…uh…yeah," he said all weak and lame. "I was about to ask Katrina to step on stage as soon as I found what instruments were available on the grid."

Mark realized he was exposing Carlos for the fraud that he was. "Well look, we're going to get out of your way. And like I said, whatever you decide, we can work around. I just want to go up and meet the lady on the light board, what's her name…Robin?"

We left the three of 'em down there in a state of confusion, and I don't know about Mark, but I wanted to ask, what kinda show are y'all putting on if some simple shit like that got by ya boy Carlos? We climbed up to the booth and introduced ourselves to Robin. Up close she didn't look half bad. She had a round baby face and shiny, curly hair pulled back with a bandana.

"Hello Robin, I'm Mark Berens, the director of *A Gentlemen's Journal.* I think Adolph might've told you about us."

"Oh hi! Yes he did, and from what he said, you guys got a pretty good show."

"Thanks a lot. I was just telling Carlos down there that we didn't need anything complicated, basically lights-on and lights-off. We could even work around what he's focused."

"I know," she said with a big sigh. "We been here for two hours already trying to hook up his uh…vision! But we aren't any closer now than when we started. If he wanted to light parts of the stage, I could've done that from here with the lights the way they were. But…he's the boss, so we got to go through all this."

"Well, let me put your mind at ease now," Mark told her. "All we need is to fade out between scenes, and enough lights so we can find our way around in the dark. Now, if you could light only the parts of the stage where the actors move to, that would be nice. But if not, no problem."

"You got a script?" she asked.

"Got one in the car."

"Well, if you just mark the cues, and leave the script with me for the rehearsal, I can do the rest."

"Great!" Mark said. "I'll get you a copy within the hour. And Robin, you seem to know what you're doing. So, I trust whatever you can come up with."

"You got a deal, Mark," she said. "I wish Carlos the Magnificent was this easy to work with," and we all laughed.

Well, the rehearsal the next night went just as easy for us, and just as complicated for them. First, let me tell you about their show. They called their show *Street Scenes,* and I guess the title was appropriate. Now, Mark had sometimes felt insecure because the structure of our show was so loose and free flowing, not following the acts and scenes you find in most plays. But our shit was tight as a blueprint compared to theirs. They had a cast of about ten people, but each one only had one or two talents. Like one woman could sing, but she couldn't dance worth a damn. One brother could dance but he couldn't put two sentences together and make it sound interesting. Then another brother would appear and deliver lines like he was Reverend Leroy or somebody, then disappear 'til late in the show. There was no camaraderie between them, and everybody was going for theyself like, I got mine; you get yours. It was more like a talent show than a play. And sometimes it looked like they were more into prancing around, being seen, and jacking off on the audience than trying to communicate a feeling or some kind of message.

Their show started out much the same as ours did with each character introducing themselves with a one-liner. You know, the ladies would come out and say something sassy like, "I am Mother Africa and I gave birth to the race of humans," then they'd snap their fingers or move their head from side to side with their hands on they hips. The guys would pimp in all cool and suave, and say something like, "On my back was built a nation of millions, and my hands carved a country out of the wilderness." It was very dramatic, but they had no follow up.

You'd hear Robin cue up some scratchy recording of Leontyne Price singing *Swing Low Sweet Chariot,* and the dancing babe would come out and do this fake ballet step that would change every time she performed it. Then the guys would come out and sing *Chain Gang* and act just like Brute Negroes. Maybe after that, the singer would come out dressed like Aunt Jemima and sing *Motherless Child* or some other gospel tune. And the show would end the same way it started.

I guess they were trying hard as they could, but to me it was the same ol' shit: rag-headed mammies, angry brutes, house niggas, field niggas; niggas, niggas, *niggas!* How come when there's a black play this is what everybody expects to see? Even the black people. That's one thing I liked about Mark's play; it showed that there are other images and other problems that blacks have.

Other times, one of the actresses would slink to the edge of the stage and deliver a line to me, Donell or Jeff like this was supposed to make our dicks hard or something. And we found that Carlos wasn't as much a director as he was a gang leader, keeping folks from stepping on each other' lines, and dishing out stage time to the gang.

They were supposed to run a tech rehearsal first and fix whatever problems they had, then we'd do the same. Then, we'd do the dress rehearsal together without stopping, like on opening night. But man, it took them over two hours to get from start to finish that first time. It was always something: the lights wouldn't be right, the music wasn't loud enough, the dancer couldn't find her way in the dark, or some trifling shit like that. It was damn near eight o'clock when we got our first tech run.

They didn't know what to make of us because when Jeff and Karen, Bonnie and Donell finally showed up, we were more like family than the gang they looked like. We hugged each other and clustered back stage after we'd worked out dressing room arrangements. Sitting quietly in the audience reviewing the new lines Mark wrote, we tripped out at this circus they were putting on. When we finally did get on stage, we were so low key and hassle free that they were all shocked and embarrassed, like we had cheated them or something. Oh, we stopped several times so that Mark and Robin could work out light cues in the booth. And we had to change some of the blocking because of that pole on stage, or because of the new lines, but we schooled the hell out of them, showed them how a real show should be. You could tell we had an effect on 'em because they dropped all that excess bullshit when we did the final run through, and the program was just about as polished as it could be. Finally we were ready for opening night. Well, as ready as we was gonna get.

18

The Black Drama Festival

I don't know about Woody, but the ten days the show ran was a blur to me, one night's performance running into the next. Oh, there was plenty that stood out, but if you asked me when something might've happened, I'd be hard pressed to tell you for the most part. During the week, I stayed at Woody's father's house (we were both too scared for me to stay with Belinda), and some nights I drove back to Maryland. I was a zombie at work because even to this day, I can't remember anything I did. But I must admit that at the time, it was one of the biggest adventure of my life.

I was impressed with both of the shows. No, *Street Scenes* wasn't as well constructed as ours, but it certainly got the audience in the mood when we took stage. And after the first weekend, our sense of team spirit and camaraderie infected even them. We'd sit in the audience and encourage them, and they'd do the same for us.

A Gentlemen's Journal really came together, and seeing it performed let me know that it was finally completed, no more rewrites, no additional blocking— nothing. Finis! The audience was very moved by the poetry and the emotion that the actors were able to project. Each of the three characters had distinct personalities displayed in their monologues. The first character was Mitch. Jeff Wiggins played him, and when he finished, the ladies who weren't crying wanted to take him home.

> Physical pain? Injury? Sickness?
> I'd take them any day over a broken heart.
> At least when you're recuperating,
> You're not by yourself.
> Even a bum in the hospital gets at least one visitor,
> Even if it's just someone emptying the bedpan.
>
> But when a man's honor is hurt,
> He finds little comfort, few listening ears.
> And when a man's heart is broken,
> Where are the Lonely Heart's Clubs for him?
> Who's there ready to wrap him up in their arms,
> Ready to say: I told you so, son...
> But come on home.

His consolation reminds him only
Of how much of a fool he has been,
Admonishing him: Be strong brother,
C'mon take it like a man.

And when a man's spirit is broken,
His heart ripped and torn from him,
His life without structure or reason,
If he survives at all,
He suffers quiet and alone.
And no one ever knows.

Jeff Wiggins had just enough restraint to pull this one off. On the last lines, he would let his voice waver and crack a little, and the audience just ate it up. I actually heard somebody sniffling one night.

Donell Robinson played the second character, Tony who's all flash and glitter; I mean, talk about type casting.

I thrive in the dusky shadows
And wrap them about like a cape.
I stalk the clubs and cabarets
Impressing everybody with my style

I become that fantasy they all wish to be
And portray those scenes locked away for so long.
The women seeking lust and desire,
Wanting to hold me here or kiss me there
Oooh baby, that feels so good!

But fantasies aren't for real
They don't feel, they don't cry,
And they don't need.
And when the real me emerges,
Full of tenderness and vulnerability
I am drowned in an illusion of my own design.

Donell wore the character like a suit, and was sensual enough to make it work. From what I could gather, the audience liked the narcissism and the gall. Still others found him delightfully comical.

The rough character of the three was Raymond, played by Woodrow. Since he created the part, I guess he had a fondness for it, and he performed it with playful menace and vulgarity.

I've finally decided that just for a day,
Just for one small cluster of eternity,
I will indulge myself in all the selfish,
Rude, obscene, completely outrageous acts
That have been forbidden to me for so long!

Won't be rational, consistent, or particularly sane,
But will be loud and arrogant, allowing the basest me
To take a peek at the world while I'm passing by!

I will take all my manners and sorrow,
And pack them tightly in a Mason jar,
Lock it in the darkest crevice of my basement,
And I won't feel guilty about nothing!
I will eat all the junk food I can find,
And not look a vitamin square in the face.
I'll burp, belch, pick my teeth,
Roll over on one hip as I sit at the table,
Release a choral fart,
And smile cause it smells so good to me!

Then at midnight, I'll retrieve that jar
Marinating in the dark all day,
Stir in ample amounts of:
I'm terribly sorry, What got into me,
Mix it up well
And drink hard, bitter gulps in preparation for tomorrow.

Our actresses portrayed different companions in the men's lives, and Bonnie Standifer was so good, they actually thought she was two different people. Karen Malone was as good, but the *redbone* issue popped up again. While waiting to use the restroom back stage, I overheard two ladies from the Liberty Company.

"I hate that high yellow bitch."

"Yeah, she definitely thinks she's Miss It. You see how all these niggas follow in behind her like a pack of dogs. Just like her shit don't stink."

"I'll betcha that's a weave she got on. Nobody's hair is that long. Especially nobody black!"

I was surprised because I knew Karen was as down to earth as anybody. And as often as I had seen her, I knew she wasn't wearing a hair weave.

That Friday, *The Philadelphia Bulletin* sent a reporter to review the play. Adolph had told us the reporter would be coming, but we just didn't know when.

He wasn't difficult to spot, this white man in a group of predominantly black faces, and the fact that he sat in the first row with a pen and pad didn't help him either. It was unnerving, and I found myself checking his reaction at every scene. I just hoped the cast hadn't seen him because I'm sure it would've made them as nervous as I was. On Saturday afternoon, the review came out, and like so many other incidents since I started this play, it had a big effect on me.

To me, the review was supposed to be part of my posterity. I'd heard other artist compare the creative process to child birth. There's the conception, the incubation, the labor and the birth. Then your offspring outlives you and takes on a life and purpose of its own. I'd always laughed at the comparison thinking it was demeaning to both mothers and children, but when I sat nervously Saturday morning waiting for the review, I understood it more clearly. Sure, this was only a play but it was *my play,* and whatever this newspaper would print would be an historical record, a judgment of what I had created. And it would be on the books long after I died, as long as they kept records. And I was anxious to see how history would regard my creation.

When Woody finally got a copy of the newspaper, we searched hungrily for the review. We should've suspected something from the article's title, *Black Drama Festival Doesn't Fulfill Need.* The reviewer was John Campbell, a staff writer and part time theater critic. He was lukewarm about *Street Sounds* describing it as, "a collage of writings by a host of black writers and like any other collage, it is part paste-up job and part art." He identified the outstanding performers and called the dancing to *Swing Low Sweet Chariot* "a sentimental and endearing favorite. Some of it soars and some of it doesn't?" But when he got to *A Gentleman Journal,* he was downright vicious. And after we read it, we were just devastated!

"The play that comprises the second half of the evening is *A Gentlemen's Journal* written by Mark Berens and Woodrow Tyler, a one- act play that is so awash in individual scenes it would capsize if it were on water. It is hardly even an exercise in theater, much the less a black play. Three characters, unlucky in love, embark on a personal odyssey of self discovery and expression. If it weren't for the subject matter, *A Gentlemen's Journal* could easily be an industrial film. The heights it reaches are just about the same, the floor-molding. One character likens his life to a basketball game, 'And when the ball is about to go into the nets,' he effuses, 'I feel like I can do anything!' Stirring words perhaps in the gym, but this is supposed to be theater. When there is such a pressing need for social commentary and the plight of society's underclass, it is absurd that The Drama Center is producing such lightweight work."

Well, uh…I was numb. I couldn't understand his viciousness. He said nothing about the audience's reaction, the dialogue between the women or any of the production value. Instead, he took pot shots at the play. I didn't know what to do. At first, I wanted to write him and ask how did he know what a black play was? Who died and left him in charge of blackness? But just like before, Woody convinced me to let it go; that it wouldn't do any good except make this John Campbell guy feel more important than he really was.

"Well, Mark," Woody explained, "when you're telling the truth and dishing out shots in your play, you gotta be able to take a few shots too, even if they're cheap shots."

"But he had his own agenda, Woody. He came to the theater with his head already full of expectations of what a play should be. And how can he possibly know what a black play is? He's white."

"I don't know, Mark. Seems like you were trying to convince me of the same thing just a few weeks ago."

"That was different. Everybody who saw the play enjoyed it; Adolph, the audience, even The Liberty Company knows we have a good play."

"I'll tell you you what it is. When you say *black play,* everybody expects to see niggas shuffling along, still lost in slavery. And when you have the balls to show black people as just people, and not as slaves, not as mammies, and not as angry bucks, it pisses folks off big time. That's why *Street Scene* didn't bother him, but he found it necessary to dog us out like we was criminals or something. We gave him an image of black people he wasn't ready to see. How dare we put on a *black play* and not talk about racism and all that other shit. What the hell did we think, that we were free and equal or something?"

I didn't feel like hearing Woody's ramblings about race relations, especially now. Hell, if I hadn't been in this damned Black Drama Festival, I would've gotten a fair shake, wouldn't have to be all tangled up in this racial bullshit. I was furious because on some level, I knew Woody was right.

Weeks later, I would come to grips with the review and what it meant. I would realize that first of all the press is not fair, and just because you can get your opinion published doesn't mean it's not a shitty opinion. But most importantly, I would learn that if I continued to do theater (or anything else for that matter), it would have to be for me, for whatever pleasure I got out of it and to hell with posterity and the press, because neither one was fair or accurate. I would understand all this later, but that night, it was a shot to the heart.

The review had a strange effect on both casts. Our actors were understandably hurt, and I thought that Carlos, Zavier and the Liberty Company would really act smug and superior now. Either that or they would patronize us and damn us with faint praise even further. But they were just as offended as we were. I saw in them a genuine admiration for our show that I didn't realize they had, and having *Gentlemen's Journal* assaulted like that hurt them as much as it hurt us; maybe even more because they felt guilty for getting the praise that should've come to us. I guess it was survivor's guilt. After that night, we became one cast, and the espirit de corps was strong between us; as strong as it has been in any other play I've done. Unfortunately, it did nothing for our energy level that night, because we gave the worst performance of the entire run. And wouldn't you know it, that was the night that everybody from work decided to come.

Of course, Linda Courtney and Thom Cooper, the office bookends, drove up with a car full of people each. And it was clear where the battle lines were drawn. The people who rode with Linda were kissing her ass for promotion, and those who rode with Thom were kissing his. They all complimented me after the show and said how proud they were. Obviously, they hadn't read the review; or if they had, they didn't know what kind of play they were looking at anyway. I doubt that any of them had ever seen one before. Thom Cooper wanted to get in on the fun, so he invited the whole cast out for dinner and drinks, on him. Oh, that would really give him brownie points at work.

"Don't nobody wanna hang out with that strange muthafucka." Woody said when I put the offer to the cast. Of course, he was right.

Craig Dempsey came too, but he drove his own car and lingered behind the office groupies to congratulate me alone.

"Well, what did you think?" I asked him.

"Hell of an effort, Mark. Just one hell of an effort."

"Did you like it?"

"Well…" he sighed again in that way I didn't like. "It was imaginatively staged, the poetry was touching, but I didn't like some of the portrayals we'd talked about before."

"Like what?"

"Look, Mark. I don't want to rain on your show. Tonight's your night to celebrate and feel proud about a great accomplishment. I'll give you a critical exegesis when we get together again. As a whole, it was a tremendous success. Took a lot of guts and a lot of heart. And I'm proud of you." For some reason, that last part sounded good to me. He shook my hand heartily, clapped me on the shoulder and was gone.

Well during the run of *A Gentlemen's Journal*, I guess I felt as wide a variety of emotions as you can get from one experience. I mean everything: joy, sadness, hurt, disillusionment, camaraderie, frustration, accomplishment, the whole works. And I figured I'd felt it all until one evening after the play. I couldn't believe who was waiting in the audience for me when the theater had emptied. It was Gregory Martin Berens, my brother.

"Greg, is that you?" I asked him as I was gathering my briefcase to leave. "What are you doing here?"

"I came to see your play. What do you think?" He looked great and he gave me a big hug. Greg had always been stockier than I was, and now he was sporting a *Miami Vice* style beard and moustache.

"You drove all the way up from Seymore Johnson Airforce Base to see my play?"

"Yeah, don't look so surprised. Actually, I was here visiting Stephanie in Jersey and Mom told me about the play, how you're written up in *Variety* and everything. So, I thought I'd swing by and check it out."

"So what did you think?"

"I don't know that much about black plays, but it was entertaining. I mean, I laughed a lot and I didn't go to sleep; and the audience seemed to enjoy it."

"Well, it's good to see you, Greg. Looks like you put on a few pounds, and I know that beard is not military issue. You on vacation or something?"

"No, Mark. I'm discharged."

"You're what? I thought you were going to retire in the military. A lot has happened the past two years hasn't it? Mom told me about you and Stephanie breaking up, but not this. What's going on?"

"Well, that's one of the reasons I came this way. I wanted to sit down and have a long talk with you, little brother.

"About what?" I said suspiciously.

"Look, is there somewhere we can go to talk privately for a couple of hours?"

"Like where, Greg?"

"Well, did you eat yet?"

"I was about to pick up a burger and drive back to Maryland. I've got a shift to pull tomorrow."

"You're not going back tonight are you? It's almost eleven o'clock as it is. Look, I was going to crash in town anyway and leave first thing tomorrow. Why don't you let me buy you dinner, and I'll sport for a hotel room. Then, we both can leave fresh tomorrow. How does that sound?"

I was skeptical because this wasn't like Greg. First of all, Greg would never have asked me what I wanted to do. He would've just told me what he was going to do. Secondly, I felt he was up to something, like this invitation was to manipulate me somehow. Hell, that's how it had been in the past. But I was so intrigued, I said yes. He followed me in his car to the Holiday Inn that I'd stayed at when it was too inconvenient to stay with Woody. We parked, checked in, and finally sat down to dinner in the hotel's restaurant, all his treat.

"I don't know how much Mom and Dad have told you about what's been going on with me." He ordered coffee and I had a beer.

"Well, Greg. You know that I only talk to Mom a couple of times a month, and she just said you were having problems with Stephanie. Dad never says much to me now anyway, other than hi and bye, but no one's said anything about you being discharged."

"It came as a surprise to me too. I'd always expected to retire from the Air Force, like Dad did."

"Yeah, I know."

"But, Mark. I never really was that satisfied in the military. I didn't know it then, but I do now. It was just a place where I could get what I wanted, a way to please Dad and make him happy."

"No, I never knew that."

"Well, it all caught up with me about a year ago; didn't seem like anything was going right. I fell into a deep depression, was drinking too much, not getting enough sleep, and then one night, I'm still not sure what happened, but I lost it. I hit Stephanie. Hurt her bad. This time she left me and pressed charges."

"Say what?" This surprised me, and then it didn't. I knew what Greg was capable of, but I never thought he directed it at anybody but me.

"Oh, yeah. We had fights before, but not like this. Well...I was arrested and locked up for criminal assault. And sitting there in that cell forced me to realize that I needed help, that I couldn't go on like this."

"So what did you do?"

"I floundered around with the military shrinks for a couple of months until I got discharged, but nothing eased the depression. Some days Mark, I swear to god, I couldn't even get out of the bed. And for the first time in my life, I actually thought about suicide, became obsessed about it, started thinking about different ways I could do it, how I could just end it all, and wouldn't that be better than all this? I guess you've got to get down like that before you're ready to do any good. Thank god my shrink knew about this rehab place in Arizona. It was an intense thirty day treatment program, and they saved my life really."

"Rehab? But you're not an addict are you? What, you're an alcoholic?"

"No, that's what I wanted to tell you. I'm a survivor, Mark...an incest survivor." He must've seen my mouth fall open because he went on to explain the obvious question. "It was Dad. When we were kids he used to molest me. I...uh, didn't know how to deal with it, so I struck out at you."

"Molest you how, Gregory?" I couldn't believe this so I got pissed. "This is what they told you?"

"It's the truth, Mark. Nobody told me; I told them. When you were still a baby, Dad used to make me have sex with him. He stopped after a while. I'm not sure why, but by then the damage was done."

"So, why are you telling me now after all these years? What do you want me to do?"

"I don't want you to do anything...except listen. I want to apologize to you. I abused you when we were kids, which is probably why you don't call me now, and I don't blame you. But I just want to say that I was wrong. I feel bad about it, Mark. I had no right. I was just striking out."

"So, I'm just supposed to forget it? All the times you'd wake me up slapping me; when you'd pour piss in my bed, all the whippings I took on account of you. Just forget all that and let's be friends now, because you said so?" The anger in the words surprised me, like someone else had spoken them. Gregory dropped his head for a minute, and when he looked up again, I could see tears on his face.

"Mark, I didn't tell you this to hurt you," he said with shaky composure. "I've hurt you enough already. If you still hate me or don't want to have anything to do with me, that's fine. I guess I got it coming, but I just wanted to apologize, to tell you if there's anything I can do to make amends, you just say the word?" He dropped his head again, and I heard him sob quietly. I didn't know this Gregory Berens. I'd seen him cry before, lots of times, but never like this.

Like, I remember once when Greg had broken the ceiling light in our bedroom. He was using the bed as a trampoline, showing me the flips and somersaults he could do that I couldn't. On one bounce, his hand reached up and accidentally pulled the fixture from the ceiling, and it crashed to the floor in a million pieces. Greg warned me that if I told, he'd beat me up. So, when Dad finally asked us, I stayed silent, figuring a whipping from him would be preferable to some of the abuse that Greg might retaliate with. Dad beat us both. He snapped his belt from around his waist, folded it double, and lashed us. We screamed and hollered like he was killing us, hoping our exaggerated trauma would satisfy him. When he finished and left the room, Greg looked me in the eye defiantly, and he stopped crying just as suddenly as he had begun; you know, like he had just flipped the "off" switch to his tears.

Well, that wasn't the Greg I was looking at now. These tears had no "off" switch. And before me sat a vulnerable, penitent man who I didn't even recognize. My anger lessened, but I wasn't ready to forgive him either. I could see that yes, he might be sorry for what he's done to me, but that was his pain, not mine; he'd brought it on himself. And whatever he might be going through now couldn't be any worse than what he put me through then. So, if he wanted to bawl his eyes out, go right ahead. But I also realized that if Greg's remorse was genuine, then his claim of being molested must be genuine too.

"You still didn't tell me why you had to be discharged," I filled in the awkward moment with a question.

"It was just that military way of life," he said, regaining himself. "It was part of my problem. You know how the military is. You can never measure up. There's always something to prove. As soon as you make one promotion, they have another obstacle for you. I just couldn't take that constantly trying to prove myself day in and day out. It broke down everything I was trying to build up for myself. So, I just chucked the whole damn thing and asked for an early out."

"What did Mom and Dad say? What did Stephanie say?"

"Oh, it drove them crazy; I was expecting that. But when my discharge papers came through, it felt like a weight had been lifted off my shoulders. I felt free in a way I've never felt before."

I don't remember what we ordered or what we ate. All I remember is looking down to a plate of half eaten food, and Gregory leaving the waitress a tip as we went up to our rooms. The next morning I was still tired, so I called into work and took another sick day. I certainly didn't feel like making that drive now, and after I rummaged through the little overnight bag I had stashed in my car, I showered, shaved and thought about what Greg might have said to Mom and Dad about all this (if he'd said anything at all), and how they might have reacted.

I thought about Dad molesting Greg, about them engaged in some unspeakable act; about Mom standing ignorantly (or idly) by. It was not an easy image to conjure up. Then, I thought about all the abuse Greg had perpetrated on me, and I got angry all over again. My stomach boiled and screamed bloody murder. I had to sit down there on the toilet just to compose myself. In a bolt of blue rage I lined them all up and struck them down; Steven Berens, negligent father and incestor; his wife Catherine, accomplice to the fact; their son Gregory, molester and abuser; and finally Mark Berens, victim, sap, stooge. Why did Greg have to bring up all this shit? Why now, after all these years? And could I even trust him to be telling the truth?

I realized that it all made sense, that it would certainly explain a lot; like why Greg always seemed to be Dad's favorite. If I had molested my kid, I guess I'd be so guilty that he'd be my favorite too. Greg's revelation was like pushing the equal button on a calculator. Then after a while, I didn't feel anger or shock or outrage. I just felt sorry for us; sorry for our whole damn family.

When Greg finally awoke, it was awkward being around him. I told him that it must've taken a lot of guts for him to say what he did. He thanked me, but there was still this wall between us, because despite all that, I still couldn't forgive him, couldn't forgive Dad either. That would happen in due time...if at all. So, we said our farewells and he drove off to Jersey, as I went downtown to lose myself walking the streets of center city Philly.

All I could think about was how glad I'd be when this damned play was finally over. I couldn't take much more of this adventure.

19

After the Festival

Well, thanks to Mark Berens, things weren't the same after the play. First of all, I had tasted the big life. Naw, I wasn't trippin' about being a superstar or no shit like that. There's a helluva difference between South Street and Broadway; even I could see that. But I knew it would be hard for me to go back to a rinky-dink theater group after this. I mean, where do you go from here? I damn sho' wasn't going to some place like the Liberty Company with some crazy-assed director like Carlos Hernandez on god-knows-what-kinda ego trip.

Even doing the play again at the Drama Center wasn't hyped no more because we did that already. Plus the fact that didn't nobody make no money, nobody but Adolph that is. The deal was that the artists would split fifty-fifty with the theater which sounds good except the artists were the cast and crew of both plays. This means that Adolph got as much as the Liberty Company and the cast of *Gentlemen's Journal* combined. Then when you divide that amount between fifteen actors and tech people, you could see that individually we didn't get shit. Some nights we would barely get enough for a meal and car fare, maybe.

Adolph paid each cast by check every other day which usually amounted to under a hundred dollars. I think the biggest check our cast ever got was $185.00 split between six people for two days. So that let me know right there that the next time we did a show, we'd have to do a better job with the business end of things. For one, our play has got to be full-length or we cut ourselves right out of the picture financially. Now, we did this show for fun, for exposure and experience. The next one we'd have to do for profit too, or why even bother going through all this so somebody else can make the money?

We didn't have a cast party neither. Everybody was so relieved that it was finally over that we just weren't in the spirit to celebrate. Besides, every night before curtain our cast and the Liberty Company would have a mini-party anyway. We'd bring our little coolers and box lunches. We'd go around to the deli and order some take-out, then we'd sit backstage and bust on each other about how somebody mighta fucked up last night, or how somebody in the audience reacted. Now that I think about it, it woulda been pointless to have a cast party anyway.

So, I discovered that hangin' out with Mark Berens, writing and producing *A Gentlemen's Journal,* and performing it fifty-eleven dozen times had changed me. It raised my expectations about myself. It raised them even beyond what I knew what to do with. Another change I can credit to Mark (or blame his ass for) is that his visit to Belinda's fucked up things between us way beyond repair.

"Well Woodrow, I'm not stupid," she told me one night after the play. "It was real obvious why Mark didn't come back. I don't know where he stayed, but wherever it was, it couldn't have been any more convenient than staying with me; or why did y'all bother to come by in the first place? So, I know what the reason was."

"And what was the reason, Belinda?"

"Obviously you didn't want Mark telling me any more of your little secrets. I mean, what else could it be?"

"It could be a lot of things, but you're so convinced that all men want to dog you out that you ain't ready to believe no other reasons anyway. Could it be that maybe Mark felt uncomfortable here? Or that maybe he stayed with somebody in the cast? Or that Mark had other friends in Philly? Could that be it?"

"Well, that's what I hear you telling me, but to be honest with you Woody, I don't know what to believe anymore. I don't know what's the truth or what's a lie?"

"Just because some whiteboy comes up in here with an ass-backwards story, you don't trust me now? You gonna let some trivial shit like this come between us?"

"See, that's another thing, Woody. Whenever something bothers me it's 'some trivial shit.' But when I catch you in a lie, I'm supposed to just let it ride and forget about it."

"Why you keep saying I lied?"

"You said you have a degree and you don't. That's a lie Woodrow, plain and simple."

"I told you what that was all about. All I gotta do is pay the bill and I'll have my degree."

"Then why couldn't you just say that to begin with?"

"Look, Belinda. I'm not gonna sit here and argue with you all night. You know what kind of man I am. Hell, I ain't gotta prove nothing to you. *If You Don't Know me by Now*...you know how the song goes." That's when I made one of those grand exits, stage left. Went to the closet, started throwing shit in my duffle bag, and I left her sitting on the edge of the bed. Later, I realized that I played the wrong card because after that, she cut me off like the phone company. When I saw her at work, she was real polite and would always speak, which just pissed me off all the more, but she wasn't calling me, and I damn sho' wasn't calling her, especially not after the dramatic exit I made.

A few days later, when our tempers died down, I tried to crack on her in the canteen. I kinda ambushed her while she was sitting alone drinking coffee.

"You sho' look good sitting by yourself, young lady." I said in my smoothest voice. "You with anybody?" She looked up and saw it was me.

"Naw, I used to have a man but he don't call or come around much anymore." She was just as cool as I was.

"Well, sometimes it takes a man a few days to warm up again once he's shut his motor off. Sometimes he needs a little time to figure out what he's missed. You know what they say, 'Absence makes the heart grow fonder.'"

"Yeah, they also say, 'Out of sight out of mind,' and besides I got a new man now, an eight year old named Jamal who comes by all the time. He gives me more love and affection than men four times his age; and with a lot less bullshit too. I think I'll keep him around. What do you think?" She smiled without any bitchiness, drank the last of her coffee, and left me sitting at the table all stunned and stupid.

So here I am back on the roller coaster again. Just a week ago I was soaring high, and now I'm living back with my Pops and Timmie, sitting around work all day bored; no lady, no show and no prospects. Damn this up-and-down shit is worse than drugs! So, I had to decide whether to kick the habit and not do any more shows, and not deal with any other honeys (yeah, fuck that, right?), or was I gonna find a new thang. But the next time, I wanted to do it right and not make the same mistakes.

One night, I'm sittin' at home watching *PM Philadelphia* on TV, couldn'tna been more than a week since the play closed, and they doing this story on the local comedy scene; you know, showing all the clubs and interviewing some of the new talent. I looks up, and I see this peasy headed brother with a big sambo grin, and realize that I know this dude! It's my boy Scottie Jackson from high school. We both sat the bench together on the basketball squad. There he was headlining at the Comedy Club, giving interviews on TV, and here I was sitting in my drawers watching him. And the brother was funny as hell; I was shocked. Where was I when all this went down? How was it that Scottie Jackson of all people was now packing 'em in at the Comedy Club? Come to find out he had an agent too, and was lined up to do some TV sitcoms and maybe even a movie. I leaned forward and turned up the volume cause I couldn't believe this.

Scottie was slick as greased ice; he was witty, well-dressed and articulate. I recognized some of them corny old routines he used to do in the locker room, but more polished now than I ever seen him. Said he got his start by showing up when the clubs had amateur night, when anybody could just get up and do whatever wild shit they wanted for three minutes. Said he just kept showing up, first this club then that one until he got better and better, and finally one of the owners approached him and wanted to be his manager; claimed the whole process took about two years.

Well, kiss my black ass. While I'm spinning my wheels at DelState, fuckin' around as a security guard, Scottie was on his way to the big times, and I don't mean South Street neither. I felt cheated and frustrated like the time Charles Patterson used to bully me around. I can remember thinking after we fought, damn is that all I had to do? And that was the feeling I had when I saw Scottie on T.V.

The more I thought about being a comic, the more I liked it. It was a clean way to do a performance. No props or sets or dealing with a crazy cast and crew. No rehearsals or production worries neither. Just take your ass up on stage, work your show and collect your paycheck. Didn't have to split it with Adolph or the Liberty Company or none of them. Yeah, stand-up comedy; I was like, damn I coulda had a V-8!

So, I go into research-mode for the next few days checking the paper, making phone calls, trying to figure out who's doing what where. I found out that the best place to start was at The Comic Works. It was the first club to have an amateur night, and it was the easiest place to get on stage. The only problem was that it was upstairs above the Persian Flower Restaurant down in Society Hill. Brothers needed a pass to go to Society Hill, didn't they? Well, if Scottie got up in there, it wasn't that damn restricted. Before the next week was out, I showed up for their weekly amateur night. And buddy, if you thought the theater scene was full of whacked-out characters, check this out.

I fell up in there about nine o'clock on Thursday when the headliners would show up. The open mike began at ten. The guy at the door would sign you up if you wanted to perform, and would collect the cover charge. He was bald with frizz on the sides; looked like Bozo musta looked on his day job. The $15 cover got you two drinks. But damn, $15 to see people crack jokes? And when I walked in the club it was just like on T.V. They had a small stage with a brick wall as a backdrop, a microphone, a follow spot, and even a piano. There were about fifteen or twenty tables with the little candles burning inside of shot-glasses, and folks had their drinks sitting around together in groups of four or five. At first, I couldn't believe what I was smelling. Then, I looked around, and at the next table whiteboy was all fired-up, sitting there smoking a big-ass Rastaman joint right out in the open. I looked back to see if this was cool, then I peeked another couple pass a joint on a roach clip between them. I thought Bozo or somebody would bust in any minute, but didn't nobody do nothing. Oh, like that, huh?

I copped a squat at a nearby table, ordered a drink, and checked out the show. The comedy wasn't half bad, no worse than you see on Johnny Carson or one of them variety shows; but like theater, seeing it live made it funnier. Plus, you didn't have time to get bored cause in five minutes somebody else was up on stage. They had every kinda comedy you could imagine up in there: jugglers, ventriloquist, dudes in clown clothes, even one guy called The Amazing Whiz who brought out this barrel of props and junk. He'd pick something at random like a toilet plunger, then he'd just go off. Some of it was funny and some wasn't, but he was running his mouth so damn fast that eventually you'd laugh at something.

Then there was this intellectual, Lenny Bruce type who was so cool he just knew his shit didn't stink; and he tried to make you feel stupid, like you were just too fuckin' dumb to understand his humor, you asshole. Once or twice I remembered seeing somebody from local T.V. but couldn't place their names or what show I'd seen them on. Sandwiched in between the club's comics were the headliners that they actually paid to perform. Now, these guys were good and had been on the *Tonight Show* or had opened for *Earth Wind and Fire* or somebody, and their comedy was so relentlessly funny that it just over-shadowed everybody else there. Yeah, pay these dudes, I thought.

Somewhere between my second and third gin and tonic, the amateur night started, and you've never seen such an endless line of pitiful, no-personality-having, non-funny losers in your entire life. At first, I didn't get it. How could these guys ever think they were the least bit funny? I mean, when you stood up there for exactly three minutes until they cut off the lights and the microphone on your ass, and when absolutely nobody so much as chuckled, wasn't that a clue that you weren't funny? So, why put us through all this? Then it occurred to me that obviously these people were so desperate for attention, they'd do anything whether it was funny or not. Hell, that didn't matter because they were too busy jacking off on the audience.

Now, I can't say this was true about everybody cause a couple of the guys were funny as hell. I mean, you could tell they had potential. They'd tell a hilarious joke, but their timing would be off; there'd be too much dead space between jokes or something like that. And I guess this was the only place you could practice, but I never knew what the words "simpleton" and "buffoon" really meant until that night. So, I left 'round about midnight when I just couldn't take it no more.

I left the comedy club, but the experience didn't leave me. After seeing this group of "comics," I figured I could do at least as good as they did. I'd be on the bus or at work and find myself thinking about some joke or some stand-up routine. I'd think about how I might dress on stage or what expressions I might use. It certainly made those long hours at work go by more quickly. I would sit at the security desk for my entire shift and scribble down my ideas on paper. Then when I got home by myself, I'd stand in front of my bedroom mirror and practice. I always knew I could make people laugh in a conversation whenever I wanted to, but I wasn't as sure about an audience. The timing and vibe are completely different. Sooner or later though, I knew I'd have to leave the comfort of my bedroom mirror and take my ass to one of them comedy clubs.

I also realized that with only the three minutes they gave you, all you really could do was go for the funnybone and the cheap shot; that's all there was time for. But theater was different; there was something more dignified than a comedy club. In fact, theater has to be the classiest gig you can get. I mean, when people come to the theater, they come for just one reason; to see and hear what you got to say, and that's all. Nobody's there to serve drinks, or get up and dance, or fire up a joint, or crack on some honey. They just sit there and listen. So even though I liked comedy, I wasn't ready to give up theater either.

Then, it hit me like a lightening bolt. Why not combine the two? Sure, why not? They managed to combine theater with everything else; dance, music, mime and poetry. Why not stand-up comedy? Lets see…for a plot line we could have this story about a struggling comic, somebody young and raw, somebody like me! The stage could be set up with a mike and spotlight, and the main character could come out and do a stand-up routine to open the show. Then, just as the audience would be getting used to the comedy, the next scene would be set backstage in his dressing room where we could see his private life. And sandwiched in between the dramatic scenes could be even more stand-up routines. Yeah, this is a great idea, I thought; a one-two punch that the audience couldn't resist. If the acting didn't get 'em, the comedy would. I even had an idea for a title, something catchy like *Laughing Through the Tears,* or even *Laugh 'til it Hurts.* Yeah I like that last one better.

But to make the whole thing work, I had to be convincing as a comedian first. And second, we had to have a good script to go along with it. Well, if Scottie Jackson could become a comedian in two years, I figured it would probably take me only a few months. And while I was doing that, Mark Berens could be writing us a script. I couldn't wait to tell him about the idea. I knew he'd be as hyped about it as I was.

That's when I found out that Mark was in the hospital.

20

Mark Recuperates

I'm still not sure what happened. I had apparently been running on caffeine, nicotine and nervous energy because the doctor said I was suffering from dehydration and exhaustion. I only stayed in the hospital for two days, but they advised me to rest for another week at home or I'd end up right back in the emergency room. The last thing I remembered was being at the office carrying a stack of claims from my. I remembered feeling dizzy and a bit nauseous, and then shivering like a cold burst of wind had just blown through. The next thing I knew, I was being lifted off the floor onto a stretcher, and someone was telling me not to move until we got to the emergency room. Everything blurred together then, people moving in slow motion, strange lights crossing the ceiling, and the clinical sounds in the emergency room giving me the creeps. I wasn't fully aware of what had happened until the next day when a nurse explained everything to me.

It's still hard to believe because I don't remember feeling sick; just tired. And certainly not sick enough to be admitted to the hospital. So, there I lay flat on my back with an I.V. needle spiked in my arm. The whole scene was humiliating. The fact that I had been so negligent about myself in the first place embarrassed me; and that I had to depend on somebody else for my everyday needs did very little for my manly pride. I guess it's that military training coming back to haunt me.

Lying on your back for two days gives you plenty of time to think about things. Since I was in the hospital, I had obviously fucked up really bad. So, I spent most of my time trying to understand when and where I went wrong. First and foremost was that drama festival. I was so busy trying to be *the man* and taking care of everybody else, that I forgot to take care of myself. If that wasn't bad enough, constantly being on the road, working days and rehearsing nights prevented me from ever getting completely rested. And to top it off, the bomb that Greg so kindly dropped on me kept me upset for days. Whenever I'd think about it, I'd get upset all over again. With all that going on, it's a wonder that I'm not dead.

The nurse said my blood pressure was up near 200 which is crazy for someone my age. That's when I knew that something had to change. I just couldn't afford to abuse myself any longer. I wasn't quite sure what, but when I got back on my feet, I promised myself never to take another fall like this again.

And the hospital is the worst place in the world to get better because someone's always disturbing you. If it's not the nurse, then it's the janitor or some other staff person. And I swear, there were people visiting me from the office that I didn't even know. I was thankful for their concern and all, but I didn't feel like entertaining them. Didn't they know I was in the hospital? Plus, when most of them came by, I got the feeling that the visit wasn't about me anyway; that they had some agenda of their own, and I was just a convenience. It wasn't until I finally got home that I managed to rest at all. That's also when I realized what kind of hole I'd dug myself into.

I had squandered all of my paid sick days on the play, so any additional time off would come out of my pocket. I was just lucky that Craig Dempsey knew why I was taking so many sick days or I probably would've been fired. That put me in a financial bind because all the bills I'd postponed during the play were now coming due. The credit card bills could wait, but the car insurance and the utilities had to be paid. In addition to that, my rent would be due at the end of the week, and I knew that racist asshole Harlen Passwaters would be looking for any excuse to evict me. I didn't know where the money would come from. After moving here and then doing the play, I only had a couple hundred dollars left in the bank anyway. I had expected to get paid for doing *Gentlemen's Journal*, but after we got our cut from Adolph Grumann I realized that it had actually cost me to do the play. Well, something had to give, but I had to consciously put these problems out of my mind, forget the stress, and try to get back on my feet. If I was going to be stressed out and worried, I might as well go back to work and get paid for it.

So, that's what I did for the next few days, just sat around sleeping, eating, watching videos and listening to records. I made sure to always have a glass of fruit juice or water nearby, and I even cut down on my smoking. I've never had much problem entertaining myself because there's always some novel to read or old movie to watch. I decided not to call Mom and upset her. God knows, she already had her hands full with Greg and Dad.. Besides, I was supposed to be relaxing and reducing stress. Mom used to say, "There are no boring times, just boring people," and I'd always believed that, but three days of this "relaxing" was giving me a bad case of cabin fever. I wanted to get out, talk to somebody, do something.

One evening I phoned Craig Dempsey and invited myself over. I was still fascinated by that studio of his, and I wanted to distract myself by playing around at his keyboard. Maybe I could write some more lyrics for him. He'd also promised me a critique of the play, but we never got the chance to talk about it at work. On the phone he sounded glad to hear from me and eager for me to come over. I was tentative about driving because I wasn't sure if I'd pass out at the wheel or what, but I made it with no problems. He greeted me at the door with a double-fisted hand shake, a hearty clap on the shoulder, and a big smile. I was a little surprised by this display, but I enjoyed the welcome just the same. In no time we were in his kitchen, drinking coffee and deliberating on what he did and didn't like about *Gentlemen's Journal*.

"Well, before I start criticizing, let me say I'm impressed that you wrote, directed and produced a play on your own. I still don't think you realize what an accomplishment that is."

"Yeah, yeah. You said that already," I joked. "Quit beating around the bush and tell me what you think."

"The part I had problems with was the character of Raymond, the rough guy in the cast."

"Yeah, what about him?"

"His scenes just didn't ring true. Where did you get his character from anyway? Who's it supposed to be based on?"

"That's one of Woody's creations. He suggested the character and told me about these scenarios that he claims actually happened."

"Happened to who?"

"I don't know, to him…one of his friends…"

"Well, I'm not sure that Woody was being honest; not so much with you, but with himself. The motivations behind some of the actions just weren't realistic."

"For example?"

"The scene that stands out the most is the one you get so many complaints about. When Raymond and his lady friend fight, he forces himself on her, and she gives in after such a big protest. Well, things just don't happen like that. It looks like a rape scene really, especially the way they play it. I mean, when she slaps him, she's really offended."

"I agree, Craig, but I only wrote it like he told it to me."

"See, if she's angry enough to whack him like that, then it can't be romantic at the same time. It's more about control and intimidation. That's what a rapist wants from a woman, not candlelights, wine and affection. No wonder so many women objected to the scene. You're masquerading a violent act as romance, and it's just not true."

"I see your point. If somebody mugged me, then tried to pretend he'd done me a favor, it would infuriate me too. I never thought about it like that."

"That's the problem with collaborations, Mark. There's a chance that you're writing about experiences you don't understand, and you might end up portraying something that's not true"

"Well, what's going on with Woody that he would tell me something like that? You know, that scene has always been uncomfortable to watch. Woodrow says the emotion comes from Karen. He believes that she's been assaulted before, and the role was some kind of weird therapy for her. Do you think Woody might've done something like that too, and this was his way of justifying it to himself?"

"Woody's your friend, Mark. I don't know the man. Maybe he just got the story wrong like you did, and he doesn't understand the message he's sending. Or maybe he *is* acting out something he's done already, or something he's capable of doing. Who knows? I would suggest that if you're planning on performing the play again, you should re-write that part."

"Craig, the way I feel, if I *never* perform that play again, it'll be too soon."

"Took a lot out of you, huh?"

"Man, I've been exhausted, dehydrated, overworked, hospitalized and damn near bankrupt behind that play. But you know, I've got to admit that it was worth it. I wouldn't have missed this experience for anything. I learned so much. If I never do another play, I did this one, and no one can take the accomplishment away from me."

"Yeah, I know it must've taken a lot out of you. Don't forget that I'm your boss, and I know that you've used up all your paid sick days for another six months. How are you doing financially?"

"It's rough, but I try not to think too much about that now. I'm supposed to be recuperating, remember?"

"Look, why don't you let me help you out a little bit?"

"What do you mean?"

"I was thinking that maybe I could give you a couple hundred dollars to tide you over. You can pay me back a little each month until you get back on your feet."

"Frankly, Craig, it would be a godsend for me right now, but are you sure you want to do this?"

"The company's got too much invested in you already. Besides, who's going to help me with my songs?"

"But you know what they say about lending money to friends. We might end up as enemies or something."

"That's why I'm going to send you a form to sign the minute you come back to work. It'll be a *payroll deduction authorization.* That way I can get my installments even before you do. We got a deal?"

Craig saw that even though I was cautious, I was damned thankful for the offer. "I don't know what to say but, hell yes! And thanks, Craig; thanks a lot."

"Look Mark, if you need help, you need help," and he reached for his checkbook.

Soon after, we were in his studio again pushing buttons and turning knobs, and he showed me how to record some basic tracks. Don't get me wrong, I'm not a musician like he is, but I did play the trumpet back in junior high, so I had a rudimentary understanding of music. And with the synthesizers and keyboards, that's all you really needed; that and some ideas. In no time I was laying down drum beats and bass lines so I could improvise enough of a melody for Craig to do the rest.

At first, I feared that doing anything creative like this would cause me to relapse, but this was different than the stage play. This was relaxing and playful, and didn't seem like work at all. Craig didn't have that manic urgency and drive like we had. He had nothing to prove, and for him, just going through the process was more important than the finished product, or any review of some confused journalist. I believe that if nobody ever heard his songs, it would suit him just fine.

"I've got an old friend who works with Baltimore Parks and Recreation," he said. "They have a program for inner city kids where they perform children's theater through out the community. She wants me to record a soundtrack that the actors can sing to. They want to do a musical without the expense of hiring a band. You ever do any assignment writing?"

"Not really," I said. "What kind of music does she want?"

"Basically, they improvise a script from popular fairy tales like *Cinderella, The Wizard of Oz,* stuff like that. Maybe they'll update the language and the characters, so it's pretty loose stuff. We're not talking grand opera here, just some catchy tunes that the kids can sing."

"Yeah, I guess I can do that; doesn't sound like a lot of pressure or stress."

"Aw no, really it's a lot of fun and the kids just love it. You should see their eyes light up. I'll tell ya, Mark, children make the best audiences. They're not the least bit critical; the whole show seems real to them, and they're so appreciative. You'll see."

That night we knocked off two cute tunes for a production of *Cinderella.* One was about the Wicked Stepmother entitled *She's So Mean,* and the other one Cinderella sings called *I Miss Him So.* Between Craig's voice and mine we made some pretty impressive demo tapes.

"Do you think we ought to copyright these songs before we send them out," I asked him.

"What for?"

"I don't know, just to be on the safe side."

He chuckled when I said that.

"What? Do you think that Motown or Capital Records might be sitting in the audience?"

"Not so much that, but just in case something comes up in the future. You never can tell."

"Well, Mark, this show won't be touring the United States, and there definitely won't be a cast album recorded. After it's over, the actors and everybody else will probably continue on with their lives and these songs will never be heard again. But if a copyright form will make you feel better, go right ahead."

I felt really petty after he said that. Obviously, I still had some unrealistic ambitions for the songs. And really all Craig wanted to do was just have a little fun with the kids (you remember *fun,* don't you Berens?).

That little respite was just the tonic I needed. I felt much stronger and returned to work even sooner than I had planned. I took things easy for the first few days, but to tell you the truth I was glad to get back. I'm not sure about this theory of sitting at home like a potted plant, doing nothing and expecting to get stronger. Everybody at work treated me like a fallen warrior and offered to do things for me. It was annoying at first, but I appreciated the attention. I didn't have to buy lunch or dinner for about a week after I returned because Becky Bates or Beth Coren, or somebody else would always bring in a casserole dish, a wedge of cake, or a bucket of goulash for me to take home. Bob Maronni gave me a five-meal gift certificate to Sizzlers from him and his wife. Had I known that passing out would make me this popular, I probably would've done it sooner.

Maronni took a liking to me. He'd seen the play and was impressed; thought I'd brought a little excitement to the office. We didn't become close buddies because he was too involved with his wife and that pack of banshees she'd given birth to, but he was a good mate to have around the office.

"Yo, Berens!" He called one afternoon in the canteen. "Did you get the lunch that Beth Coren made for you today? This is three days in a row, and I think she's sweet on you."

"Well Bob, I've got to admit she's looking better and better all the time. That little leather outfit she had on the other day was hot as hell."

"She's got the two shapeliest bazooms on this floor. Man, you better get you some."

"I just might do that. What's the story on her, anyway? How come she's not with someone already? I won't get the space-herpes from her, will I?"

"Naw, chief, I wouldn't steer you wrong. She's just the opposite, real quiet. Not shy, but just quiet; you know, like she's knows something that you don't."

"She's not one of those religious freaks is she?"

"Not at all. She can have a good time with the best of 'em, but she's just not desperate for a man. Jim Paxton tried to hit on her and she brushed him off real polite like. But you know Jim. He just couldn't take 'no' for an answer. So, she blasted him up one side and down the other; then smiled and walked away like nothing had happened. She can be a hot little thing when she has to. If I wasn't married…Well, the deal is that she lost her fiance about three years ago, and now she just won't take any bullshit from these office Romeos, but I think she likes you."

"Me? Why me?"

"I don't know, Mark. Ask her. I guess it's the fact that you're not the Romeo type. You came in here like the Lone Ranger, the adventurous artist type, and apparently that turns her on."

"Well, cool! I just might have to check up on Miss Beth Coren."

"Go get 'em tiger. Oh by the way, some forms came for you from payroll today. They're on my desk whenever you want to get them."

"Yeah, those are the forms that Dempsey wanted me to sign."

"Craig Dempsey? You and him are getting real tight, aren't ya?

"He's showing me around the local theater scene. Plus he writes songs; got a nice little recording studio in his home. We might collaborate on a childrens' play for Baltimore Parks and Rec."

"Well, you want to watch yourself with Craig Dempsey, Mark."

"What do you mean?"

"Rumor has it that he's gay."

"Craig Dempsey? Gay? Get outta here! He's divorced and got a kid already. He can't be gay?"

"Why do you think he got a divorce? Now don't get me wrong, Craig is a good guy and everything, but just check out the situation for a minute. He's single, you never see him with anybody, he lives alone, he's the most private person in the office, and I've never heard him so much as talk about any ladies. Have you?"

"Well, you can say that about me too, and I'm definitely not a faggot."

"Look, I'm just trying to warn you, buddy. It's nothing to worry about really. Everybody here gets along with him just fine, way better than Thom Cooper or that snooty Linda Courtney. But I'm just telling you so you know what the deal is, and so you can act accordingly, okay?"

Well, this was just great! Just what I needed to hear. I finally get back on my feet only to get hit with another bomb. Is that why he was so friendly to me, and so quick to loan me money? I was pissed, and I felt seduced and slimy. It was suddenly clear why Dempsey was so stand-offish at work, and everything that Maronni said certainly made sense. I was glad that nobody knew how close we really were because what would they think about me?

That put a definite damper on our collaboration. We were supposed to get together again that next weekend, but I canceled out; told him I was tired and needed some more rest. He bought it, but I could tell he was suspicious. I really did enjoy Craig's company, but I couldn't trust him now, and I certainly didn't want to owe him a damn thing. The only other place I knew that I could get the $600 dollars he'd lent me was from Greg. He'd told me if I needed anything to just ask him, so I did. I called him in Jersey where he had apparently patched things up with Stephanie. He was glad to hear from me when he answered the phone.

"You say you were in the hospital? Why didn't you tell anybody?"

"I was just in for a couple of days, so I didn't want to worry you. It was just a case of exhaustion from doing that play."

"I bet you didn't tell Mom about this did you?" he asked. "About a week ago, she had been trying to reach you. She figured you were out of town or something."

"Why was Mom trying to reach me?"

"It's about Dad, Mark. He's been sick. She said he's been having seizures. They're doing tests on him now, and the doctors think it's a brain tumor."

"Damn, when it rains it pours. Brain tumor? That's pretty serious."

"Yeah, I guess so."

"So have you talked to him yet, Greg? Have you told them what you told me?"

"No, Mark, not yet. I'm not ready to talk to either one of them."

"Well, do you still plan on telling them?"

"I'll tell them when I'm ready, but right now, I'm just taking care of myself, and trying to mend fences. I'll confront them in my own time. But you didn't call me to talk about Mom and Dad, did you?"

"No, I didn't. As a matter of fact, I called to ask you a favor."

"Just name it, little brother."

"Well, being in the play and in the hospital put me in a hole financially. If you've got it, I could really use a loan for $600. I should be able to pay you back a hundred a month until you get it all."

"No problem," he said to my surprise. Had I asked Greg for anything in the past, it usually came with a lecture or some incrimination. "Are you sure $600 will be enough?"

"Yeah, that ought to be fine. And thanks, Greg. I owe you one."

"No you don't. I'm just glad I could help you out. And Mark, maybe you should call Mom and see how she's doing."

"Okay, I will."

That was one task done. As soon as I'd get the money from Greg, I could pay off Craig and not have that hanging over my head. The next unpleasant thing I had to do was call Mom. Talking to Mom had always been easier than talking to Dad. Whenever we needed something even as kids, we'd tell her first and she'd relay the message to him. After I left home, it was even more difficult to talk to him because deep down inside, I guess I wanted him to feel guilty for how he had neglected me, how he'd given Greg all the attention, and let him get away with so much. I guess my delinquent years were really my attempts to punish him. Whenever I'd call home, he would wish me luck, tell me to be careful and automatically give the phone to Mom. I didn't expect things to be any different this time either.

"Hi, Mom. Greg told me you'd tried to call. I've been out of town a few days," I lied.

"Oh hi, baby!" She'd called me *baby* ever since I could remember. I guess even when I was 75 years old, I'd still be her baby. "I'm so glad to hear from you. Greg told me about your play; he said it was very successful and that he was proud of you. I hope everything went okay for you son."

"Yeah, Mom. Things went fine. I understand Dad hasn't been doing too well though."

"No, Mark. It seems like trouble has a way of sneaking up on you when you least expect it." She didn't know the half of it. "It started a couple months ago. Your father was working in that garden of his, and the next thing anybody knew he was getting up off the ground; claims he stumbled and fell. Then he frightened me something terrible one night at dinner. He fell across the table and overturned the meal onto the dining room carpet. This time I called an ambulance, and they took him to the hospital to run some tests. They seem to think it's a brain tumor and want to do surgery, but we want to get some other opinions before we do anything serious like that."

"That's a good idea, Mom. How's he doing now?"

"He's on medication which seems to control his seizures, but he's groggy most of the time. I would let you speak to him, but he just fell asleep."

"That's okay. How are you holding up? Is there anything I could get you? Anything you need?"

"Not really. Your Aunt Catherine and Louise Addleman from across the street keep an eye on me. They visit me almost every day, but I would like to see my two boys. I get frightened from time to time, but we'll get through this somehow. When do you think you might be coming home?"

"I don't know, Mom. I'm still getting on my feet myself. Doing that play kind of wore me out, so it won't be for another few weeks." I wanted to tell her that I was too broke and too tired to travel anywhere, but I just left it at that.

"Seems like all the men in my family are doing poorly these days," she said. "I guess you heard about your brother. About his discharge and how he's trying to patch thing up with Stephanie. I just don't know what's happening with my boys."

"Well mother, you've got your hands full with Dad right now. Me and Greg will get by just fine. Don't worry too much about us. You do whatever you have to do down there, and we'll get up with you as soon as we can."

"Okay son. I know this is costing you, so I won't keep you. But Mark, come visit us soon. Your father asks about you two all the time. I'll call you the minute we find out more about his condition. Bye bye, son."

"Good night, Mom."

Mom asked a good question. What was happening to our family? Finding Dad in this condition had upset me too. I felt sorry for him, but I couldn't forgive him for what he'd apparently done to Greg, and then to me. I wanted his approval, but I wanted his apology at the same time. Hell, I didn't know what I was feeling about him. Dad had never been sick a day in his life. Even when he had the worst flu, it never put him in the bed. And the thought of him disabled and convalescing like that disturbed me. Because if Dad could go down, then I guess anybody could crumble, especially me.

I didn't want to relapse behind this, so I turned my attention to another problem, Craig Dempsey. Anger was a more familiar foe, and much easier to deal with. So, I scripted in my mind what I would say to Dempsey once Greg's check arrived.

21

Woody Does Stand-up

After that night at the comedy club, seems like all I thought about was comedy. I'd be checking out every situation to see if I could make a joke or sketch about it. I wrote enough to fill up two legal pads, and I knew Cool Will and Tim thought I was crazy from the times they heard me practicing in my bedroom. But what could either of them say because they weren't doing much better than I was.

Pops was laid-off from work until he could get his blood pressure down. He went to the doctor to renew his prescription, and they almost shit a brick when they saw how high it was. Daddy knew his pressure was up, but he just kept ignoring it and doing stupid shit; like he would eat ham and eggs fried in lard, get a headache, then turn right around and take his medication, like it was gonna do some good. I mean his pressure was up so high that sometimes his nose would bleed. I tried to tell him not to eat like that, but he'd just remind me how stupid I was about my health, and how I'd come home hobbling and all crippled after a basketball game sometimes. They sent him home from work because they didn't want him stroking out behind the wheel. So, while he was waiting for his pay to kick in, I was the bread winner of the house. It made me wonder; damn Pops, you ain't got *no* savings? But I couldn't talk because I been working for months myself, and I didn't have none either. I was able to buy a week's worth of groceries to hold us over, and I was glad I could do it for him.

About this time Timmie was going through another one of his routines. Every now and then he'd get a job, would work fine for a few weeks, and then do some dumb shit to piss everybody off and get fired. Then, he'd start the process all over again. This time, Pops had to cuss him out for disrespecting the house; and I can't say that I blame him. All Pops asked was that we be cool, and we could stay up in here rent free, and I'll be damned if Timmie couldn't do that. Daddy told me that Tim had some hooker-bitch up in the room at three o'clock in the morning. The next thing anybody knew, she was screaming and hollering at the top of her lungs. Pops say she woke up damn near everybody on the block; and because we live in row houses, it made one of the ugliest scenes you'd ever wanna see. Good thing I was at work because I woulda pimp-slapped the both of 'em behind some crazy shit like that.

See? That's what I mean about Tim. That nigga couldn't do nothing right. Seems like he didn't have no manly pride about himself, and I was losing respect for my own brother. Well, it hurt Cool Will more than it hurt me because he would blame himself for not raising us right; would tell me that if him and Momma never broke up, maybe things woulda been different. And it seems like every time Pop gets upset, he starts talking that shit about him and Momma. William Tyler always tries to play that cool, tough role; but he still got a thing for my mother. If not, then why does her name always come up whenever anything goes wrong? How come he never has a steady woman for more than a few months at a time?

I felt like telling him that it was okay how he'd raised us; that no, we weren't rich and famous, but we hadn't been thrown in prison either, though sometimes Tim looked like he was on his way. I guess the reason Pops was still hung up on Crazy Francine (that's what I always call Mom) is because he was raised by my Aunt Earlemae. I never knew my grandmother, but I knew her sister Earlemae who raised Pops. She always spoiled him, fussed and fiddled over him 'till he was ripe for the picking. Francine was fast as a stolen car when she met Pops, and even though she was a crazy bitch sometimes, she had Pops' nose wide open. I'm still not sure what it was about her that he couldn't resist, but they always had this serious passion between them. I mean, they lived together with a passion, they fought with a passion, they even split up with passion. So, although they hadn't been together for years, they never really broke up, not completely. For a long time Momma would leave to go live with somebody else for months at a time. She'd get herself another boyfriend for a while, then out of the blue her and Pops would get back together again. So, this make-up-to-break-up routine went on for years 'til neither one couldn't take it no more. Plus the fact that they both drank too much. No, fuck that, Momma was a straight-up alcoholic.

And she always loved to mess with Pops' head. I remember whenever she came back to visit, it would all be calculated to irritate Daddy some kinda way. Like one time it was my birthday, and she showed up with her new man to take me to the zoo. She came in with some greasy headed pimp on her arm.

"Oh hi, William," she said to Pops. "This is my fiance Cleveland Jackson. We've come to pick up Woody and take him to the zoo for his birthday."

I heard them from upstairs; couldn'ta been more than nine or ten years old. Mom always dressed nice; it took her two hours sometimes just to get ready to go check the mail. She had the fancy dresses, the mink stoles, jewelry, the whole hook-up.

"Will, you did remember Woodrow's birthday, didn't you?"

"Yes, Francine. We celebrated already."

"Really? What did y'all do?"

"Why don't you ask Woody?" Pops said, then he disappeared into the back room.

"Woody!" Mom called. "C'mon, honey. You ready to go? Me and Mr. Jackson want to celebrate your birthday."

I ran downstairs knowing Mom had some big flashy present for me; she always did.

119

"Happy birthday, baby! This is for you," and she handed me a box that was damned near big as I was. "It's a race car set. Mr. Jackson thought you'd like it, so we bought it for you."

"Thanks, ma. Wow, it's great!"

"And see that big car out the window? Well, we're getting in that nice Electra 225, and we're gonna have some fun today."

"Where we going, ma?"

"First, to the zoo, and then to the Dairy Queen or wherever you want."

I can remember her acting all dramatic, raising her voice, and looking back to where Pops was to see if he'd heard her. So, Momma and me and this Mr. Jackson dude, all piled in the car and that was all the attention I got that day. After that, I felt like I was in their way. And it would always bother me to see my mother up under him, kissing and hugging him and carrying on like that. I wondered whether it was my birthday celebration, or was it his. When I finally got home, Cool Will was cooler than ever. He never questioned me about what we did (oh, but Momma would), but I could feel his hurt. That's why I don't like going out with my Mom now. You never know what-the-hell's gonna happen, or who she might be hooked up with this weekend. And that's why I don't understand why my Pop continues to let this hurt him, time and time again.

I knew one thing, I was ready to move out of this house. I was tired of Timmie's bullshit, tired of Pop's heartache, and tired of living in the same bedroom with the same spaceship wallpaper that I had when I was a kid. That's why this comedy thing was so important to me, and why I really got wrapped up in making my debut at one of the local clubs. I thought about it all the time now, and I treated the whole thing as a script so that when I'd go on stage, I could be a character other than myself.

In the mean time, I called Mark and told him about *Laugh 'til it Hurts.* He agreed that the idea was on the money, but he wasn't all that enthusiastic about it. I guess if my ass had just got out the hospital, it would be hard for me to be hyped about it too. He said he could help with the script, but he didn't want a repeat of *Gentlemen's Journal.* I'd have to give him some time to get back on his feet. Well, that was cool with me too because I didn't want a repeat of *Gentlemen's Journal* either. So, while Mark was getting better, I could get started on my comedy skills. Who knows, maybe I could just be a comic so well that doing a play wouldn't even matter.

I was down on Market Street at a store called The High Style Shop trying to hook up a decent wardrobe one payday, and believe it or not, I got into a fist-fight with some crazy nigga up in the store. It was like a flashback from my high school days. Hell man, I thought I was through scraping and fighting, but obviously not. The store was empty except for me, a security guard, and maybe a couple of customers. I didn't notice anything wrong until I was at a rack looking at some shirts, and this crazy brother came up behind me, sighing and moaning, like he's all disappointed. I turned around to find that he wasn't no wimpy looking dude either. He didn't say nothing, so neither did I until I took my stuff to the cashier to pay for it. I'm standing at the cash register, my stuff's on the counter, and the cashier's folding it up to put it in a bag. All of a sudden I hear somebody behind me screaming.

"I'll be goddamned! You mean I gotta wait behind your lazy ass again? Why don't you get the fuck outta my way!"

I turned around, more surprised than anything, and I asked him, "Yo, man, you talking to me?"

"You the only slow-assed bitch in here, ain't you?"

"What's yo' problem?"

"You the problem, muthafucka. You in my goddamn…" and before that silly clown could finish his sentence, I went into automatic attack mode and sucker punched him in the eye before he even knew what was happening. It was a reflex to me because, where I come from, if you jump to somebody that strong, the only thing left to do is go to blows. And since he was obviously already psycho, I was gonna make sure that he was the victim and not me.

After that, seems like we were fighting in a dream (or a nightmare), but I remember that he wasn't as easy to take down as I thought. Instead of falling to the floor when I rushed his ass, he took two steps back, pivoted, and used my momentum against me. Well, I wasn't gonna let this big ape ram me to the floor, so I grabbed one of the clothes racks to get my balance. The rack fell over and clothes went flying everywhere. We tumbled to the ground and wrestled free of each other. I saw that he was trying to find a clothes hanger or something to use as a weapon, but before he could even reach for anything, I got up on all fours, lunged at him like a linebacker, and hit him with my shoulder and forearm as he tried to struggle to his feet. He fell back against another rack and knocked it over. I heard somebody scream and found myself crawling along the floor up his leg. All I wanted to do was grab his fuckin' head to see what kinda sledge hammer it would make when I slammed it into the floor. Before I could reach him, three guys appeared from nowhere and pulled me off him.

They separated us, but by then we were like two pit bulls on leashes, huffing and puffing, frustrated because we couldn't finish killing each other. We stood with the three men between us and talked trash until the security guard called the police from outside. I guess they were patrolling the streets or something because they damn sure got there quick. When the cops came in, I was still in attack mode and wasn't ready to answer no bullshit questions, especially when this guy was clearly in the wrong. If the cashier hadn't stood up for me and explained what happened, I don't know what they woulda done. But as it was, they just waited for us to cool down; took him out through one exit; and later took me through another and barred both of us from the store.

When I got home, my fist was swollen where I tried to knock out that crazy fool. My shoulder and arm were aching and sore. I felt really stupid for fighting like some hoodlum. I tried to think of a way I could have avoided it altogether; but when I couldn't come up with an answer; what the hell, might as well make a comedy routine out of it. See? That's how things were for me; always some bullshit or some heartache to deal with; if not at home then out in the streets; a constant reminder of how my life was going nowhere. That's why I had to make a success at something, goddammit; and the only thing I could think of was performing.

There really wasn't nothing left for me to do except finalize some sort of routine, take my ass to the Comic Works, and see what kind of response I could get. I wished Mark coulda went with me, but after our last conversation I knew he probably wasn't well enough yet. So, I asked my boy Andrew to make the trip with me. I mean, me and 'Drew go way back, and I took him along for moral support. He'd seen *Gentlemen's Journal* and had been begging me ever since if there was something he could do. When I got dressed in my all black outfit (the one I had to kick some ass to buy), I headed off to Comic Works with Andrew.

I don't know what I was thinking about. Yeah, me and 'Drew are tight, but he wasn't used to hangin' out with all these white people in Society Hill, and the second we stepped into the Comic Works I could see him get all defensive and angry. I do it myself when I'm in a strange place or don't know what the situation is; most brothers do. But I certainly didn't need to deal with him when I'm about to go on stage. That's when it occurred to me that I'd made the mistake of confusing 'Drews friendship with Mark's talent, and if 'Drew is so much of a critic and artist, how come we ain't collaborated before now?

Before, when I met Bozo the doorman at Comic Works, the whole vibe was different. I threw on my white voice, and pretty much put him at ease. But when me and 'Drew fell up in there this time, I could see his guard was up, wondering whether or not we were dangerous. Plus the fact that Andrew was giving him some serious attitude.

"Tonight is when you guys have amateur night, right?" I asked him. "I'd like to sign up to perform, if it's okay."

He looked us up and down, back and forth and asked, "Have you guys ever been here before?"

"Oh yeah, lots of time," I said trying to put him at ease again. 'Drew didn't say nothing which was probably cool. "The last time I was here, I think the Amazing Whiz was headlining wasn't he?" I gave him thirty dollars to show that I knew what the cover charge was, and his guard went down a little bit.

"Well, have you ever done stand-up before?" he asked as he ran a pencil down a list that looked like it had a thousand names on it.

"If it'll make me get on the program any faster, yeah I'm a star," I told him.

He smiled and asked again, "What about any previous stage experience?"

"I performed in the Drama Center's Black Drama Festival a few weeks ago. Did you get a chance to check it out?" He nodded no, and I said, "Look buddy, if you put me on stage, I'll guarantee you'll laugh."

He smiled again and wrote something on the list and let us through. We strolled in, sat at a table not far from the stage and ordered drinks.

Tonight, they had a different group of headliners than before. These dudes weren't superstars either, but every now and then you'd remember a face from TV, or one of their jokes would ring a bell. The audience laughed their asses off, but soon the comedy got duller and cornier because the regulars were starting to perform. I found out later that most of them were the club's groupies who'd show up anytime the doors would open. They'd laugh at each other's routines so they could keep the illusion of being funny to each other.

Drew didn't say nothing the whole time until he got frustrated. One of the regulars was a dorky Woody Allen type who told these neurotic, pitiful kinda jokes. You know, the kind where you couldn't tell if the audience was laughing *with* him or *at* him? He was joking about being a failure with the ladies, and gave one of them Rodney Dangerfield punch lines: "I don't know what's wrong with me!" except his was more sad than humorous. Before I knew anything, 'Drew blurted out, "It's because you ain't the least bit funny, man!" I was *so* embarrassed, but I couldn't blame Andrew cause he only said what I was thinking. Then, the same thing happened with this guy that happened with Putnam the opening night of *Hair*. His whole character was just wrecked. He forgot his routine, started stumbling, and babbling and shit, then looked at us and begged, "Please don't heckle me, okay?"

Well, the crowd blamed us, the only two niggas in the house. 'Drew was embarrassed for saying it, the comic was embarrassed for blowin' it on stage, and the crowd was pissed at us for saying what everybody else was trying to ignore. And when it was my turn to go on stage, I knew the audience probably wouldn't be friendly.

Shortly after that, folks started leaving. I knew it was because the comedy was getting cornier, but I felt guilty anyway. By this time 'Drew just gave up on being entertained. He'd finished at least four drinks, and his head was in his hands. I just hoped he didn't pass out on the table; that woulda been the ultimate insult. As we waited and waited, more and more people left, and I was shocked to see the same boring guys who came to amateur night the last time. And the sad part about it was they weren't any funnier now than they were then.

That's when I realized that this part of the show wasn't about comedy, not really. It was about business. The comedy part was just an excuse to collect money from these losers; and I was right behind them, waiting like a damn puppy to get on stage. When they finally called my name, it was almost two o'clock in the morning! I swear to god, there were only three or four people left in the whole place, and one of them was Bozo the doorman, and the other was a busboy cleaning off the tables. Somebody was hangin' around in the hallway and backstage, but you couldn't actually call them an audience.

I remember nudging 'Drew as I went up, and he said something like, "Damn, it's about time," as he woke from his coma. When the performer in me saw the spotlight, the stage, and the microphone, I immediately got stage fright. I thought about Mark Berens the opening night of *Gentlemen's Journal* because my leg was twitching so damn bad, I thought I was gonna fall flat on my face.

As I got to the mike, I said some shit like, "Good evening ladies and gentlemen. I'm Woody Tyler, and I guess I got the hardest job in the world. I gotta make the tables and chairs laugh, ha ha!" I heard somebody giggle, and the doorman laugh out loud. "First, I'd like to do some impressions. This is my impression of the first black president."

I mimed stepping to the podium to deliver a speech, then I did a slow motion routine of some victim being hit by a barrage of bullets complete with vocal sound effects. And where each one hit, I would jerk my body with a stunned look on my face. I heard the doorman really laugh this time.

"My next impression is of me coming home to greet my girlfriend." I took a pause, whistled, and said, "Here Lassie! C'mon girl, good girl. Sit! Now, roll over. Okay, play dead." I got the same response as before, but I didn't do half the jokes I had planned because it was pointless now. The purpose of doing it live in the first place was to have an audience so you could play off of their reaction, but with a one-man-audience, I couldn't even do that. When I finally finished, I was ready to get outta that place, but believe it or not there was still one sad soul after me. He had waited for me, so I felt kinda obligated to be a good sport and wait until he was finished too.

Bozo came over and introduced himself as they switched on the house lights to close the place down.

"Woody Tyler, I'm Marshall Stevens in charge of talent here at Comic Works, and you don't have a bad act there. Those impressions were funny as hell."

"Thanks, but it's kinda hard to tell without an audience." 'Drew was so thankful to be outta there he was heading down the stairs already.

"I know, but you have to come back a couple of times and work your way up on the rotation," said Marshall Stevens matter-of-fact; just like waiting for hours to perform to an empty room at two in the morning was as easy as taking a piss. "Come back a few times, pay a few dues, and you'll have an audience before you know it. Then, maybe I can be your manager, take all your money, and leave you strung out on drugs." He chuckled and so did I. "Check us out next week, okay?"

I smiled, but I didn't know whether he was serious, or did he stroke everybody like that to keep the paying customers coming back. I knew one thing; if I did come back, I wouldn't show up before midnight, and I wouldn't even be back unless Mark Berens was with me. 'Drew is my boy and all, but he couldn't tell me shit about improving my comedy. Hell, I might as well had Lassie up in here for all the good he did.

Even if Marshall Stevens was telling the truth, I didn't know how many more times I could get up there for just one or two people. I guess I'm just not that desperate. Then, I thought about doing *Laugh 'til it Hurts*. Maybe I could improve the comedy by performing it in the play. Maybe I could get better each time we performed like we did with *Gentlemen's Journal*.

At any rate, Mark Berens better get well soon because I couldn't do much more without him.

22

Mark Makes Some Changes

"Hey, Mark. Come on in. I got some coffee brewing, and I'll power up the studio in just a few minutes," Craig Dempsey said as I walked through his front door.

"Uhm...no, Craig. I didn't come over to work today. I just want to sit down and talk for a few minutes."

"Oh, this sounds serious," he said. "What's the problem?" We walked into the kitchen and sat opposite each other at the table.

"Well first, I wanted to give you this," and I handed him six one hundred dollar bills, crisp and neatly folded in half. Craig inspected the cash quizzically. "I ran into a little money," I said, "and I thought I'd pay you back so you wouldn't have to wait."

"I really don't need it now, Mark. If you're strapped for cash, I told you to take your time and pay me back."

"No, I think it's better this way."

"Fine. Whatever you say, but I get the feeling this isn't just about paying me back."

"No, you're right," I said with a sigh. This was turning out to be more difficult than I thought. Where was all that anger and righteous indignation I felt a couple of days ago? "Look, this is not easy for me to say, so I'm going to come straight out and tell you. There're rumors going around the office about you that upset me, and I wanted to ask you face to face."

"What kind of rumors?" he asked coldly.

"Well, Craig, I've heard that you're gay."

"Who told you that?"

"It doesn't matter. I'm asking you here and now, are you gay or not?" He didn't flinch and stared at me emotionless.

"Yes, I am. Why? What difference does it make?"

"What difference does it make? I thought we were friends. I didn't know you were like that. Why didn't you tell me to begin with?" I sat back in the chair hurt and disappointed. Craig didn't say anything, but sat stonefaced with his arms folded on the table. After a few seconds he spoke.

"You didn't answer my question, Mark. What difference does it make?"

"It makes a lot of difference," I said agitated. "I don't know who you are anymore. I don't know if I can trust you, if I can turn my back on you, or what."

"So that's why your gave me this?" He raised the money and I nodded. "Well, you know who I am all right. I'm the same Craig I've always been," he said as he stuffed the bills in his back pocket. "You're the one who's changed. I didn't mention my sexuality because it wasn't an issue; you didn't ask me. Besides, Mark, have I ever put my hands on you? Have I ever so much as looked at you the wrong way?"

"No, because I would've smashed your face in if you tried that stuff with me."

"Like I said, nothing's changed but you. And let me ask you; if I've never approached you before, what are you so damned scared of now, huh? You think I'm going to rape you just because now *you* know?" Then Craig got pissed, and of course, I didn't know what to say to him. "You straight boys kill me. It's not me you're afraid of, Mark; it's you. Since you know I'm gay now, that just terrifies you, doesn't it?. And rather than deal with your own feelings like a grown man, it's just easier to attack me, right? But let me put your mind at ease, buddy. You're a nice friend and all, but you *don't* make my dick hard, okay? You're too young, too skinny, and way too immature to be the least bit attractive to me. And even if you were, the last person I'd want to get involved with is a terrified little straight boy." He stood up slowly, regained his composure, and continued. "Look, thank you for repaying the loan. I'm going back to the studio now, and try to relax. As always, you're welcomed to join me if you like. If not, then you can let yourself out, and I'll understand." And he left me sitting there at the table confused and dissatisfied with the whole scene.

That was a crucial moment in our friendship because I actually got up to leave. But when I reached for the doorknob, there was a finality to it that I didn't like. Had I left, it would've been all but impossible to come back later, especially as a friend. So whatever business I had with Dempsey, now was the time to do it. I lit a cigarette, helped myself to a cup of coffee, and contemplated what he'd said to me. I guess too, I was hoping that he would reappear in the kitchen, but no luck. All I heard from the back room was a blues organ as it filled the house with a bittersweet melody.

His logic was inescapable. That's probably why it was so hard to accept; that I could feel so strongly about something, and be so wrong. I reviewed his questions; had he ever touched me or even acted gay around me? No. Will he start now? No, I don't think so. Does this change anything between us? No, not unless I want it to. Then what was I afraid of?

The first thing that came to my mind was my days back home years ago. I remember how me and Greg as kids used to play with each other's privates when Mom and Dad weren't around. Nothing serious, mind you. We'd just inspect each other to see if one had something the other didn't. Then when I got older, Greg showed me how to masturbate, and what strokes to use. I even remember him grabbing my adolescent penis to demonstrate the proper grip and pressure. "And if you use your left hand," he'd say to me, "it feels like somebody else is doing it." I never thought much about those incidents until the issue came up again when I was in the barracks.

I'd become buddies with an airman named Don Reed. Ours was an unlikely friendship that ended one evening when we were drinking in his room. We got to talking, and the next thing I knew Don Reed had asked me did I want a blow job? I mean, just like that. Well, I cussed him out; called him every faggot in the book and we never even spoke to each other after that. But the fact of the matter was (it took me a while to admit this to myself) if he'd given me a blow job right then and there, it would've been fine. Hell, I was horny; all I wanted to do was come; and better his lips than some syphilitic hooker's I might find off base. The results would've been the same.

It scared me that, *A:* I had a history of incidents that could be described as gay, and *B:* I've already admitted that I could actually allow another man to blow me, given the right circumstances. The fact that I've never even touched another man, nor the fact that I've slept with so many women since then, didn't carry much weight in this equation. I was already disgusted with myself for the feelings, and I guess Craig was right; I feared that he might awaken some monster in me.

The other part of the equation was that I'd developed a lot of affection for Craig Dempsey. I valued his company and advice, but it never felt homosexual before now. In fact, it felt very masculine. No, not in a sexual way; but you know, the way you feel about a coach, the guys in your squad, or the fellas on the basketball team—that *esprit de corps* kind of masculinity. And wasn't it ironic that the support now came from a gay man?

When I'd finished my cigarette, I knew what I had to do. I walked to the studio and tried to pick-up the friendship I'd momentarily laid down. He saw me out of the corner of his eye, and continued to play.

"What do you think about this blues song for the children's play?" he asked me.

"No, it's too sad. Play something else." I told him, and he did.

After that, not much changed. Craig never showed any anger or reproach to me, and I realized why he had been strictly business at work. Had he not been so private and we'd gone through this episode, everyone would've sworn that we were fucking each other, I'm sure. But as it was, Bob Maronni, Beth Coren, Becky Bates and the rest thought we were just acquaintances. Besides, could being gay by association be any more difficult than being black by association?

This was about the same time that Woody had begun to bug me about that play of his. We'd spoken before about it, but either he didn't understand me or he just didn't give a damn. I'd explained to him that I was recuperating, that I didn't want to start another production of anything right now; especially nothing like *Gentlemen's Journal* where I had to do everything except act in the damn thing. He told me that he didn't want to repeat *Gentlemen's Journal* either, but I knew he didn't understand what I meant. He went on to tell me that he'd actually done a comedy routine on amateur night at some club, and wanted me to drive up there the next time he performed so I could critique him. Yeah, right! That's just what I needed was another midnight run to Philly, but you know how persistent Woodrow can be.

"C'mon, Mark. All I'm asking is that you drive up here one Thursday night and check out my routine at Comic Works. You don't have to do nothing but sit there and listen."

"Why can't you just tell me over the phone?"

"It's not the same and you know it. You can't critique a performance unless you see it."

"Sorry, buddy. I'm just not up for the drive. I used up all my sick days already. I'm hocked up to my eyeballs, and by the time I drive back here, I'd be too tired to even work the next day."

"So what, you can't help me on this one at all?"

"Sure, I can help you, Woody. It's just that you'll have to take the lead on this one because my tank is empty. I'm too tired to even come pick you up."

"What about the weekends?"

"That's when I catch up on my rest. No go."

"Tell you what, Mark. I'll take the Greyhound there and back. If I do that, can you at least pick me up and drop me off at the nearest bus station?"

"Okay, but what do you want to do when you get here?"

"Work on the play, asshole. What do you think? I got the characters, the plots, and the conflicts. I just need you to write a good script for me. What's the problem? If I can ride that dog into town, you can at least help me with the script."

"I told you, Woody. I'll be happy to help you, but I don't want to write the entire script myself."

"Damn, what you so scared of? You don't like black people no more? You done got *new* on me, Mark Berens?"

"I just got out of the hospital, and I don't plan to go back. I don't want to write my *own* play now, let alone yours. I'm cutting back on everything, and if you can't understand that, then I don't know what else to tell you."

"Aw, boy! Ain't nothin' wrong with you. You just scared. Look, the weekend's on me. I'll bring us some killer weed, and you won't even have to drive if you don't want to. All you gotta do is read a little and write a little. You can do that can't you?"

"We have to makes some changes if we're going to try this again. I need more work from you, and I need more support."

"Like how, Mark?"

"Well first, you gotta bring me something written down. Don't make me write the whole thing from scratch because I'm going to mess it up. These are your characters and your plots, not mine. See? That's the way we did it with

Gentlemen's Journal. I always had something written down before we ever got together."

"Okay, okay. I'll write the shit down."

"But it's more than that, Woody. I need more support from you on the production end. If this is *your* play, then you've got to direct it, make up the rehearsal schedule, worry about how the cast will get there, and all that other happy horseshit. You've got to be the go-to-man if you're going to be masquerading as a partner. And besides, sometimes I don't think you trust me, Woody, especially when it comes to business?"

"What are you talking about now, Mark?"

"You remember what happened with that copyright form? We both sat down and went over each part, line by line, and I thought the form went out as *our* decision. But when it came back wrong, it was all *my* fault. And furthermore, I was a piece of shit for having made the mistake in the first place."

"Well, Mark. You did fuck it up."

"No, Woody. *We* fucked it up. That's exactly what I'm talking about. It's not the mistake, it's the distrust, and you've distrusted me from the very beginning."

"Well, can you blame me? You saw how the form came back."

"Woody, why is it when you make a mistake, it's just a mistake, but when I make a mistake, it's some kind of failed hostile takeover?"

"Well, its not..."

"And how do you think that makes me feel, huh? I'm trying to take the lead, get the job done for both of us, and all my partner can think is that I'm some evil whiteboy trying to fuck over him."

"I didn't know..."

"That's why you've got to get your face in some of this shit too, Woody, especially with your own play. Then when you make a mistake, we can talk about you like some sorry piece of shit, instead of me. And by the way, what did you ever do with the copyright form anyway?"

"I still got it. I haven't sent it in yet..."

"I rest my case. Look, if you're ready to work on the script at least as much as I do, and if you think you can trust a whiteboy like me, then bring your lazy ass on down. Just make sure you get here on Saturday before noon and give me a call when you get in."

23

Woody's Weekend

It took that damn bus forever to get to Harford County. Seems like it had to stop at every hick town between Philly and Maryland. And the people who rode on the bus were the biggest collection of society's rejects that you'd ever wanna see. I guess if you didn't have it together enough to either own a car, or know somebody who did, you were a loser to begin with. And to be packed on a bus with a gang of them just gave me the creeps. There were the old ladies on welfare who sat at the front near the driver. Then there were the broke students or poor farmers trying to get to their relatives so they could have a place to stay for a few months. At the back was where all the criminals hung out; the convicts on parole; the alcoholics, passed out with a bottle in a brown bag; and bums back there hiding so they could smoke a joint or take a needle or something. You might even see an Amish family riding the bus with their weird-assed selves. I sat at the back too, so as soon as the bus got on the highway, I could slip in that stanky little bathroom with the blue toilet water, lower the window and fire up a joint. And I wasn't the only one. There was a line to get in there by the time we crossed into Delaware. It got so bad that the bus driver didn't even care no more. He was probably afraid that we woulda kicked his ass if he came back there talking too much trash.

It wasn't even noon yet when the bus pulled up to the side of this convenience store which doubled as a bus station. I called Mark from the pay phone there, and I was glad when his big Bonneville pulled into the gravel driveway ten minutes later.

"Thank God, I finally got here," I told him and threw my duffle bag into the back seat.

"How was you trip?" he asked.

"Weird as ever. I thought I was gonna go off like Daffy Duck inside that bus. You want me to drive?"

"Sure." He tossed me the keys and got in on the passenger's side.

"Where do you wanna go first?" I asked him. "I'm hungry myself; where can we get something to eat?"

"We can go to McDonald's; or if you like, we can go to someplace like Sizzler's or Bonanza's. Or we can just get a few groceries and go home. If there's something you want, you better get it while we're out because there's nothing in the refrigerator."

"Tell me where the Sizzler's is and I'll treat you. Then we can stop and get some beer and soda after we eat. And like I said, Mark, your money ain't no good this weekend. I just got paid and them dollars are burning a hole in my pocket." We pulled out of the driveway and headed down a two lane road that led to Route 40, the main strip where everything was.

"You got anything to smoke?"

"Yeah, I got some good shit all rolled and ready to fire up. I smoked one on the bus, so I'm already buzzed. But I don't like smoking when I'm driving, especially since the last time up in Philly I got stopped by a cop. He could've arrested my ass, but he just made me throw a joint out the window and gave me a ticket. Since then, I don't light up anything until we get there."

"Well, this is my car," Mark reminded me, "and I don't care. So light the damn thing up."

"Here, you take the whole stash then." I gave him about ten joints I had rolled at home, and he put them in his cigarette pack.

By the time we got to Sizzler's we were tore up. Mark tried to hurt me with his order. He got a T-bone and shrimp, but I was just glad to see him enjoy hisself on my dollar. We both had the munchies by then so we ate like we were starving boat people or something. I didn't even care if people were staring at us. Hell, I didn't live here, and when I'd leave the next day, I didn't have to see these crackers ever again in life.

I ate 'til my stomach hurt, and then we piled into the car and went to Mark's trailer, way out in Honkieville, U.S.A. I was just hoping that we wouldn't have to run into those Klansmen he lived with again. On the way, we picked up a few bachelor's supplies; a twelve pack of Genesee Cream Ale, some chips and cookies, and a bucket of Kentucky Fried for later.

On the way to his crib, some shit went down that I think drove a wedge between me and Mark. He swears that it didn't, but I could feel it. He acted different after that.

"Why are you driving so slow," he asked me.

"Because the last thing I want to do is get stopped by some redneck cop, with the car all lit up with marijuana smoke."

"What? Is he going to lock us up for a few joints? I got stopped once in Delaware," Mark explained, "and I knew he could smell the smoke coming out of the car, but the cop didn't say a thing, just gave me a warning. I even got smart-assed with him and complained about him stopping me in the first place."

"Yeah, that was you. When a cop stops me, I do anything he asks me to do, and I grin and shuffle while I'm doing it. Because a lotta times, they're just looking for some reason to fuck with a brother. And no matter what goes down, I'm gonna be in the wrong. If a cop and a black man go to blows on a deserted street, who's the judge and everybody else gonna believe? So with me, it's like, oh officer you want a blow job? Just whip it out, sir."

"That's bullshit," Mark said all indignant.

"That's because you's a whiteboy. If you were black, you'd be on your knees, just like me, making 'O' shapes with your lips."

"I drive this road all the time, and I've never seen any cops out here. We haven't even passed another car except that brown Caprice back there. And if a cop is going to stop us, he has to stop them too. We're all going the same speed." He lit up a cigarette and stuffed the pack in his shirt pocket.

No sooner than he said that, I looked in the rearview mirror and saw the grill of that brown Caprice flashing red lights at us.

"Damn Mark, it's a cop! What did you do with them joints? Throw 'em out the window." Mark turned around and saw the flashing lights on the unmarked car behind us.

"Don't worry," he said. "I got it," and he tucked the cigarette pack, joints and all, into the crotch of his jeans. "He'll never find them here."

I pulled to the side of the road and looked again in the rearview mirror to see Officer Rambo step out. This dude had on a green tee shirt, camouflage pants with a matching cap, and combat boots. So, I already knew he was trippin' big time. He walked slowly towards us with his pistol half drawn from his holster, and as he reached the driver's window where I was sitting, he flashed his badge with his free hand. It read: *Maryland State Police.*

"May I see your driver's license and registration, sir?" He bent to look through the window, and his blue eyes were as cold as February. I handed him my license. He looked at it, then looked at me. He looked at it again, and looked back at me.

I turned and asked Mark, "Where's your registration card?"

"It's right here in the glove box." Mark reached to open it.

"Just hold it right there," Rambo said nervously. "Keep your hands where I can see them. Is this your car, sir?" Mark nodded yes. "Then let me see your license too. And please, remove the registration card from the glove compartment nice and slow." Mark obeyed and handed it to him. "Pass them completely out of the window so I don't have to reach in." his hand still gripped that pistol of his. Then he said, "Have you guys been smoking marijuana in there?"

"No, suh!" I said with the biggest Uncle Tom voice I could find.

Mark looked at me disgusted. "I'm smoking cigarettes," he said and took a drag, filling the car with smoke.

"I know marijuana smoke when I smell it," the trooper shot back. "You guys think we're stupid, don't you? You think all cops are stupid." Neither one of us said a damn thing. "Well, you just sit tight. I'm gonna call in your license, and then I'm gonna take this car apart," and he walked back to his brown Caprice.

"Mark, listen," I said, "this muthafucka is crazy. I told you to throw them joints out the window, but it's too late now. I hope you got 'em shoved up your ass somewhere, because he's out to get us. Now, you let me handle this, okay? You don't say shit, and you don't do shit because god knows what kinda trip he's on." Mark gave me that disgusted look again, but his silence told me that he would be cool. Rambo reappeared at my window.

"You guys check out all right, no warrants or outstanding tickets." He was a little relieved, but his hand stayed on that gun. "Where are you guys on your way to?"

I spoke up. "I just got off the bus from Philly, officer; and we're headed to Mark's house."

"Where do you live?" he asked Mark.

"At the Chesapeake Trailer Park on Route 44, just like it says on the license," Mark said all smart-assed.

"What's in those bags back there?"

"Just some beer and snacks; that's all." I said.

"Step out of the car, please." he told me and walked me around between the two cars.

Being a security guard myself, I knew the routine, and I tried not to excite this guy who was obviously on some mission from god. I remembered getting stopped in my Pops' car, and when the officer saw my security badge, he just grinned and told me to go on; no warning, no ticket or nothing. Even if I had my badge, I don't think it would've made much difference to Officer Rambo here, because he was convinced that we were dangerous, and Mark being white didn't matter nowhere near as much as me being black.

He turned my pockets inside out, and pat me up one side then down the other. If that wasn't humiliating enough, I actually saw him wave to a carload of people as they drove by. You know, like he had just bagged his nigga for the day. I knew the song and dance, and I thought my cooperation would somehow chill his ass out a little bit, but it had the opposite effect. I guess he figured if I was so knowledgeable about "assuming the position" that I must've done this before. So, he never took that one hand off his gun. All the while he was watching the car to see what Mark was doing. Then in the middle of this, I saw Mark Berens reach into the bag in the back seat, pull something out, and fiddle with it in his lap. Rambo saw it too, and he got sho' 'nuff crazy then.

"You stay right here," he ordered, satisfied that I wasn't strapped. Then he prowled up the passenger's side with his gun fully drawn. I knew what was happening. He didn't know what Mark was doing so he assumed the worst. My heart beat so fast 'til it was clicking in my chest. Rambo glanced back at me, but by that time I had took myself out the line of fire. I sat my ass on the ground by a nearby telephone pole, and laced my fingers behind my head. I thought; Damn, Mark! I told you not to do nothin'. The cop crouched and eased up the side of the car so Mark couldn't see him in the mirror. In one motion he reached for the door, flung it open, and pointed the gun at Mark's temple. Cigarettes flew everywhere.

"Freeze asshole, freeze!" he screamed as he gripped the pistol with both hands and inched it closer to Marks heads. "Let me see your hands! Let me see your hands, now!"

Mark was absolutely terrified. He threw up his palms, ducked like a naughty child, and sputtered, "Wha...what? Don't shoot, mister. I was just getting a cigarette!"

"I told you to keep your hands where I could see them."

"Okay, okay. My god!" Mark realized for the first time just how serious this shit actually was, and I couldn't help feeling sorry for him.

The cop stood him up in the doorway of the car and searched him the same way he searched me; and when he couldn't find anything, he went to work on the car. He looked under the seats, under the floor mats, in the cracks of the seats, in the ash tray and the glove box. He even popped the trunk open and searched it too. Mark sat back in the car, and I heard them mumbling to each other.

Rambo was pissed that he couldn't find nothing, so he walked back to lecture me. I didn't feel like hearing anything he had to say. But he went on to tell me that he knew we had been smoking weed, and that we had lucked out; that if he had found anything, he woulda arrested the both of us. No, he wasn't even gonna give us a speeding ticket which was the excuse he used to stop us in the first place. He went on to explain how this highway was a notorious drug alley into Baltimore, and that a black man driving a white man in a nice car was a profile for a drug deal (a used Bonneville? C'mon!). That's why he was so suspicious.

This joker held us up for damn near an hour, and he still wouldn't let us go without lecturing me some more on how bad it was for us to smoke marijuana; how we were contributing to organized crime; and how expensive it was. All the while I'm thinking; yeah, yeah, yeah. I finally interrupted him.

"Excuse me, officer. But if you're through with us, can we leave now?"

"Yeah. Just a minute...I'll get your license and registration."

When he returned, his whole attitude had changed. Oh, he's Mr. Friendly Policeman now; wants to be our friends. I knew he was just feeling guilty. Sure, we was smoking weed in the car, but we weren't no dangerous criminals, and we damn sure didn't deserve to be dogged-out, hassled, and terrified like this for an hour. He knew that shit like I knew it.

When we finally drove away, I swear to god, Mark Berens was a different person. He was quiet in a way I'd never seen him before. I remembered the last time when he had discovered racism he never knew about. He at least struck out, got mad and said something. Not now. The car was as quiet as a tomb. I couldn't think of a damn thing to say. I mean, what do you say to someone who just looked death in the face and walked away?

That incident obviously fucked up the entire weekend for us. Mark tried to be friendly and polite afterwards. He pretended to listen to my ideas about the play, and laugh at my comic routines, but there was no fight left in him. Whereas before, he would tell me that I was crazy or full of shit; that weekend, I couldn't even get a rise out of him. And I knew that a Mark Berens without his passion couldn't write a script, or critique a performance worth a damn.

Here's what I think happened. Mark was just tired of dealing with niggas. And since I was a nigga, he was tired of me too. That's not to say that we weren't still cool. I don't think you can go through what we been through and not feel something for each other. It's just that having to collaborate with another black person became too much for him. He got tired of always looking over his shoulder, tired of not getting a fair shake, just plain tired of going through all the bullshit that black people have to go through everyday, especially when he didn't have to. And since he realizes now that what he doesn't know about racism can kill him, he just gave up on ever being close to black folks again. Oh, he would continue to have black friends, but it would only be on that polite level, all detached and uninvolved. And to be honest, I can't say that I blame him.

But just because he gave up on me, I hadn't given up on him yet.

24

Mark Visits Home

Woody probably didn't know what was wrong with me that weekend, me being so quiet and all. But I didn't know what was happening myself. I mean the incident with Officer Rambo, as Woody called him, forced me to acknowledge a whole lot of stuff that I had been trying to deny. Woody had said it all along; racism is routine, and obviusly there were some unwritten rules that everyone seemed to know except me. And having looked down the business end of a .45, not knowing whether I was going to live or die, had humbled me. And yeah, I guess at that moment, I would've done just about anything to keep this crazed gunman from blowing my brains out. Even in the Air Force, I had never faced death in such an arbitrary, senseless way before. And it wasn't that I was guilty that had brought me so close to death, it was because of an act of friendship, because my association with a black man fit some criminal profile they had.

I felt like a sap in Woody's presence. The trooper proved to be the very same white devil that I had tried to defend earlier, and it made me feel kind of guilty; you know, for my race, for white people. But even more than that, I felt betrayed and lied to. How could I not have known the situation was this bad? Did other white people know too, or was it just me? And if I was so dead wrong about this, what other little secrets didn't I know about. It shook my confidence. That's why I was so silent and dazed for the rest of that weekend. I mean, how do you go from believing in the American system so much that you're ready to put your life on the line for it, to where I was now—doubting if freedom and justice even existed at all. And if it does, it's so arbitrary that you can't depend on it. Certainly not enough to die for it. And did it change my opinion about black people? Well, what do you think?

Suddenly, all the racial nonsense that went on at DelState made more sense. I could see why blacks were so distrustful of whites, and why race was the first thing they thought about in any situation. And if this had rocked me like it did, what must it be like to have this nonsense hanging over your head all the time, day in and day out, constantly? I felt a kinship with black people while at the same time realizing they could never feel the same about me. And all the guilt, self pity, disillusionment, and sheer anger was too much for to me to deal with all at once. I couldn't be a collaborator now. Hell, it was hard enough to figure out how to continue to be Woodrow's friend and still feel safe.

I couldn't explain any of this to Woodrow. So, we never really spoke about it. I have no idea what he thought was happening with me. He probably thought I was just being a whiteboy again, the way he explained all of our other differences. But that's not the only thing that had come between us. Woody had changed toward me too.

It seemed like we couldn't just be friends and hang out anymore. Everything was about writing that damned play now. I mean, every time we'd talk on the phone, sooner or later the topic would come up. And after a while, I just got sick of hearing about it. It made me feel like he wasn't interested in having a friendship anymore, that all he wanted to do was to use me, and to hell with everything else. Forget the fact that Mark is recuperating and burnt out. Forget the fact that Woody wouldn't share the work load with me—just write, dammit! Finally, I had to tell him.

"Look, Woodrow. We need to take a break from this play for a while, okay? I'm just not interested right now. So let's just go back to hanging out again. Remember when we could talk on the phone for hours about anything? Remember how you used to come to the trailer for a weekend and we'd have a great time with only two joints and five dollars between us? What happened to those times?"

"Well, I thought you'd be recuperated by now, Mark. Damn, how long is it gonna take? Besides, you need to get back into it as soon as possible. That's the only way you're gonna recover. Just like getting back on the horse after you fall off."

"Read my lips, Woody. The answer is no! I'm not working on anybody's play. Do you get that? Damn, what's wrong with you? You've been bugging me so much that I don't even want to talk to you anymore because I know we'll be fighting about that damn play again. Is doing that play more important to you than our friendship?"

"Of course not."

"Then give it a break, okay?" After I said that, there was this sigh of resignation and a few moments of silence.

"You're right, Mark. I guess I was getting a little crazy. But you know me. Once I get a notion in my mind, I bust loose like the Schlitz Malt Liquor Bull. I guess I was laying it on kinda thick."

"Well, thank you."

"But I was just trying to do like you said, and take the lead."

"Woody, badgering me is not the same thing as taking the lead. There's other stuff you can be doing without me."

"Okay, tell me."

"Well for one, have you sent in the copyright form yet?" The silence on the other end of the phone told me his answer. "Have you written down any scenarios? Any dialogue? Anything?"

"Aw, Mark. You know how I am with writing. Man, that shit drives me crazy. Besides you got that over me, anyway. I told you a long time ago that you're a better writer than me. Mark, you're a better writer than anybody I know.

Why do you think I be doggin' you like that? Now, when it comes to acting, or creating characters and story lines, or pumping up the cast, that's where I come in. But I guess you'll always hafta do more work than me because you know about all that production shit. You got more skills in that than I'll ever have."

"Is that a compliment?"

"Whiteboy, please!"

"Well, Woody. You're going to have to wait until I'm able to give it to you. You can't just make me write for you, you know. I can't even make myself do that. So, just give me a little time, okay? I'll be ready to go before you know it."

"You got it, buddy. I won't fuck with you about the play no more until you say the word. Swear befo' god."

I guess I needed to hear that he respected and valued the friendship. I needed to hear that he trusted me. And with that said, things seemed right between us again. All the racial tension, the suspicion, and our status in the collaboration seemed settled, finally and amicably.

And it was a good thing, too because things at home had taken a turn for the worse when I talked to Mom the next day.

"Hi, baby. How're you doing?"

"Oh hi, Mom. I'm just fine. You don't sound so good."

"Well, I guess I don't feel so good, Mark. We finally got the results of your father's tests, and it's not good news. All the doctors are saying the same thing; it's a tumor and we should have the surgery done as soon as possible."

"What does Dad think about it?"

"Well, at first it was the hardest thing just to get him to go to the doctors. You know how stubborn your father can be sometimes."

"Yes, I do."

"Then he woke up a couple of weeks ago, and found one of his retirement check stubs. He said he didn't remember being retired. Didn't remember his retirement party, his gold watch, nothing. It scared him something terrible. When I explained it to him, I think most of his memory came back. After that he got really motivated to go to the doctors. It was his idea to get the test finalized and to have the operation done."

"So, when is the surgery?"

"He's waiting to get on the schedule now. There are only a few brain surgeons in this area, and we're trying to pick the best one from what Dr. Riggs has told us. Your father's really scared, but he's determined to go through with this."

"Well, what are his chances, ma? What can go wrong?"

"Mark, you can't get much more serious than brain surgery, honey. Anything could happen; he could be paralyzed, he could have a stroke, he could even...die on the operating table. That's why I'm calling you, son. I sure wished you and your brother could be here. Your father wants to see you two real bad, and it certainly would be a comfort to me."

"Well, mother…"

"Just the other day he was going through all his old papers, his accounts and his will. He wanted me to know where everything was in case he didn't pull through. I told him, 'Steven, I don't want to hear all this now.' But he insisted, and I guess he was right. Now he wonders if he'll ever see his boys again."

"Did you call Greg?"

"Yes."

"Well, what did he say?"

"You know, I don't understand Gregory, Mark. He said he wouldn't be able to come. Didn't give any reason, just insisted that he couldn't visit for a while. When I finally told him that this might be the last time he'd be able to see his father alive again, he just said, 'Sorry, mother, I can't come now.' I don't know what's going on with him anymore. Maybe you could talk to him, Mark."

"Me? I don't have any influence over him."

"Mark, you'll be able to come won't you?"

"Well, yes…but…"

"But what, son?"

"Mother, I didn't want to worry you about this before. I figured you had enough on your mind, but I'm kinda broke. I'm able to make ends meet, but I just don't have enough cash on hand right now to pay for plane fare, especially not on short notice where I can't get that two week discount."

"Oh, we'll send you a ticket. Why didn't you call before if you needed money?"

"I can only come for a couple days. I took all my sick days doing that play, and if I take too much more time off, my job's in jeopardy."

"However long you can stay will be fine. We just want to see you again before your father…you know."

Mother couldn't even finish that last part. And I must admit that it scared me too. Dad being sick was one thing, but going under the knife was serious. And I certainly wanted to see him again, and I wanted to be on hand for Mom if she needed me.

I couldn't understand Greg, though. If Mom didn't know why he wouldn't visit, he obviously had never told her what he'd told me; was still carrying that grudge about Dad. I don't know, to hold back on them now seemed somehow dishonorable, like neglecting your parents in their hour of need. It just didn't seem right. So, I gave Greg a call.

"Hey, Mark. What's up kid?"

"Everything's fine with me Gregory, but Mom and Dad aren't doing so hot."

"Yeah, she told me."

"I'm going to fly out and see them."

"You need any help getting out there?"

"No, they're going to pay for it."

"I'm glad you're going out there, Mark. It'll be good for them."

"Well, if it's so good, how come you won't go?"

"Oh, I guess you've been talking to Mom."

"Yes, I have. She says that you just flat out refuse to come. Why are you punishing them like that?"

"I'm not punishing anybody, Mark. I thought you understood that. I'm just not ready to deal with Dad now. I'm still trying to heal and get myself together; and until I do, I don't have much to give anybody."

"You're still holding that grudge against Dad? Greg, you should put that behind you now. Mom needs you, and Dad needs you. Don't you think you're being a little selfish here?"

"Look, Mark. What's happening to Dad is not my fault. I can't save him, and I can't save Mom either. So, I don't understand why you're trying to put all this on me. The fact is I just can't stand to be around Dad, not now. If I went home, it would only make things worse for everybody, not better. Why can't you understand that?"

"Because this might be your last chance, Gregory. If you don't see him now, you might not have another chance. It won't kill you to go down there and help them through this. Tell me, how will you feel if Dad dies on the operating table, and you never see him again, huh?"

"Don't you think I've thought about that? You think this is easy for me? But here's what bothers me, Mark. The hurt and pain between me and Dad is not my fault. I didn't abuse him; he abused me, remember? And now that I'm all broken down, everybody wants me to forget my pain, forget the fact that I need help, just fuck it that I'm fighting for my life too. I'm supposed to get over it. I don't wish anything bad for him. I hope to god he pulls through this. He's my father too, goddamit! But I can't help Dad or anyone else until I help myself first."

"Why can't you explain this to Mom then? Let her know like you let me know."

"Mark, I owed you. That's why I had to apologize. I had wronged you, and I was trying to set the situation straight as best I could. But between Dad and me, if anybody's got some explaining or apologizing to do it's him, not me. And how can I visit Mom and tell her without telling Dad too? I'll probably confront him about it one day, but it has to be when I'm ready, not when you or Mom are ready. And if Dad dies before I can say this to him…well, I'll have to find a way to deal with that, won't I?"

Well, I had done all I could do. If the man didn't want to go home, he didn't want to go. I couldn't force him. I did feel kind of sad for Mom and Dad, though. And yes, I felt a little sad for Greg too because if he had this much trouble confronting his own mother and father, something had to be wrong. I guess I never realized how wrong until now. Hell, I didn't realize a lot of things until now.

I didn't have to do much explaining to Craig Dempsey to get a Thursday and Friday off so I could have a long weekend with them. The following week, I was on a plane to St. Petersburg, the last place I'd lived before I left for the service. I hadn't been home in a couple of years so it was pleasant to see both their faces again. I just wished it was under different circumstances.

For some reason, when I saw them both at the airport I could see the resemblance between me and Dad more strongly than ever. I had his facial features; his eyes, nose, and chin; his coloring and height; but I had mom's lean build. And I could see for the first time why, when I was a kid, that strangers would muss my hair and smile when they'd see us together. But for some reason, noticing the resemblance wasn't comforting; it was eerie somehow, like looking into a distorted mirror. Mom wasn't in as bad shape as she sounded on the phone, but she did look tired and out of spirits, which I guess was understandable.

Most of the day Thursday we spent checking Dad into the hospital. We filled out insurance forms and authorization sheets, and answered two hours' worth of questions. I could see what Mom was talking about with Dad's memory. Most of the time he would be fine, the same old hyperactive Steve Berens. But then it would take him a disturbingly long time to answer a simple question. He'd struggled to remember the city he was born in, or when he was discharged from the service, or his age. Dad was never good at showing emotions and that hadn't changed, but there was a sadness and a resignation on his face that I'd never seen before. But he couldn't hide the fact that he was glad to see me.

The evening was so ordinary that it bothered me a little bit. I don't know what I was expecting, but Mom just fixed some chicken and rice, we ate it, watched a little TV, and that was it basically. We reminisced for a while, but the night didn't have the drama I expected. I wanted some sort of closure, a tying up of loose ends, some acknowledgment of affection. But whenever I'd try, it was so awkward and foreign that I went back to the idle chatting with Mom. Dad took his medication and went to bed. Not too long after that, me and Mom followed.

The next morning we packed Dad's supply of toiletries and a change of clothes for his hospital stay, and except for a slight nervousness in the air, you would've thought that we were all going on a weekend camping trip. Everybody was so busy trying to avoid the obvious. We got him checked in bright and early because the surgery was scheduled for seven o'clock. The only thing that exposed our little charade was when they wheeled Dad from his room into surgery. It was also the time when Gregory's absence was most conspicuous. Dad reached up and gave Mom the biggest hug I'd ever seen them share. He kissed her soundly on the lips and assured, "Don't worry, Katie. I'll be all right, but pray for me anyway." Mom forced a smile and said, "I will, Steve. I will."

I grabbed him in a hug and tried to put a good face on our apprehension, "Don't worry about us, Dad. You just work on beating this thing, okay?"

The nurse wheeled him from the room and it was the last time I saw my father as a whole, functioning man.

The operation took over ten hours, and pacing the waiting room for those hours to pass was excruciating—just horrible. What a sickening feeling of helplessness and anxiety. Mom would check with the receptionist every forty five minutes or so to get the same answer. I thought she would get tired of us after the first four or five times, but she always kept her composure. By noon, neither of us was hungry enough to go to the cafeteria because we had been drinking that black acid in the waiting room that was passing for coffee. But by two or three o'clock, we both thought it would be a good idea to grab a bite. I was ravenous and ate a couple burgers, a healthy order of fries, and a slice of lemon meringue pie. Mom just picked at her salad.

Finally and mercifully, the receptionist informed us that the surgery was over, that Dad had made it through, and that we could talk to the surgeon as soon as he cleaned up.

"Mrs. Berens," he called as he walked in the waiting room. "Your husband came through nicely, and he's resting in post-op now. You can see him in an hour or so, but he won't be conscious quite yet." He spoke in an official sounding voice trying to put us at ease. "The tumor was about as big as a hen's egg, and it's a good thing we found it when we did. He couldn't have gone on much longer like that. But unfortunately, it had grown around an artery; and to remove it, we had to temporarily cut off the blood supply to his brain. There's likely to be some paralysis." Mom's eyes widened when he said that. I was just numb by then.

"How much paralysis?" she stammered. "Will it be permanent?"

"It's too soon to say, Mrs. Berens. It's much like a stroke. His recovery could be full or partial, dependent on a lot of factors. But it's just too soon to say."

"Will he be all right?" I asked.

"Oh, he should pull through this just fine. The worst is over, but what his exact condition will be, and the extent of his recovery? It's just too soon to say," he repeated. "You'll be able to see him in an hour or so, but don't expect too much for another day or two," and he disappeared the way he came in, leaving us empty and frustrated.

I drove Mom to a nearby shopping mall to try to get our minds off Dad, but it didn't do much good. We stopped at an ice cream parlor and pushed mounds of frozen yogurt around in our bowls, and then we left. When we returned to the hospital, I dropped Mom off at the door and parked the car. The nurses inside said that we could see Dad, but he was not conscious yet, and that he wouldn't come around for a while. When we walked into post-op where he was recovering, neither of us was prepared for what we saw.

His body lay motionless and strapped down to a bed enclosed with metal rails. His head was capped with white bandages, and every orifice on his face seemed attached to something; to an oxygen mask, or to the tubes and pipes of the machinery that hovered over the bed like Death. They told me that this was my father, but I couldn't believe it. Nothing of the man I knew lay there. The scene was shocking. Mom walked nervously around the bed looking for some part of him to recognize. Then she affectionately took his hand in hers, rubbed it and pat it a couple of times and said, "Get the car, Mark. It's time to go home."

I was glad to leave. It reminded me of when I had been hooked up like that weeks earlier. And hearing the click and hum of the machinery gave me the willies. When I got to the car, I started the engine, but I couldn't do anything else. I don't completely understand why, but I sat there with the engine running, and I broke down and cried like a baby. No, I don't mean tears trickling down my face. I mean doubled-over heaving, and uncontrollable sobs that were confusing in their depth and intensity. This went on for a full ten minutes until I got it together enough to turn off the engine, climb from the car and light a cigarette or two. When I finally picked up Mom in the lobby of the waiting room, she took one look at my face, and she knew what had taken so long.

I slept soundly that night. I guess sleep was my best escape at that point. The next morning we called the hospital before we arrived to make sure that Dad had made it through the night all right, and to see if he was even conscious enough for us to visit. The nurses said he was. When we arrived, one of them was attending to him, checking the machines and tubes he was hooked up to. There was little change in his appearance.

"Is he awake?" Mom asked because neither of us could really tell.

"Oh yeah," she said too cheerily, "he's been awake for a while. Mr. Berens, your family is here. Can you wink to them. C'mon now, wink to show them that you're awake." She apparently saw something that we had missed. "See there," she said. "He's speaking to you. Yes, he got through the night fine, but the doctor said there would be some paralysis on his left side. If you grab his right hand he should be able to wave to you."

Both Mom and me inspected his hand trying not to look horrified, searching for any sign of movement. We saw Dad give a thumbs-up. It was a weak gesture, but clearly a familiar signal of Steve Berens. Mom grabbed his hand much the same as she had done the night before. Then it was my turn to hold his hand, but soon he shook my grip loose. Holding him like that was apparently too intimate, and it embarrassed him. But seeing that, and seeing his thumbs-up was a relief to me. It let me know that yes, my father was still there, somewhere in those mounds of tubes, bandages and dead weight; and he was just as neurotic as he'd always been. It was the reassurance I needed.

I flew back to Maryland the next morning promising that I'd return when I could. But their ordeal was just beginning. Dad would need weeks of rehabilitation and therapy to be well enough to even come home. And the uncertainty of his condition still wasn't easy to deal with. He would probably never walk again or regain movement on his left side. And the surgery didn't guarantee that he'd be free from those seizures either. His memory would continue to play tricks on him, but I knew that somehow he'd be himself again. At least that's what I told myself.

Returning to Maryland was just what I needed. Believe it or not, I was glad to see that office and my co-workers. The old grind felt good; it felt like home, and in no time I felt fully recuperated, strong and raring to go. I realized that in the past few months fortune had delivered some savage shots to my emotions, to my self esteem, to my wallet, and to my health. And look; I'm still standing! Not much could be worse than what I'd been through. But never say never because Woodrow Tyler still had a big surprise for me.

25

Woodrow's Last Stand

Mark told me over the phone that his Pops was having surgery and that he would have to fly home for a weekend. Like I said before, we still kept in touch because we was like that. But I knew that our relationship had cooled off. I didn't want to mess with him about it, but we did have this serious conversation after he got back.

"Yo, Mark. This is Woody. What's up?"

"Not much. What's up with you?"

"I just called to make sure you're doing all right. After our little cops and robbers scene last time, I was kinda worried about you, buddy."

"Well, it did shake me up, Woody. Every time I think about that crazy asshole, I get pissed all over again. But no, don't worry about me. I'm doing fine."

"Mark, you gotta learn how to chill out, bucko. Don't take things to heart so much. I mean, like with the play. You didn't have to put your guts and spleen into it like that."

"That was not guts and spleen, Woody, it's called *heart,* and maybe you should try it sometimes. But you're right, I do have to make things more balanced, and since I got back, I've been thinking more and more about doing the play?"

"For real?"

"Well, I'm not ready to start writing yet, but I've been thinking about organizing the production a little better; you know, so that we can make a profit this time, so we can spread the work around, and maybe get some help with the expenses. Make it more like a business. That way, I won't get so burnt out, and it'll free me up for the creative stuff. After all that's why I started doing plays in the first place."

"Glad to hear that. What kinda stuff did you come up with?"

"First of all, we could try to get some other investors. If you, or your friends, or somebody in the cast wants to put up their money, or donate their salary from the show to help the production, we should share any profit we make based on how much they've invested. Next, we should have specific job descriptions, and pay people according to the work they do."

"What kind of job descriptions, Mark?"

"Whatever jobs need to be done; actors, writers, directors, tech-crew, publicity, like that."

"So, let me get this straight. You're saying that if we had used this system for *Gentlemen's Journal,* for instance, the way you're describing it, you woulda probably made more money than me because you woulda worn more of these *job descriptions* you just came up with, right?"

"Well...yeah. I guess so, especially if you count all the money that I spent on the cast for travel and meals during the rehearsals. That's assuming of course that we would've made any profit."

"But damn, Mark. Why you gotta count it up like that? Like you're keeping a running tab, marking down every little thing and charging for it. It's like you're hung-up on money now or something."

"That's not being hung-up, Woody, that's called *business.* The more work you do, and the more money you invest, the more profit you get—business plain and simple!"

"But we're supposed to be in this thing together. It's like you're trying to cut me out now. Why you gotta be make them little petty distinctions?"

"Woody, I'm not trying to cut you out of anything."

"But the way you're trying to arrange it, you'll always be making more money than me, and if that's not cutting me out, then I don't know what you call it."

"If I'm always doing more work and investing more money than you, then why shouldn't I get more of the profit? You can't conduct a business like a friendship. I mean, at work you punch a clock and get paid according to what you do, but when I ask you to do the same thing, then I'm the evil whiteboy again, trying to take advantage of you."

"That's because you know whatever goes down, I'm gonna be there to back you up. If I got money; you got money. If I got a place to stay; you got a place to stay. If you do more work this time; I'll do more work next time. That's what I'm talkin' about, not no little bullshit ego trips or power plays."

"Oh, so you think all this is just a power play, huh?"

"Mark, all I know is here I stand again with the short end of the stick, and there you stand again with everything in your favor. So, you tell me what the deal is."

"I call myself helping you to produce your play. You *asked me* for help, remember? I didn't want to do the damn thing in the first place. Woody, you're still convinced that I'm out to cheat you, aren't you? On some level, you still don't trust me, and I guess you never will."

"Well, what am I supposed to think?"

"You can think whatever the hell you want to think, okay? But I'll tell you this, all this suspicion really hurts me, Woodrow, especially since I've already proven myself to you. I put my health, my job and everything else on the line for us—for me and for you—*everything!* What else do I have to do before you can trust me—*die?* So look, we don't have to be collaborators, we don't have to be partners, we don't even have to be friends if we've got to go through another conversation like this. This shit just rips my heart out. I've got to go..."

147

Click!

I shoulda known something like this was gonna happen. Andrew tried to warn me with that copyright form, but I couldn't see it then. When we started off, it was just me and Mark; buddies, partners and equals. But now when money comes into the picture, he's the man and I'm his fuckin' underling or something. But when he was pumping me for story ideas, or needed somebody to proofread his scenes; or when the play was crashing in flames, I wasn't no underling then. I didn't know Mark was like that. But, hell no, I wasn't about to accept no shit like that; even if I thought he was right. And if he wants to act like a bitch now, cool. I've dealt with bitches before.

Not too long after that, Cool Will was in the hospital hisself. It was his blood pressure again. I remember when he first checked in, it was like the Tyler Family's Fucked-Up Reunion. Seems like we can't get together as a family unless somebody's sick, dead, or dying. All of us were there, Timmie, Aunt Earlemae, Crazy Francine and her nigga-of-the-month. By the time Mom got there, Daddy had been checked in, and we were waiting for his pressure to go down so we could visit him. Then here come crazy-ass Francine, all late and wrong. She was half drunk already and was all loud and dramatic, doing embarrassing shit like badgering the receptionist and cussing out the nurses who didn't know what the hell this crazy bitch wanted. It took Aunt Earlemae to shut her up. If I had said anything to her, it woulda been the wrong thing. Timmie was sitting over in the corner like he didn't know nobody. I guess he was about to cry because if anything happened to Daddy, he knew that would be it for his sorry ass. He'd really have to grow up and be a man then.

We sat in there half the night, seems like. They hadn't admitted him into a room yet, but had him in one of those emergency room hook-ups until a room was ready. Finally, they let us go see him, two at a time. Me and Aunt Earlemae went in first. He was laying in bed with his legs crossed and one of his hands behind his head, chilly as ever.

"Y'all didn't have to make no fuss over me like this," he said. "I'm gonna be all right."

"Aw, William. Ain't nobody making no fuss over you," my aunt said. "We just here to make sure you're all right, that's all."

"How ya feeling, Dad?" I asked him.

"Just a little tired right now, Woody. They said I probably have a minor blockage. They want to run some tests as soon as they can."

"Look, Will. Is there anything you need? I can have Woodrow bring it back for you first thing tomorrow."

"Naw, I just need some pajamas, my tooth brush, my razor and stuff; that's all. Oh, Woodrow, look in my pants pockets and get the keys to my car. I want you to take care of if for me. Take it to work with you cause you know if Timmie drives it, it's gonna be all run down before I can even get outta here."

"Don't worry about none of that, Daddy. I'll take care of it. You just worry about getting well. I'll bring back your pajamas and stuff tomorrow, but we gonna let you go now. Mamma and Timmie want to see you."

"Is Francine out there? Hell, I thought they wanted me to get better in here." We laughed and I felt better that he could even crack a joke now.

"Well, after she jumped on the receptionist and the security guard, I guess they were glad to let her come back here," said Aunt Earlemae.

"Yeah, Dad. They figured you could handle her better than they could. Hell, all they had was a .357 Magnum."

"Lawd, have mercy," he sighed. Me and Aunt Earlemae walked out and unleashed Crazy Francine on his ass. That ought to be enough incentive for him to get better.

Cool Will was out of the hospital not long after that weekend, but the next day I dropped off his pajamas and stuff like he asked. Since I had the weekend off, and since I'd got paid and had a car, I thought I'd make a trip to Maryland and surprise Mark Berens. It would be the perfect opportunity to take him out and mend fences a little bit. I didn't know if I'd even find him at home. But what the hell, it was a nice day. If all else failed I could stop in Wilmington and catch a show or something. I knew I didn't want to spend much time at home because I would have to fight Timmie about the car. So, after I stopped at the hospital, I took off. Two hours and fifteen minutes later, I was at the convenience store where the bus had stopped. I then proceeded to drop a dime on Mark Berens.

"Yo, Mark. This is Woody. What's up?"

"Oh hi, Woody," he said all tired and shit.

"Damn, you don't sound glad to hear from me."

"I just don't feel like fighting with you, that's all."

"Ain't nobody gonna fight with you, boy. I'm calling to put some excitement in that boring ass life of yours. I'm at the bus station, and I just wanted to make sure you was home by yourself before I dropped in."

"You took the bus in?"

"Naw, I got my Pop's car. And if you ain't doing nothing, I was gonna come by and take you to see your favorite musical of all time. *Jesus Christ Superstar* is at the Playhouse in Wilmington. If you're down, we can catch the Saturday matinee, and be back before dinner."

"How much are the tickets?"

"Did I say anything about tickets? You wanna go or not?"

"Yeah, Woody. C'mon over."

"And see, now that you know the State Police Code of Nigga Conduct, if we get stopped this time, you won't get your brains blowed out. I'll be there in ten minutes."

When I got there, Mark was ready to go. I didn't hafta worry about him smoking weed in the car no more; he was cured of that shit. The drive to

Wilmington didn't take but an hour or so, and by the time we got to the theater, it was like old times again. We were bustin' on each other like back when we were students. I could even see the anticipation in Mark's face when we finally got our tickets and were waiting for the curtain to rise. I mean, he was like a little kid on Christmas morning. He had always liked *Jesus Christ Superstar;* said it was his favorite and how it was a modern interpretation of an ancient story. He said he didn't understand how a musical was put together until he'd seen this show. We'd seen the movie version together, but never a live production. Mark told me that he'd like to direct the show one day, and by the time the band cued up, he was hyped big time.

By intermission, I could tell that Mark got his passion back. I guess that's what it took. He just needed some time off, some rest and recuperation, then to see a professional play that he was already a groupie for. So on the drive back, he was directing the show, telling me how he woulda done things.

"It was a good production and all, Woody, don't get me wrong. I mean, the singers were just fantastic, but the setting was kind of corny. Now, I would've divided the stage into two sides; stage left would be the headquarters of Jesus and his revolutionaries; stage right would've been all the government characters like Pilate, Herod, Caiphas and all of them."

"Yeah, I like that, Mark. Makes the characters easier to identify."

"I wouldn't have made the costumes Biblical either. Make them more modern, and more military; you know, camouflage pants with those sheet things on their heads."

"They call it a 'burnoose.' I know because my friend's a Muslim."

"Yeah, them. And instead of crucifying Jesus, I would've used a firing squad. The crucifixion metaphor is passe, and it's too religious for a secular treatment like this."

"I see you've thought a lot about this play," I told him.

"Woody, I've directed this play a hundred times, every time I listen to the album."

We arrived at his crib in no time, and he was just as hyped as ever. And as we walked into his trailer, I figured this was as good a time as any to test him.

"So, Mark. Since you're in a creative mood now, do you have any ideas about *Laugh 'til it Hurts?*" I could see him pause. He was still suspicious of me.

"Not really, Woody. The last time we talked about it, I was a little upset to say the least. But as far as specific dialogue; no, I haven't given it much thought."

"Well, you certainly seem hyped now. Look at cha', just bubbling over with ideas. I bet you could write damn near anything now, the way you're feeling."

"Well, maybe."

"Like, if we got together next weekend, you could throw some ideas on paper couldn't you?"

"I suppose."

"Cool, I'll see if I can come back next weekend, and we can hang out some more. How's that sound, Mark?"

"Yeah, I guess we can do that."

"Aw, there's just one thing. Pops will be out of the hospital by then, and I won't have no transportation."

Mark heaved a big sigh, then broke down and said, "I guess you want me to drive to Philly and pick you up?"

"Could you?"

"Oh, all right Woody," he caved in.

That's what I'm talking about! I knew Mark couldn't resist me, that if I played things right, we would be back like before. I just didn't expect Mark to fall for it so quick. I wanted to drive the point home, and remind him that I wasn't his fuckin' underling like what he was talking about. If anything, I was in charge, not him.

"See, Mark, I knew you couldn't defy me, whining about how you're too hurt and insulted to work with me. Man, I played you like Ninetendo. Don't you know that you can't break a deal with the devil?"

26

Curtains

"You can't break a deal with the devil...with the devil...the devil..."

So, this is what our friendship had come to, huh? Woody set me up with the theater trip just so he could pimp me like a two dollar whore. I couldn't believe he'd said that. Later, when I talked to Craig about it, he thought that maybe I had over reacted and that Woody was just shooting off at the mouth again. But the words summed up everything. He had played me like a video game. I mean, what else could he mean? Of all the stunts he had pulled, I'd never known Woodrow to be so mean spirited, and so disrespectful of my feelings. No, I don't think he was joking at all. I think he had reached a new level of disrespect for me really. How could I collaborate on anything now? With me wondering when he would manipulate my affection for him again, how could we even be friends?

That night I couldn't sleep. I was having this dream of me and Woodrow, and I remember the image of him being in a darkened, room, his eyes burning red like a cat's. As soon as I stepped in, I felt trapped, caged and suffocated. I knew I had to leave, but as I reached to open the door, Woody had grabbed my hand emotionlessly, and was pulling me back into the room. The whole thing felt slimy and sexual. When I finally broke loose and opened the door, I awoke and found myself sitting straight up in the bed. There was a knot in my stomach, and there was no going back to sleep. The dream was pretty obvious, and the more I thought about Woody, the angrier I got. Here I was the sap again, the sucker, the victim.

Maybe we could go back to just being friends without working on any plays. Well, I thought that's what we were doing at the Playhouse, watching *Superstar,* and that only turned out to be a set up, a ploy to get me to do something I had already told him I didn't want to do. Besides, if Woody would always distrust me, and since I certainly couldn't trust him anymore, what basis was there for a friendship anyway? There was only one solution. Hasta la vista, baby! I had to say so long—it's all over. I knew it was the right decision because my stomach quieted, my anger abated, and I was able to fall asleep again.

I didn't talk to Woody for almost six weeks after that. I didn't want to talk to him. I would deal with him on my terms, on my time, when I was ready (a lesson I'd learned from Greg). So, for the month and a half after that, I screened all my phone calls. And if somebody couldn't leave a message, then they wouldn't be spoken to.

In the meantime, I went on living my life, got periodic reports from Mom about Dad. He was well enough to be checked into a nursing home, but Mom had trouble finding one at first. All the ones she visited were either way too expensive, or they reeked of urine. She finally checked him into one that was right around the corner from where they lived. She really raved about it. It was run by the Methodists, and the facilities were really nice. She claims they ate from antique furniture with tablecloths, and there were enough activities planned to keep them distracted if not downright busy every day. Apparently Dad's paralysis was permanent, and he wouldn't have the use of his left side again. The doctors thought that he could've done much better except he just wouldn't work at it.

It took her a while to get used to seeing Dad like that, confined to a wheel chair with his memory sketchy, but she adjusted. One day she reported that one of the nurses had pulled her to the side whispering like she had some secret. The nurse had asked Dad if he needed anything before he went to bed. And you know what he told her? "Yeah, I could really use some pussy right now!" The nurse laughed, and told him that they were fresh out, but that she would take up the issue with his wife. Mom even laughed when she told me the story, and I figured that if she was laughing again, and if all Dad needed was some pussy, then things weren't that bad. Then she told me that Greg had visited them and had stayed for an entire week.

"Well, Ma. How did you get along with him?"

"Just fine, Mark, better than ever. Gregory was in good spirits, and he didn't have any of that bitterness and anger he used to have. Oh, he would fly off the handle from time to time, but nothing like he used to."

"Did he ever explain why he didn't show up for the operation?"

"He tried to. Told me about going to therapy, his inner child, and some other mumbo-jumbo that I didn't understand, but whatever the reason, he seems happier now than he's ever been. So, I guess it was worth it."

"How does he and Dad get along."

"Couldn't be better. As a matter of fact he spent more time with Steven than he did with me. He'd show up at the nursing home every day to shave him, and help Steve do his exercises. Then they'd sit and just talk for a couple of hours."

"Wait a minute. Dad and Greg? Sitting and talking for a couple of hours?"

"I know, Mark. It surprised me too. Sometimes they would get on each other nerves, but Greg would just get up and leave. He'd never scream or fight like they used to. I never thought I'd see the day."

"Well, I guess anything can happen then."

I don't know what happened to Gregory, and I'm surprised he didn't confront Dad about all he told me, but I was glad that he didn't. And for him and Dad to sit down and talk like that, he must've had a brain transplant or something.

Back on the home front, I had started dating Beth Coren; you know, with the nice bazooms? That wasn't the only thing about her that was nice. She had a great sense of humor and she was quite playful too. Said that she had been a tom-boy as a kid, and that's why she scared off a lot of "wimps" as she called them.

153

She was as passionate about things as I was, but she was very independent too, which was just fine by me. I didn't want to get all hot and heavy with anyone either. But I'll tell you, I could have a lot of fun with Beth.

I told her once that I wanted us to double date with Craig Dempsey, that we were going to a children's play in Baltimore. She knows that Craig is gay, and she was worried a little about double dating with two gay guys. Well, when we got to the theater, Craig had brought his son as his date, and I got a kick out of seeing her sweat. We all ended up at the Inner Harbor and had a great time. Craig was right about the children's theater; it was a different experience with the kids. They were more joyous and active than any adult audience could've been. I couldn't wait for us to finish our project. Craig warned me that the next show he wanted to collaborate on would have to be copyrighted. He wanted to call in all his favors and all his resources to do a full-blown professional musical, but that would have to wait until the kids had their turn.

After weeks of screening my calls, I was finally ready to answer the phone and deal with anybody who was on the other end. It took a few days, but when I lifted the receiver one morning before work, Woodrow Tyler was on the other end.

"Mark, what's wrong with you? Why you ain't been answering my calls?" His voice was high pitched and urgent.

"I thought that was obvious. I don't want to have anything to do with you."

"I got somebody interested in the play, and you're not even answering the phone." He continued like I had said nothing.

"I told you. I don't want anything to do with you."

"Man, what are you talking about?"

"Well, Woody, this is how you break a deal with the devil." He stammered when I said that.

"Well...wha...Why couldn't you call me and tell me like a man?"

"Because this is when I felt like it. I'm telling you now."

"That's because you're acting like the bitch that you've always been."

"Well, whatever," I said, and I hung up. The phone rang immediately, and I weighed whether I should just let it ring and let him rant and rave to the answering machine, or should I answer it and let's get this confrontation over with, once and for all. I decided on the latter.

"What do you want, Woody?"

"I want to know what's wrong with you, why you won't talk to me."

"Because if our friendship doesn't mean anything to you, it doesn't mean anything to me either."

"Mark, what the hell are you talking about?"

"I'm not talking about a damn thing, Woody."

"Then tell me why you're so mad, and why you won't talk to me."

"I told you. I don't want to have anything to do with you."

"But why?"

"Because I don't want to be played like Ninetendo again, and this is how you break a deal with the devil," I repeated, but he ignored the comment again.

"Look, man. I'm talking about business; somebody's interested in doing the play."

"Well, if you're involved with it Woody, I'm not interested."

"Well, if you don't want to make the contact then I'll do it. Just send me a copy of the script. Can you do that?"

"No, Woody, I told you. I'm through with it.

"But why, Mark?" he persisted. "What's the reason?"

I could tell what he was trying to do. If he could engage me in any kind of conversation, he would still have a chance to ease my anger and show me how I was just over reacting to some phrase he had only casually tossed out. But the time for explanations had passed for me weeks ago, and I wouldn't be played for a fool by him again. All I wanted was for the conversation to end.

"You want to know what's the reason?" I asked him. "There is no reason. How's that? I'm just a crazy whiteboy, okay?" When he heard that, he knew the game was over. To go any further, he would have to discuss exactly what he was trying to avoid discussing. And rather than do that, he just giggled stupidly and hung up the phone. The dial tone buzzed in the receiver with a strange hollowness, and I knew I wouldn't hear from Woodrow Tyler anymore.

I was surprised how saddened I was, an emptiness I hadn't anticipated. I hung up the phone and reminisced about the fun we'd had, about the struggles we'd been through, about the danger and the sadness we'd felt together. I thought about how we both had grown, what we had learned, and how far we had come together.

Those were the memories I would try to keep because the lights had come down on this play.

Eartha Holley

About the Author

Eartha Holley is an English Professor at Delaware County Community College near Philadelphia. Active in the arts, he has also written and performed in stage plays and musical groups. "Often fiction can tell the truth of a situation better than nonfiction. And even though *The Color Play* is a work of fiction, all of the incidents and conversations actually happened. Characters have been created, and names have been changed only to make the truth easier to write and to read."

Printed in the United States
6800